NORA'S CURSE

A Novel

Marcus Starr

Manor House

Library and Archives Canada
Cataloguing in Publication

Title: Norah's curse : a novel / Marcus Starr.
Names: Starr, Marcus, author.
Identifiers: Canadiana 20220420033 |
ISBN 9781988058801 (softcover) |
ISBN 9781988058818 (hardcover)
Classification: LCC PS8637.T375 N67 2022 |
DDC C813/.6—dc23

Note: This novel is a work of fiction. Any resemblance to locations or persons alive or dead is purely coincidental.

Cover art: AboutLife / Shutterstock / (Picture: Tied up woman looking at a man with a knife).

First Edition
Cover Design-layout / Interior- layout: Michael Davie
248 pages / appox. 70,000 words.   All rights reserved.
Published October 2022   / Copyright 2022
Manor House Publishing Inc.
452 Cottingham Crescent, Ancaster, ON, L9G 3V6
www.manor-house-publishing.com   (905) 648-4797

Description: Nora, a young Canadian woman living in danger in Boston, is about to cross paths with the city's mysterious serial killer when she's suddenly hit with a highly unusual curse that threatens to forever change her life and lend new meaning to the old adage 'Be careful what you wish for...'

This project has been made possible [in part] by the Government of Canada. « *Ce projet a été rendu possible [en partie] grâce au gouvernement du Canada.*

For Kaitlyn

Praise for ***Nora's Curse***:

Marcus Starr's debut novel is a tour de force! Full of interesting characters, delightfully unexpected songs, and a storyline that will keep you reading to find out what happens next. I'm looking forward to reading more from this talented new author!

– Jordan Grupe, author, ***Beneath the Asylum***

"Nora, a comely Canadian bartender plying her trade in Boston, is grappling with personal issues when a stalker-killer inflicts terror on the American city she's come to love. As the killer draws ever closer, things take an unexpected turn for the worst when Nora is suddenly hit with a debilitating supernatural curse that gives new meaning to the old adage: Be careful what you wish for. Intriguing and thought-provoking, steeped in horror and humor, this is a truly captivating debut novel by Marcus Starr – and it's a superb must-read."

- Michael B. Davie, author, ***The Late Man***

"A certain Bestseller filled with horror, violence, humor, sex, drugs and rock n' roll."

- I. Murderman, author, ***Creep***

Foreword

Nora's world is about to turn upside down.

Her new lover has secrets. She suspects the worst. Why does he carry a switchblade?

Is he the notorious Midnight Rambler, creeping into women's bedrooms at night, terrorizing Boston?

Why does she keep going back to him?

A career bartender, Nora surrounds herself with bodacious characters: Kate, the luscious redhead, who quickly becomes a tour de force; Lesley, the tough-as-nails lesbian, who suspects something is wrong; and what about the old man in the hat, whispering dark phrases directly into her mind? Is she cursed?

Nora Murphy becomes trapped in her very own paradox – yes, she gets her innermost desires – but she learns the hard way: Be careful what you wish for, you just might get it.

Nora's Curse is a fast-moving thriller, drenched in dark humor, frequented by musicians, thieves, the priest, and lest we forget: the Devil.

"Everybody turns a bad trick now and then."
- **Ray Wylie Hubbard**

"Gigantic, gigantic, gigantic. A big, big love."
- **Kim Deal**

1

The trouble started after the redhead was hired.

The moment she entered the bar I knew the job was hers. Her face was pretty and round, freckled and fair. She wore little makeup. Her blue jeans were as faded as her brown leather boots, her white tank top not quite concealing her pierced belly button.

Blaze Temmerman, the manager of the Cock & Fiddle, went rushing over to introduce himself. His greasy, shoulder-length hair was in disarray. He couldn't keep his eyes off her. Especially her cleavage, which was on full display. Eyes go up, eyes go down, eyes go up, eyes go down, and repeat. I admit, she had spectacular breasts. The perfect pair. The kind of breasts that would make Hugh Hefner blush. I disliked her immediately.

I left the bar and folded cutlery, hoping to eavesdrop on their interview. It worked. While I wrapped those knives and forks into tightly wound napkins, Blaze and the redhead introduced themselves, then sat at the table furthest from the bar. She sat with impeccable posture. Blaze was slouched over, clipboard in hand, sweating profusely. His eyes were completely glazed over.

"So, Katie Campbell, it says here—"

"—Call me Kate."

"Kate—" Blaze said, then coughed. "Um, tell me why I should hire you. What makes you a good fit for the Cock & Fiddle?"

"How about I tell you a joke first... Blaze, is it?" Katie Call-Me-Kate said.

Blaze nodded.

The redhead flashed him her gorgeous green eyes. "Okay, here goes: An Englishman, a Scotsman and an Irishman walk into a pub and each order a pint. Upon getting their drinks, they each notice they have a fly in their glass. The Englishman says to the bartender 'Excuse me, mate, there's a fly in my pint, can you pour me a new one, please?' The Scotsman looks at his pint, picks the fly out, tosses it aside and starts drinking. The Irishman picks the fly out by the wings, holds it above the glass and says "Go on! Spit it out, ya wee bastard!""

"You're hired."

"Hi-ya," she said to me, moments later. "You must be Nora."

"You must be Katie."

"Call me Kate."

We shook hands.

"C'mon, I'll show you around, um, Kate."

"Great!" She smiled then stuck out her tongue playfully.

I looked away, straight to her chest. I had to laugh. Now I'm the one staring at her tits. It was impossible not to. I showed her around the pub and asked her the typical get-to-know-you questions. She told me she's completing her MSMS. I sighed. She'll be looking to run this pub by Thanksgiving.

I introduced her to Steve the cook, who was wearing a Metallica T-shirt and sneakers so old I couldn't tell their original color. His eyes practically flew out of their sockets the moment he saw her. She blushed and blew him a kiss.

Steve dropped his sausage into the deep fryer. The scolding grease splashed his arm. He started swearing and flopping about. We chuckled. As we sauntered toward the bar, I asked her if she'd ever bartended before.

"Oh, of course," she said, probably lying. "My last job was at the Bebop."

One of the barflies started catcalling; he was a bedraggled-looking man with a long face and thinning hair.

"Hey Red. Yer new here?"

"That's right, I am. You're not gonna hold that against me now, are you?"

"I'd like to hold somethin' else against ya."

A roar of approval came from the men sitting at the bar.

"Well then," the redhead said to the man, putting her face up to his nose. "You'll have to do better than that!"

Another chorus of laughter.

"All right, all right," I said. "Knock it off."

I asked the barfly if he wanted another beer.

"Allow me," Kate said.

She poured a foamy pint of Kilkenny, then handed it to the man. His smile showcased two missing teeth. Customers were pouring in. I told Kate to work the back room for now, until Lesley arrived.

"You'll get a kick out of Lesley," I said. *More like she'll get a kick out of you.*

Within minutes, Katie Call-Me-Kate approached the bar with her first order: three pints of Caffrey's, one Guinness, one Sam Adams and a vodka and OJ. As I prepared the order, I overheard some customers discussing Kate's chest size; then they started poking fun of my obvious lack of breasts, transporting me back to Grade Eleven, with all the Mean Kids teasing me and calling me names. Oh, they had plenty of nicknames for me. As I turned away, I slipped on a discarded lime and spilled the drinks all over the redhead. She screamed in surprise. Her skimpy tank top was now skin-tight and sopping wet, much to the delight of the barflies. Her large, pink nipples poked through her now see-through top, for all to see. Needless to say, all eyes were pointed at her.

"Oh my God. I'm so sorry," I lied. I could see her breasts clearly now, and a surge of jealousy rushed through me. I handed her a clean bar rag, and said, "Good thing Blaze went home. He'd have himself a heart attack staring at those pups."

I immediately regretted saying this.

"No worries," she said, drying herself off. "But, like, I'm gonna need to change out of this top."

I handed her a Cock & Fiddle T-shirt, and told her to get changed. For the next two hours, all anyone at the bar would talk about was the new waitress. She racked up quite the tips. Not bad for her first day on the job.

The customers continued to rave about Kate, often making comparisons between the two of us. Most notably, our chest sizes. Suddenly, and to my dismay, my lack of breasts had once again become the brunt of many jokes. My favorite was:

Question: How do you say small breasts in French?

Answer: Pe'tits'.

Ba-Dum-Ching. A real knee-slapper. Adding to my tribulation, she was scheduled to work with me every day this week, so I was forced to suck it up and try my best to get along with her. I'll admit, she made it easy.

"Are you seeing anyone?" she asked me, the moment we were alone.

"Sorry?"

"You know," Kate said, big-eyed and fox-like. "Some guy? Or girl? Other?"

I looked up from my chopping board, wiped my hands on my apron, and said, "I was. For seven years I was seeing a guy. A bass player."

"Like you."

Had I mentioned I played bass?

"Yes… Like me. But he got a job setting up concerts and sporting events. Cool stuff, really. He got so busy we could never find time to see each other. Then this blonde started working with him. So, you know."

I didn't have the heart to tell her it was him who broke up with me.

"That means we're both single." Kate grinned. "Hey, we're practically sisters now."

Just then the entrance bell rang and a handsome young man entered the pub.

"Nora? Nora Murphy?"

The handsome young man was standing next to the vintage phone booth at the main entrance. The booth, a popular prop for late-night drunken selfies, is an actual working phone booth circa 1950.

"Wow. You still work here? You look good."

"Who the hell is *this* guy?" Kate muttered, under her breath.

I finished chopping the limes, then I put aside my knife and looked up at the guy. It was Billy Swanker. He wore a motorcycle jacket and skinny jeans that revealed more than they ought to. He ran his hand through his sandy-blonde hair, then found a seat at the bar.

I said, "Well, well. Look what the cat dragged in."

"Hey beautiful. I was wondering if you'd be here. I've been thinking about you lately, you know?"

"Hang tight," I told him.

A woman wearing a large hat was waving me to her table. She was complaining about her cold, limp French fries. She scowled as she handed me her half-eaten plate of food. I apologized, ran to the kitchen, and told Steve to fire up another batch of fries. When I returned, carrying a steaming basket of fresh-cut pub fries, Billy Swanker was gone.

"Who was that?" Kate asked, as she placed her next order.

"Oh him? Nobody special. His name's Billy. Billy Swanker. He worked in the kitchen a couple years back. Only for a month or so. Then he went to jail."

"Ooh, how exciting," Kate said. "I think he likes you."

"Lucky me."

We laughed. Then we got slammed with the Dinner-Rush-From-Hell and I forgot all about the handsome young man.

It was a typical weekend at the Cock: busy, busy, busy. The band performing that night was superb, as always, and I made fairly decent tips. Kate made a fortune. She was all anyone talked about. She left early, while I closed up. After I counted the money in the till, tidied around the bar, scrubbed the shit and puke stains off the restroom stalls and walls, I changed two kegs, recounted the money in the till, while remembering to turn off all the lights and set the alarm. Then I clocked out.

When I reached my apartment, all I wanted to do was to slip into something more comfortable, drink a glass of red wine, then curl up next to Mr. Jimmy until I fell asleep. What I hadn't planned for was that handsome young man to be waiting for me outside my apartment lobby.

"Hey Honey, you're home,"

Billy Swanker spoke in a sly voice. His hands shoved deep in his pockets. He looked like a lost puppy. I wanted to ask him how he got my address, or why he was here in the first place, at this ungodly hour, but I didn't. Truth is: I was lonely. Then he smiled, showing his cute dimples, and my heart skipped a beat. I knew it was wrong for me to invite him in, but I did it anyway. Besides, I hadn't been with a man since being dumped three months ago. He seemed harmless enough.

Billy Swanker followed me up the endless flight of stairs leading to my second-floor bachelor pad. Mr. Jimmy, my loveable orange tabby, was waiting dutifully by the front door. He recoiled at the sight of Billy.

"Oh, hush hush, Jimmers."

Billy Swanker kicked off his sneakers and made himself comfortable on the couch. Mr. Jimmy followed him, cautiously, claws out.

"So, what's new? Got an extra smoke?"

I tossed him some cigarettes, then I went to the fridge and grabbed us some beer.

"Working," I said. "And saving for a down payment on a home. You know, grown up stuff."

He was fidgeting with his cigarette, scoping out my place; his crystal blue eyes focused on the door leading to the fire escape. He smiled as I handed him a beer.

"What's your story?" I asked. "You just show up out of nowhere."

Billy lit his cigarette. He took a thoughtful drag, then exhaled a plume of smoke that reached the back door. "I've been hanging low. Doing odd jobs. Nothing special. Thinking about getting my big rig licence. Hauling truck. You know, grownup stuff."

I made the decision right then and there. No, I didn't trust him. But he was cute, and he wore a motorcycle jacket. Plus, I'm a sucker for dimples, and Billy's got dimples down to his wazoo. Yes, I was weak. But I had every right to be. After dimming the lights, I put on my Albert King record, Born Under a Bad Sign, thinking nothing of it.

We drank and smoked and started making small talk. The next thing I know, he's massaging my neck and shoulders. I liked it. His warm breath breezed over me as he whispered sweetly, much to my delight. He started kissing me, slow and softly, starting from the lobes of my ears; then he began working his way down my neck, along my arms to the tips of my fingers. His kissing continued until my entire body was thoroughly examined. And by then, I was mush.

My eyes wandered to the monster he was concealing inside his pants. It was impossible not to. Billy seemed pleased that I noticed. He certainly wasn't lacking confidence.

We tore each other's clothes off. His naked body pressed against mine, until our heartbeats were touching. The heat permeating off him was exulting. I wanted more. He pinned me down, his hair tickling my face. The anticipation. This was my first ever one-night-stand. I hoped to get it right.

Judging from the look on Billy's face, I was. He spoke non-stop, but I paid little attention. I was enjoying the ride. Needless to say, we moaned and groaned until the soft light of the morning sifted through my pint-sized window.

Then, we slept.

The following morning, Billy Swanker was gone.

I woke up to a sandpapery tongue licking my face. It was Mr. Jimmy.

"Why, hello Mr. Jimmy," I croaked. I checked the time: 10:55 a.m. Time for his breakfast.

Mr. Jimmy was next to me, meowing impatiently, wanting off the futon. "Okay, okay. Don't get your fur in a knot."

I fed him. He ate greedily, then returned to the comfort of my futon, lying on my pillow. I made some coffee, then sat next to him. He listened attentively, as I told him about Billy Swanker. It was nice having a man to talk about, albeit a crude version of one.

I found my cigarettes, lit the last one, then tossed the empty pack onto the heaping pile of garbage beside the counter. Billy must have helped himself before he fled. At least he left me one.

"Ug, I gotta go get smokes," I told my cat, who could care less.

Mr. Jimmy stood up lackadaisically, then plopped himself onto a pile of laundry and slept. I finished my coffee, smoked my last cigarette, peed. Then I hopped into the shower, where I studied myself. Most notably my breasts. Or as Billy Swanker so elegantly described them: my itty-bitty tiny-titties. That really hit a sore spot, although he certainly didn't mean it to.

I've always been self-conscious of my breasts. Or dare I say, my lack of breasts? Having recently been dumped for a big-breasted bombshell, who couldn't spell her name without asking Google, didn't do wonders for my self-esteem either.

Now, don't get me wrong, I'm a catch. I'm pretty and petite, with long, straight chestnut-brown hair and a sweet derrière. My eyes are dangerously brown, my nose and cheekbones slight. But still. What if my breasts were bigger, like Kate's? I stuck out my chest and frowned. I'm twenty-eight years-old and I still have zero breasts. They were the only thing preventing me from being a Perfect 10. How unfair.

After making myself somewhat presentable, and finding clean clothes, I set out to buy cigarettes. Seeing how I live car-free, I travelled by foot. It's a fifteen-minute walk to the market.

You could say I got more than I bargained for. There was no way for me to know that my jaunt through Boston's Back Bay neighborhood would change my life forever, but it certainly did. In fact, everything in my life was about change.

Nothing could have prepared me for the horror that was about to take place, both in my personal life and in the Greater Boston area. A killer was on the loose; he was just getting started.

NORA'S CURSE / Marcus Starr

2

It was August 2019. Downtown Boston was bustling, the day seemed brightly optimistic.

As I made my way toward the market, my mind kept returning to the redhead. *How fortunate she was. Kate was young and gorgeous and full of zest. She makes incredible tips. Her, um, tips were better than mine. I frowned at my joke. Yes, I played bass guitar in a popular group; and I have impeccable taste in music (if I do say so myself), but that didn't stop me from being jealous. There, I said it. I was jealous. Jealous and insecure.*

Boston's Back Bay neighborhood is teeming with churches, beautiful Victorian brownstone homes and plenty of pubs. This was of no concern to me. I was busy comparing myself to every woman I passed on the street. *Big mistake.*

A gorgeous Hispanic lady sporting cleavage comparable to Salma Hayek strolled by, gabbing away on her cell phone. Three rugged-looking men wearing hard hats started catcalling; one managed to snap some pics. They didn't even notice me.

I stopped in front of a shop window, regarding myself in the reflection, and sulked. I recalled how those Mean Kids back home would taunt me. They'd chant: "There goes Nora. Flat as a door-a," or, "Lord have mercy, it's Mosquito-Bite Murphy." They had plenty of other names and phrases, too. Eventually, they settled on Pancake Nora. It took years for that nickname to leave me be. In fact, that's one of the reasons why I moved to Boston. That and meeting Tyson, of course.

While waiting at an intersection, I spotted Kate across the street. I counted eleven men and six women checking her out. Even the puppy dogs attached to leashes seemed to adore her.

Feeling hopeless and dejected, I continued my journey along Boylston Street, suppressing the urge to cry.

I stopped in front of an old stone church. A lineup of people was standing out front, chatting freely, waiting to pass through the great church doors.

A voluptuous brunette sporting more jewelry than the Queen of England, plus heels as loud as hammers, was approaching. Someone whistled at her. She tossed her hair and made a discerning remark as she brushed me aside.

Right then and there, something snapped. I couldn't stand it anymore. Always being brushed aside, never being good enough. I made a silent request to the Universe, asking—no begging—for bigger breasts. Or at least the money to pay for them. I pleaded with all my might.

As I was doing this, I bumped into an old man wearing a pinstriped suit, with wide-leg trousers and white suspenders. A sprinkling of rusty hair was poking from his pork pie hat. His face was gaunt, his nose bent. A small scar rested just below his chin in the shape of a crescent moon.

Before I could apologize, he grabbed my shoulders and started shaking me. A tremendous jolt of electricity surged through my entire body. My breathing became shallow. My arms and legs twitched, then filled with pins and needles. The ground below me shook. Someone somewhere screamed. For a frightful moment, all I could see was darkness. I was about to die.

The old man laughed deep within his chest. It was the worst sound I'd ever heard.

"YES," he proclaimed, squeezing my arms. "BIGGER IS BETTER."

He muttered something under his breath, then dropped me like a sack of potatoes.

For a moment, I could do nothing. Pedestrians journeyed around me as if I were contagious. Maybe I was. One lady huffed at me; nose pointed at the sky. I tasted blood. A stream was trickling down my nose. I wiped it with a Kleenex and watched it turn red. I was shaking as I stood up.

What the hell was that all about? I surveyed the scene, looking for the old man in the hat. But he was gone, lost amongst the churchgoers arriving in droves. I brushed myself off and shrugged. *This town gets weirder every day.*

Once I reached the market, I bought a carton of smokes and bee-lined straight home, taking care to avoid that cantankerous old man. I didn't trust him for a second. He smelled of pipe-tobacco and fried onions. Yikes. His breath stuck to me like glue. It wouldn't come off.

Every now and again while working, I'd hear the old man's voice: *BIGGER IS BETTER.*

The next morning my breasts were bigger. Not must-purchase-new-bras bigger, but bigger nonetheless. I was stone-cold terrified. *What the hell happened?*

The old man in the hat, *that's* what happened.

I pushed this thought aside. Wishing for something is one thing, but for it to actually happen is entirely different. Yet, there was something stirring inside of me. Something not right. I felt diseased and disoriented. My mind shifted to Billy. Uh oh. I must be pregnant. Ugh, why me? Why now? I couldn't think of a worse thing to happen to me.

Little did I know.

3

I showed up early for work, eager to grab some grub and a pint before my shift started.

Maggie Cunningham, a mature British lady whose father, as a child, was said to have fought Roger Daltrey and won, was tending bar. I loved Maggie dearly. We all did. She poured my pint the moment I entered the pub.

I sat at the booth next to the big bay windows, drinking my beer, wondering what was happening to me. I felt *strange*. My body was tingly. Something was wrong. I chalked it up to my overzealous imagination.

I headed to the band room, seeing who was around. Nobody was. The band room was empty. It looked all cozy, with its electric fireplace warming the miniscule stage, which will soon be swinging.

Then I headed to the dining area, at the back of the pub where the redhead had her interview, and glanced at its view of the patio.

Between the band room and dining room is a small darts area boasting a stunning Wurlitzer jukebox. I tossed a dart, trying to make a bull's-eye. But I instead hit number 13.

I sighed. Work was the last place I wanted to be today. Don't get me wrong, it's a classy joint, with enough witty paraphernalia to make even the Pope consider buying another drink. Yes, I'll admit the food is below average and not for the weak of stomach. It's the non-stop live music that makes the Cock & Fiddle truly special. There's live music here seven nights a week, twice on Sundays. It's my second home.

Sitting alone at the bar was Gordon Lester, an audacious ex-punk rocker who speaks with the sweetness and conviction of any true artist. Gordon is one of my favorite musicians of all time, and a regular at the pub. As I relieved Maggie of her shift, Gordon Lester struck up a conversation with me.

"Did ya hear about the Midnight Rambler?"

"The one you never seen before?"

"Yes!" he said, raising his hands in hallelujah. "Well played, Nora."

Gordon's long, thinning hair obscured his weathered face; his cherry nose matched his bloodshot eyes.

"Look at this," he said, in a thick Boston accent, waving a newspaper at me. "The Midnight Rambler's in town. Says here, the Rambler creeped into some woman's bedroom, sometime around midnight, and—um—took pictures of her while she was sleeping. Can you believe it? It's 2019, and we're living in an old Stones' song."

Then he laughed like a maniac.

"Another pint, Gord?" I asked him, noticing his soon-to-be empty glass.

He nodded.

By now, most of the people in the bar area were gathered around him, hanging on his every word, as they always do. Gordon loved the attention. His rusty voice grows louder and more confident with each drink.

Lesley came over to place an order. Her spiky blue hair was loaded with hairspray, her Doc Martens well-worn, her tongue danced around her lip ring while she waited.

"Hey Hamilton, what's with the redhead?" she asked, while I prepared her order.

Lesley is the only person who still calls me Hamilton; a nickname I earned after moving here from—you guessed it—Hamilton, Ontario, Canada.

I giggled, but chose not to respond. With Lesley, it's best to play it safe.

She leaned in. "Think her boobs are real?"

"Wouldn't you like to know." Kate said with a smirk, as she turned the corner.

Lesley, a proud lesbian who takes shit from no one, replied, "Hell yeah I'd like to know," and stuck out her tongue.

Kate's face flamed red. I did my very best not to regurgitate my burger. As Kate left to serve another table, Lesley turned to me and said, "Yeah. They're real."

Wednesday night is jazz night, meaning: great music, lousy tips. Lesley likes to harass the poor college kids, who show up every week looking to practice their jazz chops, drink ice water and watered-down cokes, then leave without tipping. Once, I saw her grab a young horn player by the scruff and put him in a half nelson, swipe his wallet and take his last five dollars. Before she let go, she said, "This is my tip, you noodle-playing cheapskate wanker." *It was brilliant.*

As the musicians were setting up, Billy Swanker entered the pub, and sat alone in the booth furthest from the stage. He ordered chicken fingers with fries and a bottle of discount beer. He was being distant. He hardly spoke a word. Whenever I glanced his way, he would be fidgeting with his phone or toying with his food, looking as though he were about to cry. A far stretch from the badass I thought he was.

What an amateur. You can't trust a guy who can't handle a one-night stand. This seemed obvious, even to me. So, I let him wallow in his own misery, munching away on subpar food, alone. Subsequently, he left without saying a word. But he did leave a miniscule tip.

When I arrived at my apartment, there he was, lurking in the shadows of the lobby. The glowing amber of his cigarette gave him away. Billy Swanker's face perked up when he saw me. He flashed his hard blue eyes.

"Who's the redhead?"

I ignored him. In fact, I wanted him gone. He put his arm around me, giving me his best grin. It was a dangerous smile. He made a joke, and before I could find an excuse for him to leave, he was back inside my apartment, cool as a cucumber.

He flung his shoes and went straight to the refrigerator to make himself a sandwich. He looked unhealthy. My maternal instincts were interfering with my better judgement. I asked him where he went after he left the pub. He ignored me and shovelled the food into his face. I fetched a couple beers, handed him one. We drank.

The smell of ammonia hit me straight away. Mr. Jimmy urinated in Billy's sneakers. I couldn't believe it. He'd never done anything like that before.

"My cat hates you. He just peed in your shoes."

Billy barely noticed. He ate voraciously. After devouring his sandwich, he unbuttoned his shirt and stretched out on the couch. His tattooed biceps tightened. His hairless chest was well-chiselled. His boyish face was watching my every move.

I put on a blues record, then sat next to him. I took notice as his crotch sprang to life. I'm weak. He put his hand on my knee and inched his way north. Then he kissed the small of my neck.

I melted. His lips met mine. We shared a long and passionate kiss. His breath tasted like sex.

"Where were you tonight?" I asked, for the second time.

"Oh, nowhere, really."

His eyes scampered across my living room before settling back on me. "Look at you, all tense."

He reached over, started rubbing my shoulders and neck. His fingers found the right spots. I started to relax.

"You're smooth, Billy Swanker."

His hands were ravenous, eager to explore. Within minutes, we were fully naked. This time it was me who took charge, kissing him all over, starting with his toes, then slowly and meticulously moving my north. My mouth was eager to explore.

Soon we reached ecstasy.

Afterwards, we smoked in thoughtful silence, gazing at the world outside my one and only window. It was twilight. That tranquil moment before the night is conquered by the clear light of dawn.

Then the Day People wake up.

I reached across Billy's sweaty body and turned off the lamp.

"Where'd you get them scratches?" I tried to sound casual, but was deeply disturbed by the claw marks on his back.

"What? Oh, I dunno," he said, avoiding eye contact. "Probably from you, babe."

As a bassist, I keep my fingernails short; those scratches weren't mine. Before I could speak, Billy pulled me close, jabbing me with his erection.

Oh well, I'll get rid of him in the morning.

Without hesitation or consideration, I jumped aboard the Billy Express, and rode him long past dawn. We made ugly noises, howling and hissing like street cats, until my sheets were a pile of sweaty goo, and we were thoroughly exhausted.

I loathed myself for letting him have his way with me. Billy Swanker was bad news. *How did this happen?* I was at a crossroads. Yes, he was kinda creepy, and no I didn't trust him, but damn he was randy in the sack. I hadn't realized what my life was missing until he showed up. Seemingly out of nowhere.

Billy was a nice distraction from my ex-boyfriend Tyson. I had other issues to attend to. Namely, my breasts. Suddenly, I had some. What troubled me was that although my breasts were growing, the rest of me wasn't.

"You don't like Billy Swanker, do you?" I asked Mr. Jimmy the following morning, although by morning I really meant afternoon.

Billy was gone.

I was glad. It prevented the awkward conversation that would have otherwise ensued. It wasn't as though we had anything in common. I searched for my smokes, speculating what my mother would say if she knew what I'd been up to. Here I was, a twenty-eight-year-old career bartender, having my first love affair. Before Billy, I'd only been with Tyson, who was off cavorting with what's-her-face.

But I digress.

Mr. Jimmy arched his back, then watched me fill his dish. He ate, then he retreated back to the futon for the remainder of the afternoon. What a life.

Days like today, I wish I were my cat.

4

After breakfast, I put my tip money into the savings jar.

Four hundred dollars was missing. I couldn't believe it. Who does that? If he needed the money, he should've asked. I'm doing alright for cash. My rent is cheap, and I don't drive. I might have lent him the money, if he'd given a proper reason for needing it.

I texted Swanker. It was time to end this. I hoped a breakup text wouldn't seem too juvenile. If it did, too bad. I chose my words carefully.

Yet, that wasn't what troubled me most. I couldn't ignore the trepidation stirring inside me. Something was off. I still didn't feel right. My breasts were constantly itchy and sore. They were growing. Time for bigger bras. I'd been wearing the same size bras most of my life, so this was a new experience. Reluctantly, I took a pregnancy test, which proved negative. Phew. At least it wasn't that.

It was only a matter of time before the customers started giving their two cents. My ex-boyfriend was the first person to poignantly point it out.

"Nora, did you get a boob job?

I ignored him and headed straight for the restroom. I checked the mirror, looking for lines around my eyes. Thankfully, I found none. Then I stuck out my chest. My breasts were indeed bigger. My beloved Pixies T-shirt was stretched to the max. It couldn't take much more.

I'd been secretly wishing for bigger breasts my entire life. I'd won the lottery. Why was I so worried? Who cares where they came from? Here they were. My trepidation turned to joy. I was finally a Perfect 10.

They were nowhere near the size of Kate's, but for the first time in my twenty-eight years on this planet, I actually had some. I returned to work with an extra bounce in my step.

"Do you like them?" I asked Tyson.

He was fidgeting with his bass amp, trying to look busy. He was taller than Billy Swanker, and stronger. He dressed casually and without conceit. He brushed a meaty hand over his freshly-shaved head and shrugged. His warm brown eyes showed concern.

"Um, I guess. I mean, whatever makes you happy. You look great Nora. You always look great." He moved away from his amp, twiddling with the tuning pegs on his bass head, then added, "I've missed you."

Then why'd you break up with me?

I walked away satisfied.

The late-night crowd trickles in after 9 p.m. Thursday nights at the pub were a treat. Brian Washington, an old black blues musician, performed weekly. Brian is another local legend. He comes from a lineage of incredible blues and jazz musicians. His uncle, Terry Washington for example, recorded several songs for Chess Records back in the day. His band, who scored a hit with Baby, Let Me Be Your Baby Tonight, toured all over America and Europe. His songs still get played on blues and soul radio programs.

There was a lot of pressure on Brian coming from his family. He once told me, "When I first picked up the guitar, my mother told me, 'Son, if you're gonna play that thing, you'd better play it good. Don't you go embarrassing this family!' It's safe to say, Brian hasn't embarrassed his family. In fact, he's toured with Willie Nelson, partied with Emmylou Harris and performed on the Letterman Show. How cool is that? And here's the best part: as truly wonderful a musician as Brian Washington is, he's an even sweeter person. Because of him, Thursdays were my favorite night of the week. The customers came to listen.

Kate arrived with her order. She wouldn't stop staring at my chest.

"Take a picture, why don't ya? It'll last longer."

"Don't mind if I do," Kate said, pulling out her phone. She snapped several. "Let's get one together."

She took shots from multiple angles. Then she posted the best ones on her social media apps. Oh, to be twenty-one again.

At the end of the night, just before clocking out, Kate approached me cautiously.

"Did you hear about the Midnight Rambler? It's all over the news. Scary stuff." Then she added, "You'd better be careful, Nora. Living alone and all."

I nodded, then continued changing a keg. Changing a keg is like milking a cow, once you do it a couple times it becomes effortless, but it's never fun.

She shrugged and pattered away.

To be honest, I wasn't interested in the local news. But I could no longer hide from it. This story was all the rage. In Boston anyway. It would soon become a national story.

Although the story was alarming, I was preoccupied with my own problems. I didn't give it much thought.

Work finished, and I walked home.

The only person waiting for me was Mr. Jimmy.

Later that week, I went bra shopping with Amanda, my BFF. I couldn't have been any happier. Amanda, who makes whatever we're doing fun, insisted I started showing them off.

"If you've got em, flaunt em."

It didn't take much convincing.

That Friday I had a rare night off. Amanda came over, all done up in black eye-liner, sparkling nail polish, tight-fitting black crushed-velvet dress and platform boots. We went clubbing. We certainly garnished some attention. We were getting checked out by everything with a pulse. This was something new to me.

It was late September 2019, my breasts fit into a B cup, and I was on top of the world. My world, however, would soon start to sag. Calamity was inching closer and closer, looming over the horizon.

But not tonight.

Tonight, I was on top of the world and nothing could bring me down. Not even the Midnight Rambler himself.

5

The Nashville Runaways are a couple of song-slingers hailing from (you guessed it) Nashville who ended up in Boston a few years back. They've been local favorites ever since.

The group leader is Susie St. Marie, a fiercely independent country-twanging gal born and raised in Austin Texas, who later made her way to Nashville, where she met her creative partner Naughty Taughty Trisha. This pair of outlaws are as wonderful on the eyes as they are on the ears. Audiences love them. They often ask me to play bass for them. Um, yes please.

The Nashville Runaways perform once a month at the Cock. Tonight, we were scheduled to play the late show. There is nothing better than selling out on a Sunday night in Boston. It feels like magic. Even the police presence couldn't diminish the excitement of the night, at least for everyone else. I, on the other hand, had a miserable night.

I was wearing a short skirt, lace stockings, slightly revealing top, my favorite brown boots and just the right amount of makeup. I looked great. Susie St. Marie, with her strawberry-blond hair and sexy cowgirl getup, was as fine as Tuscany wine. Naughty Taughty Trisha, a blond dish who can play finger-style guitar as good as anyone in town, if not better, was as alluring as her name suggested.

We performed every song to perfection. Cesar Rodriguez, our drummer for this particular evening, is one of the finest percussionists in Boston. His persistent flirting aside, he and I make one heck of a solid rhythm section. The trouble started during the set break.

Upon finishing my cigarette, I was accosted on my way back inside the bar by an obnoxious middle-aged man wearing a Red Sox jersey. He was blocking the entrance, and pointing at my chest. I couldn't make out what he was saying over the noise, nor did I care to, so I brushed past him. When I did, he reached out and squeezed my breast. I mean, really squeezed it. He said something stupid like, "They feel real!" The group he was with burst into laughter.

I stood frozen for a moment, letting my mind process what just happened. Before I knew it, Lesley came over and knocked him flat on his ass. That shut him up in a hurry. I've served this man plenty of times over the years. He wasn't a bad guy really, just another dipshit who can't handle his alcohol.

Before I could thank Lesley, she turned to me and said, "Serves you right for getting a boob job, Hamilton. Try and stay alert next time, why don't you? Maybe then you won't need me to save you."

"Excuse me?" I said, but she disappeared inside the pub.

I shook my head, then followed her. After ordering myself a beer, Lesley approached me, looking me up and down.

"Listen, Hamilton, you're alright for a straight-white chick. And yeah, that guy's a jerk. But it serves you right." This was as close to an apology as I could hope for. "Hey, you should come to the rally with me. I'll let you know when it's happening."

"I'll think about it."

I turned and walked towards the stage. Cesar was standing next to his drums, chatting it up with a group of women who were hanging on his every word. One woman in particular, with her amber pig-tails and the ruddiest set of lips I've ever seen on a person, was giving him the Dirty Eyeballs. Every time Cesar spoke, she would laugh and toss her head like a cheerleader. I know where she'll end up tonight. Drummers are all the same.

I don't think the ruckus from the patio was even noticed inside the pub, which was swarming with patrons. Everyone was talking over each other, telling stories, getting lit. It was a good gig. Later that evening, the cops showed up after a bunch of drunks started fighting over me. Apparently, there was a bet going around as to whether my breasts were fake or the real McCoy.

I hadn't decided yet myself.

THE NASHVILLE RUNAWAYS SETLIST:

SET ONE:

Folsom Prison Blues medley

You're Just Star Struck, Baby (Original)

Move it on Over

I Fall to Pieces

Coal Miner's Daughter

I'm Built This Way (Original)

The House That Built Me

Jolene

SET TWO:

If the House is Rockin'

Lying Cheating Son of a Gun (Original)

Ladybug, Lady Bird (Original)

Blue Moon of Kentucky

Snake Farm

Scarborough Fair

The Devil I Know (Original)

Whiskey in a Jar

SET THREE:

Mall Crawler (Original)

Big Boss Man

Crazy

Train Kept a Rollin'

You Can't Always Get What You Want

Bobby McGee

Sometimes I Don't Feel Like Coming Home (Original)

Dream On

Encore:

Angel from Montgomery

6

Monday was to be a well-deserved Me Day.

My plan was simple: feed Mr. Jimmy, fire up the coffee maker, pee, shower, smoke cigarettes, play guitar, drink wine. That was my plan. Instead, I ended up back in bed, taking nude selfies. My breasts being the center of my attention, of course. They looked splendid. How did they get this big? I didn't care. Why worry about the details, right? Nor did I worry about the constant tingling, nor the persistent itchiness, especially during sleep. They were bigger and that's all that mattered.

They weren't huge by any stretch of the imagination, but they were now a solid handful. I studied them from every angle. I even gave them names: Bonnie and Clyde. Then, I masturbated. It was a marvelous afternoon. Mr. Jimmy joined me for a nap. At some point during my nap, I was hastily awakened by my phone. It was Billy Swanker.

"You little prick."

"Who you calling little?"

"You."

"Listen, hon."

"Do not call me hon."

Mr. Jimmy leapt off my futon and disappeared.

"Okay, okay. Whatever. I'm sorry babe. Listen, you're probably upset over the money."

"You bet your hairy ass I am."

"And I can assure you, you'll get it back."

"Is that so?" I said, using my too-loud-for-inside voice. "Well then, when will that be?"

"Next week, I promise. I just needed a quick loan. And I didn't want to wake you while you were sleeping. You looked so cute all curled up."

I was gobsmacked. I lit a cigarette and let the nicotine moderate my anger. I inhaled deeply, blew a smoke ring and watched it dissolve.

"Whose number are you calling from anyway? This isn't the number you gave me."

"I know, I know. I got a new phone."

Something occurred to me: he hadn't received my breakup text (not that we were dating, of course). This was bad. How did things get so out of hand? I knew nothing about him, other than he was a warrior in bed.

"Tell me, Billy Swanker, where are you right now? Where are you staying? What's going on?"

"Still at my mom's. Same as before, hon. I'm saving up for a—"

"—Saving? Saving? You stole four hundred dollars from me. That's my rent. You know, rent? Rent, in case you don't know, is when grownups pay money to live somewhere. I know it must be difficult for you to understand that."

Mr. Jimmy poked his head out of the closet, shot me a whimsical look, then ambled slowly and languidly toward his food dish.

"Hey, don't worry. You'll have your money back next week, I promise. When do ya work next anyway? I'll meet you after work and—"

"—No way. You have my email address? Send an e-transfer."

"Can't do that. Sorry."

I was furious. Unfortunately, my voice cannot sound intimidating no matter how hard I try. I'm *that* girl, you know, the one with the omni-pleasant voice.

"Listen, you little creep. Keep the money. I don't want to see you again. Ever!"

He started crying.

Instead of hanging up, I put him on speaker phone and listened to his sad story. Every wretched word of it.

Billy Swanker's father was currently in jail for beating up his mother, again. So, Billy needed money to pay her medical and legal bills. He said his mother had suffered a fractured jaw, split lip and a sprained ankle. Not surprisingly, she was looking to have a restraining order put on the son-of-a-bitch. The rest of his story was just blah, blah, diddly blah. I didn't believe a single word of it. It seemed more likely that he was a drug addict needing a fix.

When we hung up, I reached for my guitar and wrote a country song called The World Needs a Hero (But it ain't Him). It wasn't Dolly Parton, by any stretch of the imagination, but it was good. I immediately felt better. Writing a new song is on par with reaching the pure state of nirvana. Well, almost. Let's just say it feels pretty darn good.

I put my guitar away. Then I went back to my futon and continued examining my breasts. Why were they growing? That was the million-dollar question. Best not to think about it, I told myself. I ran my fingers along my nipples, watching them spring to life. I'll need to purchase new outfits, seeing how nothing I own fits anymore.

But first I needed to settle one last score. I took one final selfie, then masturbated for the second time that day. It was a wonderful day.

I worked a typical Tuesday night at the Cock: hectic. This one woman in particular was getting belligerent with her friend. I thought she would tear her friend to shreds. She probably did, after they left. I had to cut her off. Then she went ballistic. It got nasty. Once again, Lesley came to the rescue. Nobody stands a chance against Lesley.

On a brighter note, I received several compliments on my chest; and coincidentally, made incredible tips. Bonnie and Clyde were really coming through for me. My new outfits showcased them nicely.

The band called me up to join them for their final song. I sang Hit Me with Your Best Shot, while the remaining twelve or so patrons were up on their feet, dancing and singing along, taking videos and selfies. It was a smash.

As usual, I finished up late. This time I decided to order an Uber. Although it was after 3 a.m. when I got home, guess who was waiting for me? One hand in pocket, the other clutching his cell phone? Billy Swanker, of course. Soon thereafter, he was naked, face up on my futon bed, while I rode him to Sexy Town.

Yes, I'm weak.

Billy Swanker loved my blossoming breasts, and was eager to explore this newfound territory. Billy's hands soon gave way to his lips, which were kissing in and around my tender nipples until they were firmly erect. I was delighted. Consequently, he was too.

His mighty member was pulsating stalwartly. The heat coming off of him as he stood over me was tremendous. His muscles flexed; he was looking to conquer. He removed his shirt in one easy swoop.

I lit some candles. He talked dirty, melting me with each naughty word.

In a fit of passion, we tore off each other's clothes. We were like animals, caught in the moment. And that's all it was.

Billy was gone in the morning. Three times a charm.

THE WORLD NEEDS A HERO (BUT IT AIN'T HIM)
By: Nora Murphy

I could never love a man who's down on the ground

Looking for table scraps

Barking like a dog

They say a whipped dog never cries on the outside looking
in;

The world needs a hero but it ain't him

I could never love a man over six feet tall

He'd be way over my head

Not wanting me at all

I'd always want what he ain't got and follow his every
whim

The world needs a hero but it ain't him

The Devil seems to know me

And horseshoes seem to bore me

I guess that's why I'm in the shape I'm in

Let's call it buyer's remorse

You can get back on that horse

The world needs a hero but it ain't him

Now you can't play a sad song on a banjo

But you can make this old guitar, sing a lonesome melody
So if you take me out tonight
You'll either sink or swim
The world needs a hero but it ain't him

The Devil seems to know me
And horseshit always bores me
I guess that's why I'm in the shape I'm in
Let's call it buyer's remorse
You can get back on that horse
The world needs a hero but it ain't him

Now I ain't saying there's no man right for me
If you want a piece of my heart
You'd better get down on one knee
Because my pappa raised me right
I won't lead no life of sin
The world needs a hero but it ain't him
The world needs a hero but it ain't him
The world needs a hero

7

"There's a rally happening Sunday night," Lesley said, after cornering me and Kate on the patio.

"And I know you're not working and I know you're not working, so the two of you are coming with me. It starts at eight. We'll meet here at seven, have a drink, then walk over."

It was a brisk evening. The kind where nothing you wear feels appropriate. The three of us were standing just beyond the borders of the patio, leaning against the steel fence, smoking. Lesley, whose shift had just ended, was enjoying a beer. She was with a group of women, all dressed in warm coats and knitted scarves, getting loaded.

Kate shrugged, then released a cloud of strawberry-scented curls as she exhaled.

Lesley looked at her with venom.

"Haven't you heard?"

Kate shrugged again, this time with a tinge of self-consciousness.

Lesley looked at me. Her patience waning.

"Either of ya's?"

Kate looked at me and we both started giggling.

"Jeez, would ya get a load of the Boobsy Twins, over here!" Lesley said, loud enough so that her friends at the table would hear.

Kate and I looked at each other and grinned. a silent connection was made.

"Take Back the Night," Lesley said, intentionally slow, as if we were stupid. "Is a rally. It's happening at the Parkman Bandstand, in the Commons."

She produced a pack of cigarettes and offered me a cigarette, which I accepted. Kate looked disgusted by it, and continued vaping. I glanced at my phone. My shift started in twenty minutes. All I wanted was to smoke in peace. That wish was in vain.

"The rally happens every year. I'm surprised neither of you girls know about it. Anyway, this one's gonna be a real shit-kicker."

To this, the women at the table cheered.

By now, Lesley was all worked up. "You two know about the Midnight Rambler, don't you?"

Kate looked at me and started giggling. I tried my best to ignore her, but it was contagious. I giggled too. Lesley, on the other hand, was furious. Her face tightened into a purple knot of rage.

"That sick bastard just raped another woman," she said through clenched teeth. "In her own bedroom. Happened Tuesday night. You must've heard. It's all over social media. That makes five victims now. Five!"

Kate was clearly taken aback by Lesley. Most people are, at first anyways. Her eyes met mine and we burst into spontaneous laughter. There was something about Kate that made me smile, even as I was being assaulted with spittle from an angry lesbian who's trying her darndest and makes a good point. Lesley waved us quiet. Kate composed herself as best she could, and I did too. After an awkward moment of silence, it was Kate's turn.

"Um, okay, then," Kate said, one bushy eyebrow raised. "Yours truly, and this bad-ass, bass-playing bombshell standing next to me, shall attend this rally. But like, whatever shall we wear?"

To this, the entire group of ladies broke into hysterics—shrieks of laughter and clapping—until someone yelled for another round; right on cue, Maggie Cunningham came out carrying a tray full of drinks. Everyone hurrahed.

I managed to step away from Lesley, and slipped inside the pub, which had been completely done over. Maggie, who adores the Halloween season, and has for as long as I'd known her, taken it upon herself to decorate the already cluttered pub with enough Halloween paraphernalia to bring Vincent Price back from the dead. She really outdid herself this year. The walls were covered with witches holding broomsticks, plastic jack o' lanterns with Dollar Store lights flickering inside them, vampires with fake teeth, ghosts and goblins galore; and the pièce de resistance: an orange punch bowl filled with tasty treats, sitting at the edge of the bar, within arm's reach.

Work went well; exceptionally well, if I were to be honest. Thanks to my busty new chest-pals, I raked in the best tips of my life. It was quite remarkable. In fact, I made more money in October than any other month in my bartending career up to that point.

Things started to escalate, as they often do. As time went on, I was getting hit on more often than a cheerleader at a college frat party. Far more than I thought necessary. This was something I wasn't prepared for. However, I'll admit: there were some pretty cheeky one-liners.

"Hey, nice rack. Wanna see them on my wall?"

Or:

"How much did those cost, 'cuz I gotta send the doctor a thank you note!"

Or my personal favorite:

"Nice tits. Wanna fuck?"

Even Gordon Lester couldn't help himself.

"Hey Nora," he said, after I poured him another pint. "Looking good these days. What's new? You're hair?"

This went on and on. It became the new normal. I'll admit it: I quite enjoyed it. Who wouldn't? It was fun. My confidence was at an all-time high. But what I really enjoyed most was the money. Who wouldn't? Pretty soon I'll have enough saved for a down payment on my first home. Not bad on a bartender's salary.

If only my mother could see it this way, but she refuses to. She's old and set in her ways. Worse, she blames me for screwing things up with Tyson, whom she truly adored. She won't let up about it. Ugh.

The holidays are coming. Which means I'll have to see her again. And then what? I can only imagine what she'll say when she sees me. Or, once she notices Bonnie and Clyde. She'll be sharp-witted and cruel, as always. She won't have a single nice word to say.

The knots in my stomach were unbearable. Soon I'll be forced to catch a plane back to Hamilton, Ontario. Soon I'll be face to face with my mother.

8

The rally was a smash.

Thousands of women gathered at the Parkman Bandstand, holding signs, singing songs, chanting slogans, arms linked together, all in the name of solidarity. The evening was gorgeous, the moon full, precarious. The weather was warm enough so that one could wear a short dress and long boots, or jeans and a jacket. Or go topless. There were no rules.

Prior to the event, Kate came over and helped with my makeup. She made me look fabulous. To my surprise, she handed me a card, signed by the staff at work. Including the part-timers. The card showed a stripper ready to show her goodies. When I opened the card—FLASH—there they were.

$400 tumbled from the card. I was flabbergasted. Kate was the only person I spoke to about Billy robbing me. She promised to keep it Our Little Secret. She didn't. Instead, she went and organized a fundraiser in my behalf.

I was beginning to like this redhead.

We arrived early. Maggie, who greeted us with more than just a smile, poured us each a pint of Sam Addams. Free beer is one of the many perks of working at the Cock & Fiddle. The pub was crowded, the patio at capacity.

An older gentleman, sporting a denim jacket and cowboy boots that should've been put down long ago, was complimenting me on my performance the other night.

He kept taking drunken glances down my top. The old buzzard was drooling over them, spilling his beer in the process. Lesley came out of nowhere, and told him to buzz off. He did.

Lesley put her arm on my shoulder, and motioned to Kate to come over. Lesley said, "Finish yer drinks and let's go."

As requested, Kate and I finished our drinks. But we weren't ready to leave just yet. First, we powdered our noses, primped our hair and peed one last time (one more for the road).

She kept asking about Billy Swanker. Who he was? Where did he come from? What did he do? The more she asked, the less I knew. Billy Swanker was a perfect stranger. I didn't even know his birthday.

That was embarrassing, but I shrugged it off. He was my rebound fling. That's it. We finished up in the restroom, then headed outside. Lesley was waiting for us. She lit a smoke, blew a cloud of smoke in our faces, then started walking.

We followed.

Things were about to get funky. Very funky indeed.

The women at the rally were hell-bent on revelry.

Fortunately, we were too. Droves of people were chanting and holding signs with catchy slogans: EQUALITY FOR ALL, LOVE IS LOVE IS LOVE, LOVE=POWER, NASTY WOMEN UNITE, NOTHING TRUMPS INJUSTICE, PUSSY POWER IT'LL GRAB YA, RESIST FEAR—ASSIST LOVE, RISE OF THE WOMAN=RISE OF THE NATION, SEXISM IS NOT AN ISSUE, SILENCE IS NOT AN ISSUE, and to my surprise, and Lesley's chagrin: WE ARE WOMAN - HEAR US ROAR!!!

Lesley seemed to know everybody. She was constantly shaking hands, hugging friends, handing out glow sticks and chatting with random people. She was right at home. To my dismay, Tyson was there with his new girlfriend, Stephanie, who was holding a sign of a penis with a circle and strike through it. As they approached, I pointed them out to Kate. Consequently, Kate stepped in their way, and asserted herself, as only a redhead would. Tyson's girlfriend was visibly shocked. Her walnut face crunched into a ball. Her lips smacked themselves silly.

Kate looked her up and down, then turned to Tyson. "You could do better."

"Fuck you, bitch," the girlfriend said.

"Kiss your mamma with that mouth?" Kate said to her face.

Stephanie shot Tyson an 'aren't-you-going-to-do-something?' look. His face went as red as Satan's scrotum.

"Alright, alright. Knock it off," Lesley jumped in, saving the day. Lesley gave Stephanie a don't-fuck-with-me look, and meant it. Then she dragged me and Kate to the front of the bandstand.

"What a bitch," Kate said, shaking her head. "You're way sexier than that skank." She offered me her flask. "Here, this will help."

It did. The peach schnapps warmed my insides, and I immediately felt better.

"Tyson doesn't know what he's missing," Kate said, as she took a pull from her flask.

"Yeah he does. I can see it in his eyes. He'll be knocking on my door before long."

But then what?

Lesley put her arms around me and Kate. "Do the Boobsy Twins wanna know more about the Rambler?" She didn't wait for a response. "First it was this random woman. Happened sometime after midnight. The jerk climbed a tree and sneaked into her bedroom. Then he starts taking pics of her. While she's sleeping. She wakes up and totally freaks out. He bolts out the window. I swear to goddamn God."

"Unbelievable," said Kate.

"Then you don't know Boston." Lesley said.

A group of women approached, trying to pull Lesley away. Lesley snapped her fingers. The women stopped, but didn't go anywhere.

"Anyway," she continued. "That one barely caught the news, right? But the next one sure did. This jerk comes back. To the same house no less. Only this time he, um, whips it out and tea-bags her. Like for fuckin' real."

"Get out!" Kate said, then stuck a glow stick in her hair.

Lesley handed Kate a sign, then ventured off with the group of women. They ventured off to the side of the stage and formed a circle. The guest speakers came out one by one, and spent the better part of an hour lecturing the crowd.

I tried to pay attention, but was preoccupied with self-sabotaging thoughts about my ex. Seeing him with his new girlfriend was infuriating enough to land me in some anger management course.

The woman started pumping her fists. "IT'S TIME WE TAKE A STAND. IT'S TIME WE MARCH. AS ONE!" She'd worked the crowd into a frenzy. The woman, with dull brown hair and glasses three sizes too big, stepped away from the microphone, and led the congregation southbound.

"Here we go," Kate shouted.

She took my hand, and we started marching with the thousands, taking it to the streets. The chanting grew larger and louder. Kate joined in. "TAKE BACK THE NIGHT. WE ALL HAVE THE RIGHT. TAKE BACK THE NIGHT. WE ALL HAVE THE RIGHT."

We bumped into Lesley, who was pumping her fist in the air. I tugged on her jacket until I had her proper attention,

"So, what happened next?"

Lesley looked at me with pity. She lit a cigarette, took a drag. "So," she exhaled. "That was just after the Fourth. Right? Well, two weeks later, this creep sneaks through another window. This woman was older. Like, my mother's age. And get this…"

She lowered her voice and leaned in close. "He pulls out his dick and starts crankin' it! Took some pics, too. Then he spilt.

Hence: The Midnight Rambler. Great fucking handle, I'll admit. But when I find the guy…"

Kate was flabbergasted. Her face lit up like stars. For the first time since I'd known her, she was speechless. Lesley, on the other hand, took another drag from her cigarette. Her demeanour changed. When she spoke again, her face softened. Tears swam in her eyes.

"I know what it's like." She dried her eyes on her denim jacket. "I've been there. It happened when I was a kid."

Kate reached out and embraced Lesley. Soon they were crying. Before long, I was too. Lesley was about to say something else, but was accosted by a six-foot drag queen, who came stumbling over. The pair disappeared.

"This is fun," I shouted.

Kate was beaming. Her hair tangled as the wind swept through it. She didn't care. We locked arms and were carried away by an endless sea of bodies. The march was heading south toward Boylston Street.

The sidewalks were crawling with nightlife, cheering us on. It was a colossal party. Everywhere, people joined in. A drunk woman was flashing a group of Asian tourists. A chorus of honking ensued. Fireworks filled the confetti sky. Beach balls bounced over heads.

Trouble was lurking up ahead. We were heading straight toward it.

Just outside a Four Seasons Hotel, a bloodthirsty crowd was circling two men. Both had their sleeves rolled up. One guy looked as tough as a junkyard dog, with greasy blonde hair and tattoos covering his face. The other was a scraggly man wearing an unfortunate tracksuit, yapping like a noisy neighbor, clearly strung out.

The tattooed man waved him on.

The scraggly man jumped onto a parked car. He stepped up onto the roof, released a primal scream, then ran full tilt. He lunged.

The junkyard guy made a furious fist. It was the size of football. The fist made perfect contact, stopping the scraggly man mid-air. The scraggly man crumbled like a cartoon.

"Woo-hoo!" Kate clapped me on the back.

The fight was broken up; the march moved on. Kate was pulling me onward with her exuberance. We could march fast enough. I was about to offer her a drink, when something caught my eye. At first, I didn't recognize the old man with the hat, who was standing with a group of shabby men in front of the stone church. But he recognized me.

He looked impeccable. His pork-pie hat shielded one side of his face. All he needed was a Tommy gun. We locked eyes. He snarled, then started making big-boob gestures, laughing through leathery lips. His eyes were tiny slits of yellow.

Suddenly, he changed. His face was ghost-white. His tongue forked like a rattlesnake. Eyes like pearls, swirling under the fog of night. He stretched out both his arms.

ZAP, a surge of electricity crashed through my body. I collapsed, getting trampled in the process. Knees and boots and stilettos and sneakers. I tried standing up, but I couldn't move. So instead, I laid on the pavement, convulsing, while a million pairs of legs plodded past me, chanting.

His voice entered my mind like an invisible intruder: *BIGGER IS BETTER, DEARY?*

I put my hands over my ears, trying to shut him out.

It didn't work.

YES! BIGGER IS BETTER!

My head was being crushed by an anvil. I couldn't shut him out, no matter how hard I tried. He was slithering inside my head. My breasts were burning. I scratched them, clawed them, trying to rip them off my chest. Anything to stop the burning itch. They were red-hot. When I screamed, nothing came out.

Just as I thought things couldn't get any worse, my nose started bleeding. The sight of my blood brought on a panic attack.

I closed my eyes and said goodbye.

Kate yanked me to my feet, her eyes bugging out of her head. I spotted the old man in the hat. Kate followed my gaze. She made a sour face, like seeing your father naked. Then she turned her attention toward me, and started wiping the blood from my face.

When she asked how I was, I lied and said I was fine. I wasn't. She smiled and gave me a weary thumbs up. We marched. I stole a glance over my shoulder, and watched the old man vanish into thin air. Poof. His cronies continued mocking and pointing and shouting obscenities, but soon they were lost in the madness.

The march soldiered on. I felt weird. Body numbness. I wanted to run as far away as possible. But I couldn't. I was in the middle of a rally. I put on a phoney smile and bit my tongue. Kate hugged me. Then we walked on down the road.

The rally continued for another hour. Not surprising, we ended up back at Lesley's place, where we partied long past dawn. The party was a rippah, as Lesley says. Total debauchery.

I made some new friends, including a tranny named Danny, who insisted we go on a date. Danny, with jet-black hair and all the French perfume you'd care to smell, was found an hour later, passed out next to a bowl of Skittles, wearing nothing but pink earrings, pink panties and pink panty hose. Everything was coming up pink.

Kate snapped a pic and immediately posted it on God knows how many social media platforms.

It was sometime after 6 a.m. before I found my way home. I was drunk. The grotesque amounts of alcohol I consumed made it easier to forget the nefarious old man, and his insidious taunting. I wasn't ready to accept him. Nor was I willing to accept what happened at the rally. Things like that don't happen. I must have imagined it.

I must have imagined it, I told myself repeatedly, until I pretended to believe it. This is something I'm good at, although there are a million therapists in America who would argue against this technique. But that's how I cope. I bottle things up. Until I explode.

A pancake-sized circle of puke greeted me outside the lobby. There were chunks of pineapple in it. Cute. I did my best not to gag. I stumbled up the stairs, found my keys, then somehow opened my apartment door. When I flicked on the lights, someone was inside my apartment.

Billy Swanker.

Billy was on the sofa, smoking a hand-rolled cigarette, legs on the coffee table, as if he owned the place. His hand brushed through his hair, splashing water onto his face.

"Hey hon. I had a shower. Hope you don't mind."

Before I could react, my cat started rubbing against my leg. His eyes said he was hungry. I picked him up with shaky arms. Mr. Jimmy squirmed. He leapt off me, scratching me in the process, drawing blood.

"Look what ya did," Billy walloped. "Here. Allow me."

Billy loped to the washroom, and came out carrying a bottle of rubbing alcohol, cotton swabs and a large Band-Aid.

"Sit down."

I sat, shoulders slumped, staring at the scratches.

Billy said, "Geesh. Good thing I'm an expert at this." He dabbed my wounds with the alcohol; the pain was tremendous, even in my inebriated state. "Hold still. Don't make me say it again."

I jokingly slapped his face. Being angry took too much energy. By this point, I was running on fumes. What I wanted was to curl up on my bed and pass out, and not wake up until dark.

Billy ignored me. His eyes were full of menace. Something was bothering him. He was more irritable than normal. After cleaning my wound, he tripped over the cat dish. Water spilled everywhere. I chuckled. How many times have I done that?

Billy's eyes were murderous. I was about to crack a joke, but thought better of it. He swore and kicked the dish across the floor, slipped and fell. Then he threw a tantrum, kicking cupboards, slamming doors, swearing and slobbering. I'd never seen him act like this before. I didn't like it.

He went to his backpack, and returned with a switchblade. He thumbed the lever. SWOOSH. Out comes the blade. For a moment Billy stood there, transfixed, regarding the knife like a dear old friend.

"Where'd you get the knife, Billy?"

"Oh, this?" he replied.

He held the blade plainly so I could see. It looked dangerously sharp. Clearly, this knife had seen some action. He approached without caution, grabbed the back of my hair, and pulled with the full weight of force.

"Is this funny to you?" he asked, through gritted teeth, pointing to the mess on the floor.

I shrugged, trying to escape. He forced me to my seat, made a no-no gesture, then he stuffed the blade under my chin.

I froze.

The sharp, steely edge was sinking into my skin. One sudden move and he'd carve me up like a Thanksgiving bird.

"Billy," I managed to say, my voice just above a whisper. "Take it easy. It's me, Nora. We're cool, right?"

Billy was muttering something under his breath. He sounded crazy. His knife was firmly against my throat. Billy's thumb dug deep into my collarbone, causing unbearable pain. His hands were shaking. Just as I thought the knife would plunge deep into my oesophagus, and I'd taken my final breath, the blade disappeared—Swoosh.

I sighed, then noted the fresh urine dribbling down my leg. I ran to the washroom, fighting an ocean of tears. My reflection in the mirror was deplorable. Do *not* do anything stupid and get yourself killed, I told myself. This is not the time for self pity. Tears can wait.

When I returned, Billy seemed disconcerted.

"Jokes," he said, as he casually tossed the knife into his backpack. He returned to his seat at the table, charming me with a smile.

I pretended to laugh. What I needed was a plan. Otherwise, he'd kill me. Even in my drunken stupor I knew this to be true. I dusted off a bottle of white wine, and washed two glasses. One glass declared: **Zero Fox Given**, the other: **For Fox Sake**, but the word Fox was replaced with a crude drawing of the animal. These glasses were an anniversary present from Tyson. I filled the glasses to the brim. Then I found my bottle of single malt Scotch. I poured two shots.

I smiled seductively, studying his face. I raised my shot glass. "Cheers to Billy Swanker."

He laughed. His dimples gave the appearance of a twelve-year-old boy, but his eyes told otherwise. Billy Swanker was insane. We drank. He coughed, and made a funny face. I poured him another. He's an amateur. I hoped to use this to my advantage.

I edged closer to him, tapped two cigarettes from my pack, lit both, and handed him one.

"So, Billy," I said, ignoring the overzealous drumming in my chest. "Tell me about your mother."

He did. Every last wretched word.

As he spoke, he became increasingly distracted, jumbling his words, making little sense. His legs were shaking. His fingers tapping nervously on the table, drumming to the madness of his mind. A gasket ready to blow.

Clearly, my plan needed altering. I went under the kitchen table, on all fours and unzipped his pants. Billy rose to the occasion, nearly poking out my eye in the process. I got down to business.

It didn't take long.

Afterward, Billy relaxed, stretched his long legs, helped himself to some Scotch, then spoke freely of his mother.

He had a lot to say: "Ma was young when she had me," he said. "So was Pop. Ma forced him away. Now he never comes around. Why would he? Ma trash-talks him day and night. She's a real bitch, you know. But I love her. Even after what she done to me." His voice wavered, his eyes dripping with shame.

"Yeah, Ma done terrible things to me." He gulped the remainder of his Scotch. "As a boy, she would touch me you-know-where. She said I was special. But if I ever told anyone—*anyone*—she would hurt me. She did, too. This went on and on. Until I got bigger than her. Then it stopped. But enough about Ma."

Billy bit softy onto his bottom lip, and looked at me like a dog salivating over a piece of meat. I didn't mind. That's exactly how I saw him.

He skidded his chair next to mine, and started kissing my arms, then shoulders, working his way toward my eager mouth. We kissed passionately. He unsnapped my bra. Soon my breasts were exposed. Pink and warm and plenty-for-the-taking.

Billy was in awe. "I can't believe these are yours! What's going on, babe? You used to have tiny titties. Now this. Not that I'm complaining. Are they even real?"

Billy didn't wait for an answer. His hands were insatiable. His penis sprang to life. My eyes gazed upon his prized package. Seems like Billy was ready for round two.

I braced myself. Then I found my way on top of him. Billy moaned. So did I. We bounced all night, not stopping until the commuters and birds filled the morning with song.

The next time I saw Billy Swanker, I wasn't so lucky.

9

My hangover was a bulldozer to the brain; my mouth was an ashtray; the previous night a blur. Mr. Jimmy was nudging my face, eager to be fed. I fell out of bed and cursed the furry devil. The smell of cat shit was egregious. "P.U." I told him, sprinkling a handful of treats on top of his regular food. The kitchen was a disaster. "Time to take out the trash."

I fired up the coffee maker, then scurried to the washroom for a long pee. As I sat on the toilet, watching Mr. Jimmy feast away, I marvelled at his simple life: eat, sleep, poop, repeat. I recalled the first time I met the orange fella, and it warmed my heart. He was a birthday gift from Tyson. I remember it like it was yesterday (except that I don't actually remember yesterday).

Tyson was standing at my doorway, grinning like a schoolboy on prom night. At his feet was a shiny blue box. He handed me a birthday card showing a cartoon woman and a cat. It read: HAPPY BIRTHDAY - TO YOU AND YOUR PUSSY, and when I opened the card, it read: CAT. Meowing was coming from inside the box. I tore it open. "Oh my God," I cried. Inside the box was a miniature orange tabby with the most precious green eyes and pouty face. I hugged Tyson and kissed him full on the lips, again and again. He seemed so proud of himself. "What are you going to call him?" he asked, as though the question had been pestering him all day. "Mr. Jimmy," I blurted out, a nod to the Stones' song I'd been rehearsing with the Nashville Rejects. That was the day Tyson first said he loved me.

The smell of coffee overpowered the stench coming from his litter box. This was a good thing. I poured myself a cup, while Mr. Jimmy flopped onto a pile of dirty clothes, retiring for the afternoon. My morning cigarette made me nauseous. I raced to the toilet and vomited. How long has it been since I was this hungover? I returned to the kitchen feeling worse. I washed down some Tylenol, hoping it would do the trick. Flashes from the previous night started to arrive. I remembered the rally, but everything after that was foggy. My mind was struggling to make sense of it all. Billy Swanker was here, that much was certain, and we had powerful sex. I knew this because I was sore all over. Plus, two wine glasses and an empty Scotch bottle lay on my kitchen table. The ashtray was overflowing. My kitchen floor was sticky.

I remembered Billy's switchblade. The bastard put it to my throat. He was going to kill me. I was sure of it. But I stopped him. Then he was sweet. None of this made sense. Why would he do that to me? I sighed. If Billy was half as clever as he was handsome, he'd be dangerous. I laughed at my own joke.

Amanda's text startled me: *lets do coffee!!*

I responded: *"HARD NO."*

Her reply: *"No isn't an option lol.* Followed by: *"Meet at Chuck's in 45 minutes."*

I hopped in the shower, feeling limp. I could barely keep my eyes open. When I reached for the soap, I shrieked. Eyes blinking on and off, not believing what they were seeing. This must be some kind of joke. My breasts were huge. Up until now, they looked natural. Not anymore. Yet, they were spectacular. I loved them. No matter how hard I tried not to. I couldn't stop admiring them. They were the Perfect Pair. Yes, I'm spending half my earnings on a new wardrobe, but that's a price I'm willing to pay. I wrapped my hands around the bar of soap and went to town.

Today's my lucky day. On my way out, after grabbing my phone, jacket, keys, purse, smokes and my lighter, something spilled from my jacket pocket. I did a double take. It was a bag of shrooms. Where did these come from? Then it came to me. At some point last night, during Lesley's afterparty, she had thrown her arms around me and said, "Something tells me you're gonna need these." She handed me a bag of magic mushrooms, then put her head against mine. "Remember Hamilton: microdose."

Mr. Jimmy sniffed the bag. His head snapped back. "Now, now. I wouldn't want you getting into these." I stuffed the baggie in the freezer, tidied up, then left. I made it to Chuck's Diner, slower than a month full of Sundays.

10

Chuck's Diner is your typical 50's style restaurant; with its checkerboard floors, cherry-red vinyl seats, white chrome-trimmed tables and stainless-steel backsplash, pictures of Marilyn Monroe, James Dean and pink Cadillacs clutter the walls; Elvis has been spotted eating here, munching away on a triple-bacon heart-attack burger, sipping on a coke.

True fact.

The smell of sweet summer sausage, fried eggs and strong coffee improved my mood. I love that smell. It reminds me of the happiest moments of my childhood. My father would serve up a big family breakfast on Sundays, then we'd spend the day watching football in the den. I never cared much for football, I just loved being with my dad.

"That little prick."

Amanda, who was sitting across from me, playing with the tip of her ponytail, was furious. Her big brown eyes beating down on me, as she processed what I'd just told her. She stabbed her eggs Benedict with her fork.

"Why couldn't he carry a gun like a normal bad guy?" she said; then added, "You should've called the cops."

I shrugged. I'd already told her everything I remembered of the previous night. I didn't want to beat this dead horse any longer.

"How's your online dating going anyway?" I asked, looking to change the topic.

Amanda sighed. "Shitty. All I get are dick picks. I met one guy last week, who wanted to send me videos of him—um—you know."

"Get out!"

"Seriously. Dating is harder than it used to be."

"Word."

We went to work chomping on our sausage and eggs. Meanwhile, the Beach Boys were singing a delicious four-part harmony that made me want to have fun, fun, fun. All this time, I had yet to remove my coat. I hadn't seen Amanda in awhile. I was worried how she'd react to Bonnie and Clyde.

When I did, she gasped.

"Oh my God. Would ya look at those puppies. Come on, Nora. What's the deal?"

"They won't stop growing," I said, wiping the egg from my face. "I mean, don't get me wrong, I love the extra attention. And the money."

Her cynical look rattled me.

"Something is definitely wrong," I finally said. "I can feel it. They hurt. More than usual."

Amanda reached over and placed her plump hand over mine. "Are you pregnant?"

I laughed, and told her I wasn't. We giggled.

"Nora dear, you're almost thirty. Your boobs were bound to grow sooner or later. Besides, they look fabulous."

"Almost as good as yours."

"Almost."

The waitress topped up our coffees. I surrendered my half-eaten plate. The eggs weren't agreeing with me.

"You'll get used to them," she said. "I mean, look at me." Amanda has humongous breasts. "I'm concerned about this Billy Swanker character. I don't trust him. He's not your type. You should dump his sorry ass." She gave me a stern look. "I can't believe you haven't introduced me to him yet. He'd better be cute."

"He is. It just kinda happened. He showed up out of the blue. I don't even know how he got my address. And it's not like we're dating. Just, you know—"

"—Well, at least he's not Tyson. I heard about his new hussy. What's her name?"

"Stephanie Cockburn."

"No way! That's her name? It should be Step-On-My-Cock-Burn!"

We giggled, drank too much coffee, and gossiped for an hour. I missed these moments with Amanda. We used to do this every weekend before life got in the way. I paid our bill and left a good-sized tip. Next one's on her, she insisted. We hugged, said our goodbyes, then Amanda took a bus home, while I set off to work.

Blaze had scheduled a meeting before work, and I could only assume it was bad news. I was wrong. I should've seen this coming. The writing was on the wall. Blaze wanted to discuss my breasts.

"Have a seat, Nora."

Blaze Temmerman sat behind his puny desk in his crowded office. He wore a buttoned-up plaid shirt, which desperately needed washing. He was perspiring, and blatantly stoned. Blaze fetched us a bottle of fake champagne and two plastic cups. He poured us each a glass. This was not how I was expecting the meeting to begin.

"There's been a lot of talk about you, lately, Nora. Many of the regulars have been quite vocal about it, too."

He glanced at my chest.

I folded my arms.

"They say you're doing an exceptional job around here. You're all everyone is talking about. Um, you and Katie of course. So, I'd like to make you an offer. You don't have to take it, of course, this work is not for the faint of heart. Nora, as you may or may not know, I run a gentlemen's club called Boston Manners. Nice place. And we're always looking for new recruits."

I choked, grabbed a tissue, and blew my nose.

"Sunday is amateur night," he said. "A very popular night. Turns out, the clients love seeing, um, fresh faces."

Blaze leaned back in his leather seat, placing his hands on his belly. Since his shirt only fit him standing up, much of his stomach hair was sprinkling out.

"I'll think about it," I said, getting ready to leave.

"If you have any questions or concerns talk to Katie. She can fill you in on the details."

"Right."

I left.

One thing about being a bartender, there's never a dull moment.

On a random night off, I ate Lesley's mushrooms, and spent the afternoon contemplating my life, high as balls. Something I hadn't done in quite a while. My mind drifted toward my idiot step-brother Denny, whom I haven't seen or heard from since last Christmas, when he showed up unceremoniously with his methhead girlfriend. The pair were atrocious. I stopped feeling sorry for him that night. Instead, I worried. I know a junkie when I see one. Billy Swanker, I believed, was an addict. I was sure of it. He's the same age as Denny: twenty-three, a peculiar time in a young man's life, I suppose.

My mind moved to Billy Swanker. Yes, I'm his side piece, and I'm okay with that. I wouldn't want it any other way. He's been in jail, he's got sexy tattoos, and most importantly: he's got it where it counts. But he's barely an adult. He's all hormones. One day those hormones will fade like an old pair of Levi's, and he'll just be another dude with a dick. And lest we forget the switchblade knife. Did he really put it to my throat? He did! What was that all about? I was so inebriated it almost seemed like a dream; Of course, it wasn't, no matter how much I wished it was.

I had a flashback; sudden, jarring. It was from that night. Sometime in the wee hours of the morning, on my way to the washroom, I tripped over Billy's backpack. I peeked inside, and saw a black ski mask, leather gloves and rope. It's probably nothing. That said, I should avoid him from here on in. I mean, he doesn't even like good music.

Tyson, on the other hand, had superb taste in music. He turned me on to the blues. For that I'm forever grateful. He was my first real boyfriend. In fact, he's the reason I moved to Boston in the first place. (That, and to get as far away from Pancake Nora as possible.) I truly thought Tyson and I would last forever. We talked of one day owning a little home in the suburbs, with vegetables growing in the yard and sunlight spilling into our lazy living room.

Sadly, this was not to be. What went wrong? That dirty bitch took him away from me; at least, that's what Amanda says. What did she call her? Step-On-My-Cock-Burn. Too funny.

Ahh, the drugs were kicking in. I was getting introspective. Happy thoughts, happy thoughts, I reminded myself. Time to ride the shroom wave. My acoustic guitar was leaning against my futon. I tried playing it, and failed mightily. Basic motor skills were gone. I left the instrument alone, and reminisced about my father.

Daddy died of lung cancer at the age of fifty-two. The cancer hit him hard and fast. It was tragic. I was sixteen when it happened, with a face full of acne, a mouth full of braces and zero breasts. Alas, I was Pancake Nora. That was a rough year, let me tell you. I'm surprised I made it out alive. I still miss my father dearly. I miss the way he would call me his princess, tussle my hair and tell me how pretty I was. I miss watching Bruins games with him, always wearing our jerseys for good luck. Daddy loved the Bruins. So much so that he bought us playoffs tickets one year. We flew first class and stayed in a fancy hotel and everything. Mother was furious, but Daddy didn't care. He said we'd remember this for the rest of our lives. Ah, precious memories. Who sang that? Willie Nelson? Or was it J.J. Cale?

It wasn't until my second year of college that I started finding my groove. My acne cleared, which was a relief, my chestnut-brown hair grew past my shoulders, and the sprinkling of freckles along my high cheekbones illuminated my diamond face nicely. People started taking notice. To my mother's dismay, I didn't finish post-secondary. Fate had other plans. During March Break, I flew out to Boston with some friends to catch the Bruins and Leafs in action. That's how I met Tyson.

He was working as a vendor selling peanuts and beer. He looked so cute in his uniform, I just had to say hello. Needless to say, I ordered my beer from him all night. By my third beer, he'd mentioned this pub he was performing at the next night. I could tell he was eager to show off for me. We ended up at the pub, staying the whole night. What a blast! Watching him move up and down that Fender bass was quite alluring. I knew I could learn a lot from him. I was smitten. He couldn't believe it when I said I also played bass. Soon we were dating. Next thing I know, I'm working at that very pub; and the rest, as they say, is history.

The shrooms led me back to my breasts. Why were they growing? Not that I'm complaining, but still. If they don't stop growing—and soon—I'll be in a whole heap of trouble. Something about them still feels wrong. Sometimes, it's as though there's microscopic worms roaming around in there, working some sort of voodoo black magic. It's awful. I don't notice it at work, because I'm too busy working my tail off; I notice it late at night, when I'm alone. Every time I look down, I'm shocked. I cannot get used to them. Worse, they're stealing my identity. People don't look me in the eyes anymore. I might as well be wearing the T-shirt that says: My Eyes Are Up Here.^^

I've been cursed.

Once that thought entered my mind, the shrooms began getting more intense (happy thoughts, happy thoughts). I became frightened. I knew I was in trouble. The urge to scream was insatiable. Then without warning, the old man in the hat sprung into my mind; his gristly face, long and narrow. The scar below his chin cut deep and wide, his serpent-like tongue protruding from his pale lips. I could see my reflection staring back at me from inside his pupils. I looked small, insignificant.

For a moment nothing happened. The old man simply floated behind my eyelids, taunting me. Then his face changed. His eyes were alive. I could feel his hideous breath rub against my skin, as he mocked me in his cackling caw: BIGGER IS BETTER, DEARY? YES! BIGGER IS BETTER! He smelled of rot and decay. The smell was everywhere. He was close, somewhere inside my apartment.

Something crashed.

My heart leapt in my chest, as my eyes jumped in their sockets. I was short of breath. Then came another crash. I bolted upright. My apartment came rushing into view. I looked over at Mr. Jimmy, who was standing over his food dish with a crabby face. I grinned, fed him; then let my mind mosey its way back to the old man in the hat.

It hit me, hard and fast as the truth always does. That wretched old man did this to me. He cursed me. It seems obvious now. But how? He was older than dirt. A relic. Probably a Vietnam vet whose brains are fried from PTSD. But, yes, he cursed me. Deep down, I'd known this all along. I was just hoping it would go away on its own. Well, it hasn't. I fumbled for my pack of cigarettes and lit one with shaky movements. I smoked in silence. Mr. Jimmy was now perched on top of my futon, staring at me with his loving green eyes.

"He did this to me, didn't he?" I asked him. "The old man in the hat? He did this, right?"

Mr. Jimmy blinked.

I repeated the question, only this time in my mind.

Again, he blinked.

You sneaky little devil, I said in my mind. You can read my thoughts, can't you?

He blinked.

Things were spiralling out of control. The walls were closing in, inch by inch, moment by moment. I needed to change gears, quickly, before this mushroom trip totally derailed. I found my Pixies record (the one Tyson bought me on my twenty-fourth birthday), and placed it onto my turntable. I dusted it off, adjusted the speed, then cranked up the volume.

The sound was like sex. Their music was beyond exquisite. It was profound and timeless, yet daring and cutting-edge. I marvelled at Kim Deal's coolness. She was and always will be my favorite bass player. I dreamed of the day she would enter the pub, so I could tell her how great she was. Kim Deal was the real deal.

This monkey's gone to heaven

This monkey's gone to heaven

This monkey's gone to heaven

This monkey's gone to heaven

I regarded my breasts again. They no longer fit into my hands. Impossible, but true. I started panicking. Had they literally grown in the past hour? Apparently, they had. They hurt. My entire body, in fact, hurt. I felt diseased. Those swimmers were moving around in there. Whatever they were, they were bad. Why was this happening to me? What did I do to deserve this? Why me? Then the scariest question of all came to mind: how's my mother going to react?

This thought has been nagging at me for quite some time. How will I explain this to her? Things haven't exactly been copasetic between us since I moved to Boston. To be honest, things haven't been good since my father passed away, going on twelve years ago. We only see each other on the holidays, and the holidays are fast approaching, which means I'll have to face her, once and for all. Sigh. It doesn't take a crystal ball to know how this will end up. She'll be sharp-witted and cruel. She'll call me a low-life, skanky waitress, then ask how much I paid for my boobs, in front of everyone. Then, she'll give me a long list of reasons why I should move back home to Hamilton.

Then there's her hubby: Carl the lawyer. Yuck. Carl gives me the creeps. He's a little too touchy-feely for me, thank-you-very-much. Same goes for his perverted, methhead son, Denny. Could I have picked a worse step-family? Probably not. Oh well, you can choose your friends, but you can't choose your family.

Apprehension was setting in. The shrooms were making me realize how unrealistic life can be. Life is merely a dream, a voyage into the great unknown. Then you die. All we are is dust in the wind, dude. The more I studied my breasts, the more I understood: I must put an end to this madness. This curse. Right away. If not, my breasts will never stop growing. It's downhill from here. Yes, they were my moneymakers and the money has been phenomenal; and yes, I looked spectacular, but there will soon come a tipping point: The Point of No Return.

Speaking of my moneymakers, did Blaze actually offer me a job as a stripper? Yes, he most certainly did. Should I take him up on his offer? Could I, even if I wanted to? It's doubtful. Should I discuss this with Kate? Yes. I like Kate. Kate was fun. Was I too harsh on her at first? Yes, but that's how I am. Sadly, it takes time for me to warm up to new people. I've always been that way.

My blinking phone stole my attention. Big mistake. Social media and psychedelics do not mix. I tried going online for like, one minute, then decided against it. The moment I did, I was bombarded with catastrophic news: Midnight Rambler Claims Latest Victim; Women of Boston Beware!

I remembered Billy's backpack. Had I really seen the black ski mask and leather gloves? Yes. I felt sick just thinking of it. I needed to pull my mind together. I reached for my acoustic guitar. Maybe this time I'd have better luck with her. I did. I wrote two songs. Just like that. They were sloppy and bluesy and weird and strange; they were unlike anything I'd written in the past. Jeez, I wonder why? As I put my Gibson away, I was reminded of how lucky I was for being a bass player. As a bassist, I also get to play guitar, and the guitar is a wonderful instrument. The perfect vehicle for composing music. My guitar's name is Kim. She's a beauty. I bought her the first week I moved to Boston. Let's call her my housewarming gift to myself.

As it grew later in the evening, and the shrooms began to subside, I dimmed the lights and listened to music all night. So did my neighbors. Several albums later, including every Pixies' album I own – which is all of them – I succumbed to sleep.

My dreams were ghastly: I found myself alone in a dark alley. The wind was unkind. Sirens rang off in the distance. I heard gunshots, followed by screaming. My life was in danger. I tried running, but my feet wouldn't move. A crowd suddenly appeared, chanting: "PANCAKE NORA, FLAT AS A BOARD-A; PANCAKE NORA, LOOKING TO SCORE-A." "Shut up!" I shouted in a faraway voice. Eventually, the chanting ceased and the crowd dispersed. Once again, I was alone in the dark alley.

Then the old man appeared. His twisted face was menacing. As he inched closer, his long, skeletal fingers danced along the brim of his hat. His smile was as sincere as a gambler's grin. We were face to face when he finally spoke. "Bigger is better, Deary?" His eyes were digging into mine. "Ahh yes. Bigger is better!" The crowd reappeared. Only now, I found myself on a stage dangling on a stripper's pole; the music was deafening; the lights blinding. I was naked. The crowd was ravenous. Their chanting grew louder and louder as they all joined in: "BIGGER IS BETTER—BIGGER IS BETTER—BIGGER IS BETTER—BIGGER IS BETTER—BIGGER IS BETTER—BIGGER IS BETTER—BIGGER IS BETTER—BIGGER IS BETTER—BIGGER IS BETTER—BIGGER IS BETTER—BIGGER IS BETTER—BIGGER IS BETTER—BIGGER IS BETTER—BIGGER IS BETTER—BIGGER IS BETTER..."

I woke up in a pile of sweaty sheets with those iniquitous words ringing in my ears. I knew what needed to be done. I just hoped that it wasn't too late.

WHISPERING STREET (FOR THE BLUEBIRD)

By: Nora Murphy

You know I'm gonna miss you, now you're gone
So, I'll bare my aching heart and soul
As the bluebird sings her song
Chiti—wee—wee—wee—do

I'll always look for snakes out in the yard
While an alley cat comes a rollin' by
Trying to steal your lonely heart
Chiti—wee—wee—wee—do

The summer leaves will fall
While I'm stuck here in this song
Counting all the ways today, that I've done you wrong
Lest we sleep on Whispering Street

Now, I'm going to spread my wings and fly
While I'm reaching new heights
These memories come rushing by
Chiti—wee—wee—wee—do

We built our nest so beautiful, it's true
So, one day we would raise our young

NORA'S CURSE / Marcus Starr

Then carry them off to school
Chiti—wee—wee—wee—do

Now that winter is on its way
The night reminds the day
How your soul's as white as the drifted snow
That'll crumble at her feet
And lest we sleep on Whispering Street

So I guess I'll sing this song
And let the bluebird carry on
While I'm searching for that lost chord
Somewhere, hiding in the breeze
And lest we sleep on Whispering Street
And lest we sleep on Whispering Street
And lest we sleep on Whispering Street

11

Boston in late October is captivating. The autumn leaves turn flame-red, honey-yellow and bright orange; the sun is a golden yellow sea, but the chill in the air serves as a reminder: winter is coming. Today, the weather was cold. I cursed myself for not dressing warm enough for the walk. I needed to gather my scarves and hats and gloves and warm coats once I got home.

I waited impatiently, as a row of buses screeched onto Marlborough Street. When the lights changed, I veered right and headed toward the church, hoping to find the old man in the hat. Yes, it was a long shot, but worth a try. It was 2:15 p.m. I needed to hurry, otherwise I'd be late for work.

A gathering of homeless-looking people was waiting outside the church. One man, with a cigar box at his feet, was holding a cardboard sign declaring Jesus Luvs You, then written underneath: Spare Some Change? I placed a twenty-dollar bill inside the box. The man smiled graciously, said thank you, then looked away. Beside him, an elderly woman with thinning blue hair, was shouting at teenagers whizzing by on rollerblades. One of the teenagers flipped her the bird as he sped away.

My search was proving futile. Hopelessness was creeping in. I felt dejected. This was a new low. I considered giving up and heading to work early, when I tripped over a pair of legs stretched across the sidewalk. I fell hard, scraping my knees. When I stood up, confused, I recoiled. A figure was looming over me, casting a tall, crooked shadow. It was him. The old man pointed at my chest and sniggered, "BIGGER IS BETTER, DEARY?" His sonorous voice slithered down my spine like hot soup. He loomed over me like a bad dream. His mangled teeth made me cringe; his breath smelled worse than the men's urinal at the Cock. Somehow, he was inside my head, stealing information like a hacker. His delight was explicit. Whatever he was doing to me was getting worse. His whispered words, punishing in their cruelty, grew louder and louder until I was ready to scream. "BIGGER IS BETTER? YES, BIGGER IS BETTER!"

I tried to stop him, but I was weakening. My body went limp, my mind overtaken. My legs gave out. I fainted. When I came to, people were huddled around me, asking if I was alright. I ignored them, and scanned the vicinity. The old man was gone. For a moment I did nothing. I was at a loss. Tears were circling my eyes. I knew if one escaped, there would be plenty more.

There was a commotion at the side of the church. The old man's minions were floundering about, causing a ruckus. One of them pointed at me before disappearing around the corner. I charged through the crowd after them. I was pissed off. I knew my adrenaline would soon wear off and I wanted to catch the old man before that happened. Behind the church was a half-empty parking lot. A trio of skateboarders were trying new tricks. Someone was smoking pot. Across the street was a Thrift Store. A moving van was illegally parked out front. Two strong men were carrying out a flat-screen TV, loading it into the back. The old man was nowhere to be seen. Nor were his cronies.

Feeling utterly dejected, I marched around to the front of the church, ready to leave. A long lineup of people was walking up the flight of stairs, and were being greeted by a friendly-looking priest, who was passing out pamphlets, pumping hands and kissing babies. The priest came rushing down to offer me a pamphlet. He was tall and lanky, with a razor-sharp nose and impossibly green eyes safeguarded behind a pair of horn-rimmed spectacles. He had an honest face. I liked him immediately. His long, pale robes and spectacles reminded me of Rupert Giles from Buffy the Vampire Slayer, which made me like him even more. I took his pamphlet, said thank you, then turned away and walked to work. The trip was unsettling, to say the least. The sensation of being followed was efficacious. The old man was monitoring me, whispering unkind words into the crisp, autumn air that only I could hear. Hopefully his words wouldn't kill me, or make me go stark raving mad. Or both. I wished he would leave me be. But if wishes were horses, as they say. Periodically, I pretended to check my phone, in hopes of spotting him, but I didn't see him, although I could feel him breathing down my neck. This feeling stayed with me all afternoon, like a bad dream that refuses to die.

12

"Did ya hear 'bout the Midnight Rambler?"

Gordon Lester's scruffy voice snapped me from my daydream. I'd been reflecting on the disastrous Thanksgiving that just passed. With apprehension in my heart, I'd flown back to Hamilton Ontario and visited my mother.

Big mistake. Carl the lawyer was so drunk and obnoxious, he made Denny seem mildly tolerable, and that's saying a lot. Carl is certainly not my father. I miss spending Thanksgiving with Daddy. We'd watch hockey (wearing our Bruins jerseys, of course), and throw popcorn at the screen whenever the other team scored or hit one of our favorite players. Daddy would drink beer and tell me all the reasons why the Bruins were the greatest team in the history of the NHL. This Thanksgiving, on the other hand, was a complete catastrophe. I spent the entire time on defence.

Mother: Where'd you get those boobs?

Me: They grew, Mother. Breasts do that, you know?

Mother: Nah. They're fake. Fake as that smile on your face. It's just like you to spend what little money you earn on a goddamn boob job.

Me: No Mother, you're wrong.

Mother: What's next? You're moving to Hollywood?

Me: "They're real, Mother."

Denny: "Um—can I see them? Let me be the judge."

Carl: "Can't you people shut up for a change?"

Mother: "When I was your age—"

Denny: "—Pleeeeease. Just one peek."

I looked up. Gordon was sitting on his usual barstool, reading his newspaper. His gray knitted sweater was holding on by its last thread. His messy hair coupled with his droopy eyes made him look more like a poetry professor than an aging rocker.

"Look here," he said. "You read this yet, Nora darling?"

I shook my head, poured his Sam Addams. He wasn't yet drunk, but certainly on his way. He clutched the glass with both hands and drank, savouring every drop.

"Look here. They show every place the Rambler hit. Where and when."

He went to hand me the newspaper, but dropped it instead. He left it on the floor and reached for his pint. Kate came over and placed her order: four pints, a cosmopolitan and two glasses of white wine.

"Did ya hear?" Gordon shouted across the bar to Kate. "The Rambler hit another house on the weekend. Sunday night, in fact. Poor woman woke up with the creep beside her in bed. How the hell he gets away with it in this day and age…"

Gordon downed his beer and motioned for another. He sat upright, looking me up and down.

"Tell me, Nora. How'd yer tits get so big? I mean, they weren't that big before. Not even close. Now, don't get the wrong impression, darlin'. I don't mind. I'm just askin' cuz we'd all like to know."

"Why?" I batted my eyes sexily. "Do you like them?"

There was no use hiding or denying them anymore. My breasts were nearly as large as Kate's, and that's saying a lot. Gordon went as red as wine, all the while nodding in favor. He grabbed his beer and turned to the man sitting next to him.

"Did ya hear 'bout the Midnight Rambler? The woman said he was wearing a black ski mask. Shoulda pulled it off his big fat head, and socked it to him. That's what I woulda done."

He dropped his glass; it shattered. The barflies shouted "OPA!" then returned to their conversations as if nothing had happened. As I swept up the broken glass, Gordon's words danced in my brain. Especially the part about the black ski mask.

Had I heard him correctly? What the hell was going on here? By now, the barflies were gathered around Gordon, who was clearly enjoying the attention. The volume of his voice increased as he spoke.

"Apparently, he likes them older women. At least he ain't no pedo. But still. He's a dead man. The Rambler's on the loose, folks. Everybody's talkin' 'bout it."

Just then, a group of men wearing hard hats and heavily soiled work boots stepped inside the bar, and went straight to the back corner. One man, presumably the foreman, approached the bar, rubbing his hardened hands on his well-worn jeans. He was tall, tanned and ruggedly handsome. He opened his mouth to speak, looked at my chest, then did a double take.

"Jugs!" he proclaimed.

I rolled my eyes. He looked to be about forty, and as tough as a hockey player.

"What can I get ya?"

"Jugs!"

"Hey," I snapped. "My eyes are up here." That shirt couldn't come quick enough.

The construction worker took a wad of cash from his wallet and tossed me a fifty.

"Two jugs" he said, with a shit-eating grin. "Keep the change."

He took the beer back to his table, having a good laugh as he did. When Kate took their food orders, they started chanting, "JUGS. JUGS. JUGS." One of the men started pointing at me. He handed Kate some cash.

"Um," Kate said to me a moment later, holding two twenties. "They want a pic of us together."

"Why not? At least they paid for it."

I came out from behind the bar and approached the men and the table. I put my arm around Kate. The men huddled around us. The foreman produced his phone, aimed his camera strategically, then told us to say: 'Jugs'.

Kate flashed me her bright green eyes.

"Boobsy Twins."

By the time December rolled around, Kate and I had become a thing of legend. We were on top of the world, making tons of cash and having a good time doing so. Yet, as much as I was enjoying my new found glory, and I most certainly was, I knew things wouldn't end well. Yes, my breasts have grown considerably over the past few months, but the rest of me needs to catch up. Unforeseen problems were arising. Mainly, I could barely stand up straight; and when I did, my body was absurdly disproportional. I was beginning to look like a cartoon character. That, and my back felt like someone slugged me with a sledgehammer.

Out of curiosity, I googled 'rapid breast increase' and was bombarded with porn. Better refine the search. I adjusted the settings on my search engine and tried again, but to no avail; nothing but boobs.

This was getting ridiculous. I tried another approach. I typed 'Boston wizard casts spell' and hit enter: basketball and Harry Potter. Lastly, I tried 'Boston creeper', and what came up? Plants. This was proving more difficult than expected.

Mr. Jimmy, who was carefully adjusting his posture, yawned, then returned to his afternoon nap. I made coffee, then plunked myself in front of my iPad, trying to find anything on the old man in the hat. I googled 'old man in hat': 34,079 photos emerged. This is going to require more thought. Where have I seen him before?

Answer: in front of the old church. What if I google the church? First, I'll have to remember its name. I had no clue. They all looked the same to me. I googled 'Boston churches' and over three thousand churches popped up. Who knew there were so many? I narrowed it down to the street; and after some sleuthing, found the church I was looking for: The Church of the Holy Cross.

According to Wikipedia, The Church of the Holy Cross was Boston's oldest Catholic church. It was completed in 1843, rebuilt in 1889 and again in 1947, after being destroyed by fire. There was too much yet not enough to go on. I was searching for ghosts. The more I searched, the more my anxiety skyrocketed. My best bet would be to go back to the church and keep poking around. I mean, what else could go wrong?

I checked the Sunday mass schedule. There was an early mass and a late mass; needless to say, I chose the latter. As I was heading out the door, I noticed something poking out of my purse. It was the newspaper clipping from Gordon's newspaper. Something made me dust it off and put it away for later. I stuck it next to the To Do list (which was empty), then headed out the door. Time for church.

The day was basement-damp. I trekked along the busy Back Bay sidewalks shivering and complaining, convincing myself how much better off I'd be at home, curled up next to my orange kitty, drinking coffee. Walking was becoming increasingly difficult. My back and feet hurt all the time.

When I reached the church, I took a moment to really look at it. It was stunning. How many times have I walked past it, never once stopping to take in its breathtaking architecture? (Italian Renaissance, according to the plaque at the bottom of the stairs.)

A crowd was chatting amongst themselves while they waited to enter: mothers and daughters dressed in their Sunday dresses, standing beside men in simple suits and warm jackets; teenage girls wearing expensive-looking headphones acting unimpressed, while the boys were fidgeting with their devices, bored silly. Somewhere a baby was crying. At the back of the line, a group of haggard-looking men were sneaking sips from a brown paper bag. I checked to see if the old man in the hat was one of them. He wasn't. I'm not leaving without talking to him, I scolded myself. He did this to me, he can fix me.

Feeling like a lost dog, wondering what my next move should be, I was approached by an elderly woman with lovely white hair.

"Excuse me Miss. Are you waiting in line?"

"Um—no—well, maybe."

I didn't know what to say. I certainly couldn't tell her I was looking for some tramp who jinxed me.

"Well then," she said, thoughtfully. "Why not join me? Lord knows I could use the company." She motioned me with her cane.

I introduced myself, then scoured the lineup, looking for the old man.

"Nora Murphy? Well, that's a fine name. My name is Mrs. Connolly. But please, call me Mary."

I shook her hand, which was wrapped in a white glove.

"Pleased to meet you, Mary." I was distracted, and felt guilty about it.

"I've been coming to this church all my life," she told me, matter-of-factly. "Once you get to be my age, you realize how precious life is. Yes suh."

She was clinging to my arm as the line edged closer to the entrance. Her perfume reminded me of my dear old grandmother, who passed away shortly after my father. I glanced over my shoulder, looking for the old man in the hat.

What would I say to him?

I didn't know. That was too far ahead. As we slowly ventured up the stairs, I found myself face to face with the priest. He greeted Mrs. Connelly in a way that suggested they were age-old friends.

"Mrs. Connelly! How wonderful to see you." His voice hinted at an Irish accent, his grin wide and handsome. He studied me briefly, then he stretched out a sizable hand. "Greetings Miss. And welcome. I am Father McCleary. It is my pleasure to formally meet you."

We shook hands. I smiled politely, then I followed Mrs. Connelly inside the church, where again I was struck by its grandiose architecture.

The timeworn walls were lit with large crimson candles; slivers of yellow light sprinkled through the magnificent multi-colored stained-glass windows, depicting saints and sinners from a time long ago. The poppy-red carpet, which led to the altar at the center of the church, was being trampled upon as the churchgoers found their seats in the pews. Directly above the altar was the cross of Jesus Christ; his pale and burdened eyes gazed over the congregation. The church choir, clad in ashen robes, were singing soft and sweetly, while their conductor flapped about like some prehistoric bird. To say I was feeling overwhelmed would be a gross understatement.

Mrs. Connelly removed her gloves and dipped her short, veiny fingers into a four-foot-high ceramic bowl that smelled like a swimming pool. I noticed others doing the same.

"Holy water," she whispered; then she led me to the front of the church, where she knelt and made the sign of the cross before entering the pew. I tried my best to imitate her, but I was beginning to feel like an impostor.

I scanned the room for the old man. How was I supposed to spot him sitting up here at the front? Things weren't going as planned. Anger was setting in.

"You know," Mrs. Connelly said. "I've been coming to this here church for over eighty years. Now, that's a long time."

She coughed, pulled out a pink handkerchief from her purse and blew her nose.

"Yes suh. Long before you were even a twinkle in your dear mother's eyes. The world was a different place back then, you know. My father served in the 11th Airborne Division during the war. He was a brave man. Mom would bring me and my two brothers here every week. I was baptized here, you know. I was even married here, if you can believe it?"

She had a voice that could soothe a baby. Her eyes were an ocean of secrets. I liked her, even though she was distracting me from my goal. How was it that I found myself inside the church in the first place? Things were spiraling out of control.

"Oh, how I love Father McCleary. He says this church is special. And he is correct. It is special. Oh, the stories I could tell you, Miss Murphy." She found a Kleenex, dabbed her eyes, then looked up. "Oh, it looks as though we're ready."

She placed a cold, crinkled hand over mine; the organist started pumping chords, everyone rose. I was the last to stand. Father McCleary emerged from the back of the isle, then journeyed to the altar. He motioned everyone to sit.

I was becoming unnerved. My stomach was in knots. What the hell was I doing here? What did I expect to happen? That God Herself would come down from behind the clouds and save me? I didn't think so. I strongly considered leaving, but Mrs. Connelly's grip on my hand tightened. My attempts at sneaking glances around the church proved impotent. Reluctantly, I gave up and followed along as best I could. When in Rome, right? I mouthed along to hymns, stood and sang, pretending to pray. I shouted 'Amen' at what I hoped were the appropriate times.

Meanwhile, the priest delivered his sermon with great fervor, his congregation clinging to his every word.

"For todays sermon, we shall discuss envy. Thomas Aquinas once described envy as follows: Envy is sorrow at another's good. And, we can see this to be true. Proverbs 14:30 states: A heart at peace giveth life to the body, but envy rots the bones." The priest raised his arms high above his head, and his parishioners cried out: "Amen". The light seeping through the stained-glass window gave him a ghost-like aura. "Yes, envy is indeed deadly and will destroy your soul, body and life. And before it takes your soul to the lake of fire, it will pervert your thinking, torture your mind, ruin your health, consume your body, wreck your reputation and thus, destroy your life." A murmur spattered throughout his congregation. "Let me read to you now a passage from 1 Corinthians 13:4: Love is patient, love is kind. It does not envy, it does not boast, it is not proud. Therefore, love is the answer to all your daily problems."

It was as though the priest was speaking directly to me. I'd been so consumed with bitterness and envy, begrudging Kate and all the attention she was getting, that I'd destroyed my inner peace. I'd become a bitch. Always comparing myself to others. And perversely, I was starting to miss my former self. I liked who I was. Now look at me: I'm cursed. I'd gotten exactly what I deserved. I could imagine my father shaking his head at me, saying, "You got yourself into this mess Princess, you'll get yourself out of it."

At some point in the service, the worshippers stood and walked single file toward the front of the church and let the priest put pocket-sized pieces of bread onto their tongues. Mary insisted I follow her. I did. I ate the Body of Christ, or the Host as she called it. It needed salt, maybe some hummus for dipping. The altar servers started passing out large wicker baskets, into which people were shoving money by the pocketful. Mrs. O'Connell produced a weathered pouch from her handbag and tossed in a handful of bills. I asked if they took Interac.

As the mass concluded, I congratulated myself for having not embarrassed myself with my ineptitude. The people departed the church in slow, thoughtful movements, whispering amongst themselves. Mrs. Connelly kept quiet as we headed toward the exit.

Outside, people were gathering in groups along the sidewalk, exchanging emails and soup recipes, conversing and telling stories. It was all so picturesque. This was not the belligerent crowd I was accustomed to. I helped Mrs. O'Connell down the long flight of stairs, keeping an eye out for the old man. I was about to thank her for her company, when I saw him. He was standing with his entourage, huddled in a tight circle, chinwagging.

We locked eyes. I could feel the hatred sweltering off him as his pasty lips stretched into a scowl, his eyes cunning like a fox. He removed his pork pie hat and started twirling it like a magician, letting it dance through his fingers at impossible speeds. Immediately, his vile voice invaded my mind like a thief in the night:

BIGGER IS BETTER, DEARY? YES. BIGGER IS BETTER!"

A shock raced through me, like when your microphone zaps you when you sing into it. I had to gather my strength, then I shot him a look that said bring it on.

Big mistake. He brought it on.

"WHAT, BIGGER ISN'T BETTER? OH MY, YOU POOR THING. WELL THEN, MAYBE I COULD DO SOMETHING ABOUT YOUR PURTY LITTLE KITTY DOWN BELOW." His eyes went to my crotch. "AND I DON'T MEAN THAT ORANGE FLUFFBALL WAITING FOR YOU AT YOUR POOR EXCUSE OF AN APARTMENT, PANCAKE MURPHY."

"Don't you look at him," Mrs. Connelly snapped, grabbing me with surprising force. "He's just a bitter old nilly willy."

"You *know* him?"

"Yes. Yes, I do. But that was a long time ago. Yes suh."

The old man's hat returned to his head. So did his smug excuse for a grin. He waved, then scurried off with his vagabonds. Mrs. Connelly watched him go with great interest.

"Good riddance to bad rubbish," she said.

With all my effort, I shrugged off that encounter; temporarily, at least. Once we found our way to the sidewalk, she started rummaging through her purse until she produced a business card. She handed it to me. It had her name and email address printed on it, as well as the phone number of her residence.

"Call me anytime, Sweetie. Lord knows I could use the company. I've been alone for quite some time now."

I took her card, befuddled, then I walked her across the street to the bus shelter, listening to her stories. She certainly had many. The old lady walked with a great sense of purpose, while letting her cane provide its much-needed support.

I wanted to hear more about her life. How does she know the old man in the hat? Was she ever cursed? Maybe I wasn't alone? I considered inviting her for a coffee, but judging from her demeanor, she intended to get back to her residence as swiftly as possible. When the bus pulled up, she kissed my cheek. I hugged her tightly, then helped her onto the city bus.

We said our goodbyes. The bus groaned in protest as it lumbered away.

As I journeyed home, I wondered if this was a chance meeting, or if our lives were intertwined? Was that all a coincidence?

How much does she know of the old man in the hat? Was she the person who could help me with this ridiculous predicament?

I didn't know the answer, but I was eager to find out.

EYES ON YOU

By: Nora Murphy

When I first laid eyes on you
A feeling crept in my heart
Yes, I knew right from the start
When I first laid eyes on you

So, I set out to make you mine
My love was honest and true
Your eyes were oceans of blue
When I first laid eyes on you

If I had all the answers
The meaning of it all
Yes, if I had all the answers
Maybe you'd stop by or call
I gave you all the love and happiness that money can buy
When I first laid eyes on you, I thought you'd be mine

That's when I gave you my heart
And a love that would always be true
A love that would last forever
Every day, I said this to you

We set the world on fire
You gave me the sun and the moon
When you said you'd love me forever

Again, I'm always the fool

If I had all the answers

The meaning of it all

Yes, if I had all the answers

Maybe you'd stop by or call

Because I gave you all the love and happiness that money
can buy;

When I first laid eyes on you, I thought you'd be mine

Time has a funny way of letting love linger on

If you come back home, one rainy day

Tell me every thing I did wrong

Because I gave you all the love and happiness that money
can buy;

When I first laid eyes on you, I thought you'd be mine

We went our separate ways

And I lost a piece of my heart

The flicker lost its spark

But when I first laid eyes on you

Now you're a face in the crowd

I'll catch a glimpse, and then you'll be gone

I'll turn and walk home alone

But when I first laid eyes on you

When I first lay eyes on you

Eyes on you

13

Cock & Fiddle Christmas parties are legendary.

Kate, who was my Secret Santa, bought me a flask with Boobsy Twins written on it. Naturally, the B's looked like boobs. When I opened the cap, it smelled of Peach Schnapps. It's safe to say the flask was empty by the end of the evening. That's when the trouble started.

I was Lesley's Secret Santa. I handed her a poorly wrapped present, unsure if she would like it or not. She loved it. I'd bought her the Buffy the Vampire Slayer series on DVD, complete with more bonus features then you can shake a wooden stake at. I was worried she might not want another DVD (her bookshelf was stacked with them), or that she'd stopped using them, but Lesley's tough-looking face broke into a thoughtful smile once she tore open the box.

As per tradition, Blaze was dressed in his sleazy Santa Claus costume, and he made damn sure we stayed plenty drunk. His mother Barbara, who owns the pub, is always generous around the holidays. This year, the staff received Bruins tickets, which were stuffed inside a thank-you card. I was thrilled.

Randy the hipster, who was working behind the bar, was doing his very best to provoke the Boobsy Twins into taking our tops off. Kate managed to turn it around on him; and by midnight, Randy was waving bottles of champagne over head, singing the Macarena in his skivvies. Kate snapped some videos, which she smeared all over TikTok. It was obvious that Kate had a thing for Randy, although I couldn't for the life of me understand why; with his tofu sandwiches and taintless man bun. But there's no accounting for taste. Besides, who was I to criticize someone else's taste in guys? Yikes! My track record speaks for itself.

In our drunken stupor, Kate pulled me and Lesley into an Uber and we rode off to the strip club, but not before giving into Randy's final request: a pic of the Boobsy Twins together in the novelty phone booth. With our bums inside the booth and our arms wrapped around each other, Kate grabbed my breasts, and we shouted: "Boobsy Twins!"

Here you go Randy, this one's for you.

Out front of Boston Manners, Girls! Girls! Girls! blinked on and off in brilliant blue neon lights; signs with ABSOLUTELY NO RECORDING DEVICES—THIS MEAN YOU! were plastered all over the walls, stalls and halls. I was terribly excited. This was my first time at a strip club, although I kept that to myself. The security checked our IDs twice before letting us in.

On our way toward the main seating area, we passed through a long corridor with several small rooms filled with lavender couches and funky lamps, where tall women in tight thongs were straddling horny college boys and beer-bellied men; pool tables and video gambling machines were placed close to the main entrance, as far from the stripper's stage as possible.

A group of guys were shooting pool, shouting over the music and high-fiving one another; one guy, sporting a wife-beater tank top that showcased a sprinkling of curly chest hair, whistled as we passed. Kate laughed and blew him a kiss. Lesley told him to take a long walk off a short pier.

A long, penis-shaped bar with pink lights running along its shaft greeted us. Small round tables ran along the large square room; bunches of men were sitting in shadows, laughing and carrying on; others were drinking alone, staring anonymously at their phones. A row of semi-private booths, where sexy strippers were enticing men into lap dances, ran along the edges of the room; and despite the guy in the Wife Beater shirt, most of the patrons (all men as far as I could tell) were well-behaved.

This, of course, was about to change.

Kate dragged us to the bar, where we ordered watered-down, overpriced drinks from a male bartender wearing a tuxedo, then she led us to the front of the stage.

"Pervert's Row," Kate declared, over the raging music. The stage was laced with florescent lights; two stripper poles and a simple chair were waiting in concupiscence. The upcoming stripper was standing beside the stage, arms crossed, arguing with the deejay. She wore leopard skin platform boots and a matching thong and bikini. She had long, curly hair, heavy makeup and lips like cherries.

Sitting next to us was a group of college boys chanting: "Show us your tits!" and flashing money like sailors on leave. Without warning, the stage filled with fog and the deejay introduced the next dancer.

"Allllllright Ladies and Germs, aaaand the rest of you. Please put your hands, and money, together for Miss Tess Tickles. That's right! Miss Tess Tickles – ya better get 'em checked out soon. Get ready to be tickled pink by this luscious lady. And remember folks, tipping is not a city in China, and she doesn't take credit. It's caaaash only. Here she comes now. Miss Tess Tickles!"

The stripper stepped up to the smoky stage. The music was atrocious. Miss Tess Tickles was struggling to dance along to it. Once she removed her bikini top, however, things started to improve. The college boys beside us were enjoying another round of Jell-O shooters. One stood up, shoved a fistful of dollars into his mouth, plopped himself onto the stage and waited, bills up. The stripper strutted over, got on all fours, and using her teardrop shaped tits, plucked those bills from his mouth.

At that moment, I realized I was a prude. As she stood up, she let her thong fall to the floor. Miss Tess Tickles was now full monte. Her long, curvy legs started wrapping themselves around the poles, much to the delight of Pervert's Row.

Kate shouted, "Look at her ass wiggle! And those abs. Phew! But don't you worry, we're hotter than she is. Boobsy Twins all the way!"

I considered asking why we hadn't gone to a male strip club, but didn't. By now, the other strippers were circling us like sharks in shallow water. A blonde with silicone balloons below her too-young-for-botoxed face approached us. She started grinding with Kate, who produced a wad of bills, and stuffed them into the stripper's cleavage. There certainly was enough room.

The deejay announced the next stripper. "Let's give it up once again for the lovely Miss Tess Tickles. Nooooow, let us prepare to be enchanted by the one and only: Bambi Does Boston. Bambi is a favorite of ours and yours, so remember folks, put your money where your mouth is, because Bambi Does Boooooston!"

The sweet sound of a motorcycle seared through the loudspeakers; except it wasn't a motorcycle, it was Mötley Crüe. I let out a good loud yelp. You gotta love a stripper who dances to rock and roll.

The song kicked into overdrive and Bambi did too. Her legs wrapped around those poles like two tongues touching; first slow and cautious, then with increasing intensity and intricacy. Soon, she was sliding up and down those poles like a circus acrobat, leaving little to our imaginations. She had breasts of Brobdingnagian proportions—obviously fake—and she worked them like a pro. One by one she removed nanoscopic strips of fabric, slowly revealing her hidden treasures to the lusting onlookers. The college boys beside us were voracious.

Lesley came back and put her arms around me and Kate; she kissed us both on the lips and said, "There. I had to get that out of the way."

She sat down next to us. Drinks immediately appeared. Without warning, Lesley was flat on her back on stage, money in her mouth.

Kate was egging her on. "Work it Girl! Work it!"

Bambi's bare breasts beat down upon Lesley's brittle face. Her money quickly disappeared. Lesley remained on stage as the next song came on: Strutter, my favorite KISS song; and then to my astonishment, Kate leapt on stage and started shaking her ass like a pro. Then she removed her top. Her freckled breasts started bouncing along to KISS, and the crowd was loving every minute of it. I felt a tinge of envy, which turned to shame, which quickly turned to alarm: I knew I'd be next.

I was.

Kate and Lesley dragged me onto the stage just as Cherry Pie came on. Kate, Lesley and Bambi Does Boston were now rubbing nipples like lovers in erotomania. The gentlemen at the back of the club were flocking to Pervert's Row, waving money, cheering us on.

We were a smash. Kate and Lesley ripped off my blouse and bra and launched them into the audience, never to be seen again. My tits looked spectacular. So did the rest of me. Men were jumping on stage, money where their mouths were, in hopes to get a closer look. We each took turns snatching their bills.

Things went downhill in a hurry.

By the end of Cherry Pie, I started feeling nauseous. I returned to my seat, alone and partially naked. I found my cardigan sweater and quickly covered up. I was considering calling an Uber, when I felt a strong hand grab my shoulder.

Billy Swanker.

The chains from his motorcycle jacket rattled as he sat down next to me. He seemed agitated.

"Jesus Christ, Nora. I never expected to see you here," he said, looking over my shoulder. "C'mon, babe, let's get you outta here, and go for a drive."

Was he following me?

"Don't worry babe, I'm sober. I wanna show you my new wheels."

He placed his hand on my thigh and squeezed. I pushed him away, then stood up and left for the restroom, passing Kate along the way. She was talking to the deejay, preparing to get up and dance. I had to stop and watch. There was no way I could miss this.

The lights dimmed, the fog machine exuded its minty mist, and Groove is in the Heart came roaring through the speakers. The deejay introduced Kate as Strawberry Fields, who then came strutting down the stage with all the confidence in the world. The college boys, blue-collar workers, businessmen, married men, scruffy old stragglers, strippers and waitresses alike watched in awe. Kate winked at me, then started shaking her thang. Once again, she was topless.

As Kate pranced about, the room started spinning. I had to leave. I forced myself to the restroom.

The ladies' room was immaculate, by far the cleanest I've ever peed in. I passed the vanity mirror and fancy towel rack, then hurried into the stall. When I stood up afterwards, I almost fell over. I felt queasy. I knew something wasn't right with me. Yes, I'd been drinking heavily, but I can handle my alcohol. I am a bartender after all. It takes more than a drink or six to knock me on my ass. I splashed water on my face and tried to convince myself I was fine, but I didn't believe it. What did Swanker do to me? I knew the answer: he drugged me.

Things were getting blurry. I could no longer see straight. My eyes were going in and out of focus, barely held open. I stumbled my way back to Billy. He finished his drink. Then with his arm firmly around my waist, he helped me out of the club, and I ended up inside a classic muscle car with bench seats as blue as a bowling alley. It was huge. It was a car you could raise a family in. It smelled of gym socks and cigarettes. Even in my semi conscious state, I knew the car was stolen.

Billy sped off, twisting and turning around tight corners, ignoring the sirens. I passed out. When I awoke, we were parked in a dark alley, hiding in the shadows of night.

Billy removed my seatbelt and immediately started groping me. I pushed him away, but his hold on me was unyielding. His hands were disobliging. There was a struggle. He yanked my hair so hard I would feel it for a week. I cried, begging him to stop. He refused. He punched me in the jaw and told me to shut up. I saw stars.

When I regained consciousness, he was kissing my neck and shoulders, wheezing like a sick puppy. My sweater had been torn to shreds. I tried pushing him away, but he persisted. I reached for my phone.

"Now now, Nora," he said, stroking my head. "You're not being a good girl tonight. I like it when you're a good girl."

I pushed him away and started thrashing about. I wanted to hurt him like he hurt me.

"Please don't fight me, Nora. Not tonight. Tonight, we can play a game. You like games, don't you? Because I do. You can play mommy. I'd like that. Would you like to be my mommy?"

He held his knife to my face. It's ugly, silver blade glistened under the gory light of the crescent moon. Its sharp edge pricked me as he pinned me down. A stream of fresh crimson blood trickled down my neck.

I struggled, but he easily overpowered me. I was horizontal with him on top of me. Black leather gloves enveloped my mouth, leaving me without air.

My body went limp, my eyes stayed shut. I stopped resisting. My mind found a cold dark place and stayed there. I barely budged as he did those terrible things to me. I regained consciousness sporadically, long enough to feel his hot, sweaty body thrusting itself in and out of mine, calling me Mommy while doing so. He was weeping. The dashboard was a pool of blood. There was too much to be just mine.

"Mommy, oh Mommy," he said over and over, keeping one hand over my mouth. At some point, his muscles spasmed and he went still. That's the last thing I remember.

The following day I woke up alone in my futon, feeling worse than ever.

14

I let the warm, foamy bath bubbles wash over my tortured body, as I lay naked and defeated in the tub.

The pain was egregious. My body felt like it had been beaten with a sledgehammer. I was a complete wreck. The shame I felt was even worse. Looking at my scars, it almost seemed fitting; me lying stark-naked in an old bathtub that Amanda dubbed my Psycho tub, seeing how it so closely resembles the bathtub from the original Psycho movie.

There were burn marks on my wrists, cuts on my arms and chest, my neck was stiff and I could hardly move my jaw. I guess I should count my blessings, though. The bastard may have drugged me, hauled me into the back of a stolen car to do unspeakable deeds, while I lay there like a beaten rug, but at least he got me home safe and sound. He even tucked me into bed. What a gentleman.

But why would he bother drugging me? Every time I see him, we wind up having sex anyway. It made no sense. Then again, neither do the scars on my tortured body. I knew he was dangerous, but never like this.

I slid the bar of Oil of Olay from the tips of my toes up to my knees, along my thighs, stopping at my breasts. I sighed. They've grown again since last night.

The damn curse, relentless in its punctuality. I leaned back and closed my eyes. My mind drifted to Tyson. Why would he break up with me? I still don't know. When I look for clues, I don't see any. We were lovers and best friends. We were soulmates. I blamed it on my tiny breasts. Could I have been wrong? Maybe, maybe not. Look at Stephanie, with her amazing T and A. I've always had the A, but never the T. Now look at me: I'm all T!

I'll need to order new bras, yet again. This was becoming a bi-weekly ritual. I don't buy them in person anymore. Amazon to the rescue. I moved my mind away from Tyson. That ship has sailed, as they say. If only my heart would let him go. I took a deep breath, releasing it into the steamy air, and let the bath bubbles sparkle and pop over my ruined body. Gradually, yet unintendedly, I succumbed to sleep.

I dreamed of nothing.

I was forced to take time off work. The bruises along my neck and shoulders made it impossible for me to show myself. I could barely speak due to my fractured jaw. Blaze was unimpressed. Fortunately, Randy had recently finished his exams and was off until the new year, so he gladly picked up the extra shifts. It's now two weeks before Christmas—the busiest time of year—and business was booming.

Kate was worried silly. She kept sending me texts asking if everything was OK. I lied and said I was fine. I wasn't. I was a wreck. Maybe some time off would do me good. My body and mind needed to heal. I spent my days sitting by the window, novel in hand, admiring the falling snow which served to cover up the leftover garbage from the dumpster in the back alley. I spent my nights watching Buffy reruns and writing songs on my acoustic guitar.

So, there I was, stuck inside at home with my orange tabby, waiting for my rape wounds to heal. It's a good thing my mother supplied me with an arsenal of homemade knitted sweaters. I now have an array of turtlenecks, cardigans, half-zip, sweater dresses, boyfriend, girlfriend, gender-neutral, oversized, undersized, cashmere, cable knit—in all the colors of the American rainbow: red, white and pink. Until my body heals, I'll stick with my turtlenecks.

I called Amanda. Amanda is the only person in the world I could count on at a time like this. When she arrived, she was clad in full goth garb: straight, jet-black hair, gaunt face, black lipstick, black collar around her neck, to go with her black lace dress and shoulder top. She studied my face. Her eyes darted to the bruises on my wrists, then to my swollen, puffy eyes.

She held out a deck of Tarot cards, looked me dead in the eyes and said, "We need answers, sister. Answers."

We turned off all the lights. I put on the Lost Boys soundtrack, while Amanda lit six black candles, positioning them in a circle around us. She shuffled her tarot deck, then placed them into three neat piles in front me. We sat cross-legged on the living room floor, facing each other, our wine glasses within reach. Mr. Jimmy sat perched atop the futon, studying the peculiar shadows dancing along my barren walls, with negligible curiosity.

Amanda closed her eyes. Her silver eyeshadow matched her sparkling fingernails. We sat in silence for longer than I thought necessary, until her eyes spontaneously opened.

She seemed different, as if in a trance. She placed her hands over the pile of cards closest to me, paused, then turned over the Three of Swords. She studied the card. The look on her face was discouraging.

"You poor thing," she muttered, more to herself than to me. "You are in a process of healing, but you are not there yet. You are still grieving. You are still learning. Look," she pointed to the heart pierced with three long daggers. "Your heart has been punctured by these three swords: words, actions and intent. Notice these dark clouds in the background, these are your worries and troubles. It appears you still have a long way to go. You mustn't cause others any more pain. That's the key. But worry not, your heart is strong and will soon heal. It will feel love and happiness again."

Amanda placed the card to her side and picked from the second pile, producing the Seven of Swords. "But in reverse," Amanda whispered. "Oh, dear Lord." She reached for her wine. "Secrets," she proclaimed. "Ahh, yes. Secrets. You have many. You are deceiving yourself and others. You must take responsibility over yourself, and your life. Start fresh, come clean. And you will. Oh yes, I believe you will. You will soon find your way back into the light."

Her voice sent chills down my spine. I was beginning to panic. I'd been expecting her to say something along the lines of, "You will find new love somewhere over the rainbow." I reached for my wine glass and dumped the contents down my throat, hoping my luck would improve with the next card.

Amanda continued. "One more card, Nora. What's it gonna be? I've never pulled two Swords cards back-to-back before. This is totally transcendent."

She closed her eyes, and took two unhurried breaths; her hands hovered over the third pile of cards, as I stared at her with dreadful anticipation. Her golden-brown eyes opened in a flash. She turned over the third card. It showed a skeleton carrying a scythe, and the number thirteen. She placed it neatly on the floor, directly in front of me, and gasped.

"What is it is?"

She just smiled and shook her head. Her eyes darted from me to the card, back to me, then to the card again. She picked up the card and kissed it sweetly with her painted lips.

"Death," she said, in a hollowed voice. "But not for you."

Amanda came out of her spell. Beads of sweat danced along her brow like melted snowflakes. Her wine glass needed filling, so I emptied the bottle and broke out another. We drank. We reminisced. We gossiped. I told her everything. I talked of the old man in the hat, and how he cursed me. I spoke of my steamy love affair with Billy Swanker, to her amusement. Not once did I mention Billy's knife. There are certain details a woman doesn't disclose, not even to her BFF.

We plotted our next course of action. Amanda wanted to learn more about my curse. Moreover, she wanted to catch that old man in the hat. I was surprised by her sudden interest, but happily agreed. I've always trusted Amanda. She has great instincts; and as it turned out, her instincts proved correct.

That devious old man played a much bigger role in all this than I could have ever imagined. Catching him, however, would prove as difficult as catching a cold in July.

The following morning, I put on a strong pot of coffee and began scrolling through Tyson's Instagram profile, knowing full well this would lead to misery.

It did. He had recently changed his profile pic from the one of him wearing the Bruins jersey I'd bought him for his birthday, to a closeup pic of him and Stephanie. She looked gorgeous, they both seemed happy. I wanted to gag. I searched through more of his photos. He had deleted all our pics. Seven years down the tubes. Was it even worth it?

I drank my coffee in bitter silence. Beside me, Mr. Jimmy griped. I tickled him under his chin. "I love you Mr. Jim Jim."

He looked up at me with his loving eyes, nudged my hand and started purring.

I began creeping Stephanie's Facebook profile, knowing full well this would also lead to misery, but not caring one bit. Stephanie Cockburn was tall, blonde and confident, with full lips and bosom. Everything about her made me angry, including her posh wardrobe. Her banner boasted a beautiful shot of her and Tyson walking hand-in-hand along the Charles River in mid-October. They gazed longingly into each other's eyes, while the autumn leaves blanketed the golden-crisp ground below them. Her profile picture was a closeup of her and Tyson; the camera strategically aimed so her cleavages would pop out of the pic. She had recently posted a picture of the two of them at the protest. She was holding that sign of the penis with the strike through it. I had a good chuckle at that. Then I moved on.

I was in the process of turning off this insidious device, when I came across some breaking news:

Midnight Rambler Strikes Again!

Another woman has been sexually assaulted, in a string of home burglaries that has been shocking the Greater Boston area since July. Dubbed the Midnight Rambler, the perpetrator, who has been sneaking into women's bedrooms in the middle of the night, has assaulted his latest victim, making this number six. The incident took place in the wee hours of Monday, December 14.

A woman in her 30's claims she awoke to a man masturbating beside her. He had been using his phone to take pictures of himself as she slept. The woman awoke, screamed, then kicked him off her bed. She called 911, The perpetrator stole some jewelry, before escaping through her window, disappearing into the night. He was wearing a black ski mask and gloves and a black jacket.

Authorities suspect the culprit has had no prior history with this victim. According to police chief Reggie Lewis, "His victims appear to be unrelated. Although, he knows when they are alone and when they are asleep. Clearly, this perp does his homework."

Chief Lewis claims they now have a better description of the perpetrator (sketch below). The suspect is a white male, approximately 20-35 years old, between 5'7-5'10"; roughly 170 lbs. Police are urging residents to keep their windows and doors locked at all times.

The first reported assault took place in Medford, Massachusetts, Wednesday July 8, at 1 a.m.

I stood up too quickly and almost tumbled. My mind was on overdrive. My neck and shoulders were still aching, so I popped another Tylenol in my mouth, washing it down with cold coffee. This was going to be a rough week. I looked over at my cat, who was pining for my attention. Mr. Jimmy labored toward his food dish and started meowing long and mournfully.

"You sure know how to play hungry," I told him, carrying a bag of his favorite treats.

I sighed. My apartment was beginning to smell worse than a freshman dorm. It was time for a purge. I formed a plan: First, I'd get rid of all this garbage, then pick my clothes up off the floor and pile them in the hamper, run them to the laundry room and throw them into the machine; then I'll sweep, mop, tidy, dust, wipe countertops and maybe, just maybe, prepare myself my own fancy feast.

It's not often I get this much time to myself; and judging from the look and smell of my apartment, it was well needed.

As I swept the floor, I came across Gordon Lester's newspaper clipping. It had fallen behind the refrigerator. The entire page, which had a large boot print plastered on it, was dedicated to the Midnight Rambler.

Having spent the last seven years in Boston, I've become desensitized to these types of stories. Seen one, seen 'em all. I read the article, which listed each assault in order up to that point:

Wednesday July 8, 1:00 a.m., South End

Monday July 19, 12:45 a.m., South End

Friday August 14, 1:05 a.m., Mission Hill

Wednesday September 23, 12:15 a.m., Back Bay

Monday October 26, 1:45 a.m., Belmont

I studied these dates, looking for a pattern. Finally, I spotted it. Because the incidents took place after midnight, the dates changed. The actual day—at least in Nora's World—would be the night before. For me, Wednesday July 8 at 1 a.m. is really Tuesday night. I pulled out my calendar on my phone. What was I doing that day? Working, of course. I flipped through my journal lying next to my acoustic guitar. Yes, just as I suspected: that was the night I was first greeted by no other than Billy Swanker.

Roll back Monday July 19 to Sunday and voila! Billy Swanker. According to my scrappy notes, that was also the same night I was visited by the old man in the hat. Was this a coincidence? I didn't know. Friday August 14: same. All the dates matched. Billy Swanker, it would seem, has been creeping into women's bedrooms, doing God knows what to them, then fleeing to my shithole apartment so I can finish him off.

Gross. I circled back to the internet and checked another date, already knowing what I'd find. Billy Swanker's latest outing occurred a mere six blocks from the strip club, while I was there.

The swanky bastard. Was that why he went to the strip club in the first place? Because he knew I'd be there? If so, how did he know?

Then I figured it out: Randy had tagged me in a pile of posts that night, including the pic he took of the infamous Boobsy Twins staring lustfully at the camera, my breast in Kate's freckled hand. How classy. To make matters worse, in Randy's final post that evening, he tagged me and Kate and Lesley as we headed out to the strip club. (That lamewad hadn't even gone with us, FFS.)

Billy Swanker was stalking me on social media.

Why was I surprised?

I promised myself I wouldn't cry anymore, not for me, not for Billy Swanker, not for Tyson, nor for my father (well, maybe for Daddy). I'll stick with playing music. If there's one good thing about being a musician, even a part-timer like myself, it's that it's a healthy outlet. It gives a gal something to occupy her mind and hands with. A musician can get those pesky feelings out in song, while exploring the strange and uncomfortable aspects of life at the same time.

It's how I express myself. It helps me deal with stress. Susie St. Marie has been introducing me to a wide range of notable American songsters including Dolly Parton, Lucinda Williams, Ray Wylie Hubbard (whom she claims revealed to her the meaning of life at an all-you-can-eat sushi buffet in Lubbock, one night after a gig; something to do with how to play a proper E chord); and her favorite artist of all time: Patsy Cline. There is so much beautiful music coming from this great country it can be overwhelming trying to keep track of it all.

My Gibson J-45 lets me do whatever I want to her, so I tuned her up and started fiddling around with some blues licks. I started picking some nasty grooves. Once I started, they kept coming. I wrote a meaty-beaty blues thing. I'm not great with a flatpick (that's why I play bass) but my fingerstyle is respectable. Trish has given me a few lessons and they've clearly paid off. One hour later, I managed to scratch out another tune; one quite different than its predecessor.

It was a weepy little thang, with a sweeping melody, about Tyson. Sort of. Although some of my songs are based on actual events, I allow them to take on a life of their own. Give them wings to sail on. Writing songs is unlike any other experience. That's why I spend so much time playing my acoustic guitar. Bass is what I do professionally. At home, it's my acoustic.

Once I put the guitar away, I went right back to worrying. I've got Christmas with my mother coming up, which isn't brightening my mood one bit. I'll need to be better prepared this time. Last year's Family Christmas gathering was a disaster. The highlights being when Mother got so drunk, she ended up face-first in the punchbowl; and when Denny left with his methhead girlfriend, and managed to lose his phone and keys and wallet. Incidentally, he was locked out of the house for the night.

The cops showed up at our front door sometime after 6 a.m. with Denny in handcuffs. His eyes resembled Mother's poinsettias. Apparently, he was found sleeping in our neighbors shed, doused in gasoline, his pockets lined with various narcotics. He had no ID, and his girlfriend was MIA.

But enough about my disreputable family. I can worry about them soon enough. It's time I start putting together my broken pieces. Starting right here, right now. It's time I clean my apartment, once and for all.

Night's Long Gone

By: Nora Murphy

Tiny holes in this knotted heart

Make room for despair

I should have known right from the start

But I didn't have a care

I was young and innocent

The girl with the dark brown eyes

You came along, heaven-sent

I guess, I should have realized

We were sliding toward the stars in the sky

By the glow of the setting sun

Keeping warm under the moon, so bright

I lived my whole life in one night

I lived my whole life in one night

I lived my whole life in one night

Now the night's long gone

Night's long gone

I remember walking through the park

On that endless summer day

You taught me how to fly a kite

We got caught out in the rain

NORA'S CURSE / Marcus Starr

You gave me your coat, to keep my dry
While you shivered in the cold
We held hands to pass the time
You said you'd never let me go

We were sliding toward the stars in the sky
By the glow of the setting sun
Keeping warm under the moon, so bright
I lived my whole life in one night
I lived my whole life in one night
I lived my whole life in one night
Now the night's long gone
Night's long gone

Be careful what you wish for, friends
You may get it in the end
Sunny days don't last forever
And hearts won't always mend
You only get one chance, so make it right
Your world may disappear
Beginnings never last too long, the end is always near

We were sliding toward the stars in the sky
By the glow of the setting sun
Keeping warm under the moon, so bright
You live your whole life in one night

We live our whole lives in one night

I lived my whole life in one night

Now the night's long gone

Night's long gone

Night's long gone

Night's long gone

15

Downtown Boston was a winter wonderland.

People bundle under warm coats and wool hats and thick socks and strong boots, as they headed out to the shopping conglomerates to purchase presents for their loved ones.

Winter neutralizes. It stops you dead in your tracks. Then you cast away all the extra earnings you've managed to scrape up that year and spend it on thoughtful junk.

Yes, it was beginning to look a lot like Christmas.

I spent Christmas alone, while my mother and Denny flew with Carl to the Bahamas for the week. I pictured them peeling bananas and sipping Pina Coladas on the beach, rubbing suntan oil on each other's backs, laughing and carrying on, while I sat at home, eating cold turkey from a can, drinking beer, watching the snow squall from my one and only window; all the while, my cat snoring softly beside me, dreaming his little cat dreams, without a care in the world.

It was a holiday for the ages. Mr. Jimmy, much to his chagrin, wore his brightly-knitted Christmas sweater and antlers long enough for me to snap some pics. Then he shot me a look that said 'Never again.'

The highlight of the evening was when I posted a cute pic of us wearing our matching holiday sweaters on Instagram. @BigBadVoodooDaddy commented: id like 2 stuff ur stockings full of my xmas cheer; @RacerDude said: call me santa and lemme cum down ur chimney anytime; my favorite was from @dildodude: yo nice pussy ho ho ho.

Tomorrow is Boxing Day. My first day back to work since being assaulted. Fortunately, my scars healed quickly. My mind, on the other hand, was still heavy with burden.

I'd been having recurring nightmares of that awful night in that awful car. Except in my dreams, Billy ends up killing me, slowly and methodically, carving me into little pieces with his switchblade knife.

My apartment was in ship-shape, which was encouraging, and I was allowing myself some much-needed rest. After watching It's a Wonderful Life for the one hundredth time, I curled up in a ball with Mr. Jimmy, and listened to the final John Prine album. A classic. I dozed off, only to be startled awake by my nagging phone.

Billy Swanker.

"Hey babe. Thanks for answering. I need to talk."

"Um, excuse me?"

"You're lucky I saved you last week. I think those college kids spiked your drink."

I was flabbergasted, speechless.

"Anyway, I wouldn't go to that place again if I were you. It's not safe. I'm surprised it hasn't been shut down."

"You asshole. I hate you." I started bawling.

"Well, I don't blame you. Anyway, I'm just calling to wish you a Merry Christmas. And to thank you for always being there for me."

Silence.

"Um—and to tell you that my mother died. Brain hemorrhage. On Christmas fucking morning, no less. I just got back from the hospital. I guess I won't be seeing her again until the funeral."

Now it was his turn to cry.

"Hey Billy, I'm sorry to hear that, but—"

"—I know I had no right to get so rough with you the other night. I don't know what comes over me sometimes. I really like you, Nora. Like, really like you. The girls my age are different, you know? I was hoping we could start dating, or something. That is, unless you're seeing someone new."

My mind was full of questions, but I couldn't catch any of them, so I threw the phone onto my bed, and started pulling my hair out in clumps.

All the while, Billy kept talking. I put him on speakerphone and listened to him grovel. As he was yammering on, an idea occurred to me. It was dangerous, but it just might work: I'll meet up with him in public, where it's safe; then after getting him good and drunk, I'll coax him into a confession. That way I'd know, without a shadow of a doubt, that he really was the infamous Midnight Rambler.

"I'll think about it," I said. "And I'm sorry about your mother. I know what you're going through. I remember when my father passed." That's if you're telling the truth, I wanted to add, but didn't.

"Great! Take your time. I'm starting a new job next week, as a telemarketer. But don't you worry," he chuckled. "I'll make sure your number stays off the list."

Damn you, Billy Swanker. How could I possibly be smiling right now?

But I was. He was the only person who took the time to call me on Christmas Day, although I did receive numerous text messages, GIF's, emojis and short videos. Amanda sent a GIF of the Grinch wearing a lit-up holiday sweater, trying to act sexy. To her, this was funny. I replied with a tailor-made GIF of Justin Bieber wearing a Santa hat in his birthday suit. To me, this was funny.

"You should come to the pub for New Year's Eve," I told him. "The Nashville Runaways are playing. I could probably get you a free drink or two."

"Deal! Thanks, babe. You don't know how much that means to me. Listen, I gotta run. I have to call my entire extended family and tell them the news. Merry fucking Christmas indeed."

He hung up.

I rolled over onto my side and closed my eyes. If I dwelled on this, it would destroy me. How come the only person who called me on Christmas Day was the very person who raped me? A potential serial rapist, no less. Has my life sunk so low? I've always been one to bury my feelings; cast them away to some secret island, where they can fester and rot unnoticed and unmolested. Out of sight, out of mind. This helped after Daddy passed away; likewise, with all those bullies at school. Those were rough years. I couldn't leave town soon enough. Still, I had to find out what's up with Billy. I had to know if he really was the Midnight Rambler, as unlikely as that may be.

Finally, as these thoughts began to rip my mind apart, I slept.

Alone on Christmas. No happy song has ever been written about being alone on Christmas. My life was spiraling out of control. I was a racehorse running rampant off the track. My heart was a glass house, shattered; no one, sadly, to pick up the broken pieces.

My heart was miles from mending. Because of this, I've tried to forgive myself, as best I could, for the events that would soon unfold. Life is unfair, unjust. It catches you at your most vulnerable, and exploits your weaknesses. It rips your heart from your chest, and then it hands it back to you on a silver platter, steely knives and silvery forks to stab the bloody thing with. Yes, I've made many mistakes.

Asking Billy Swanker to join me on New Year's Eve was the single worst idea of my life.

16

Boxing Day at the Cock & Fiddle was as exciting as getting a Brazilian wax, while hungover.

Maggie had decorated the pub with multi-colored Christmas balls, wreaths, poinsettias, ribbons, garland, mistletoe, the whole nine yards. I was working at the North Pole.

Much to my surprise and delight, Mrs. Connelly stopped in for dinner with some of her nursing home friends.

They certainly were a spicy crew.

"Holy Mother of Jesus, would you get a load of those gerber servers!" one of them said, while marching to her table. I couldn't help but laugh. I'd thought I'd heard them all by then, but apparently not. I brought over five glasses of water, then wiped off their table.

Initially, Mrs. Connelly didn't recognize me; she looked up at me, studied my face for a moment, then smiled.

"Oh, why hello! Nora, is it? Yes, yes. Miss Nora Murphy. Oh, I'm getting so bad these days. But when you reach my age, you'll understand why."

She introduced me to her friends: Gertrude Oliver was clearly the eldest (and cutest), all four-foot-nine of her. She was all wrinkles and smiles. Linda McNeil was sitting next to her; she had orange hair, permed, bright lipstick and a Christmas sweater to match. Abigail Martin, a feisty Latino lady with auburn hair and dazzling dark eyes, looked to be the youngest of the bunch.

Roger Huckabee, the lone male, was tall, thin and morose; he sat moodily in the corner, refusing to make eye contact with anyone.

They ordered coffees and hors d'oeuvres. Clearly, they had never tried our coffee before, it could peel the paint off a rusted bicycle. They sat in the front area, and were speaking louder than they realized, which made it easy for me to listen in.

"Do you know that Cathy Tankard is a lesbian?"

"What? No."

"Why, yes. She is. She really is."

"That can't be true. She was married to—oh, you know—I forget his name."

"Buddy."

"Yes! Buddy. She was married to Buddy for over fifty years."

"That may be correct. But I know."

"Why don't they play better Christmas music here?"

"Christmas was better back in our day."

A chorus of agreements.

"It was still called Christmas!"

Another chorus of agreements.

"Not like today. You can't even say the word without offending somebody."

Roger finally piped in. "All you ladies do is complain and gossip. Can't you talk about anything interesting? Like the Sox? They're looking to have a great season—"

"—Oh, stuff it, Roger. Nobody here cares about baseball."

"My Paul used to love baseball. He was a Yankees fan."

"Well, nobody's perfect," Roger grumbled.

"Who's the dame behind the bar, Mary. The one with the big—"

"—Oh, that's Nora Murphy. She's a dear. I met her at church."

Upon hearing my name, I went over and topped up their coffees. Mrs. Connelly tugged my sweater and asked when I'd be attending church again, saying how she could really use the company. I was not prepared for this question, so I dodged it, all the while trying to ignore my nagging conscience. I really should go back, if for no other reason than to check up on the old man with the hat. I'll have to face him again sooner or later. Sooner would be better.

Abigail ordered a glass of white wine, spilled almost the entire glass, then insisted on cleaning it herself. I politely refused. When I bent over to wipe up the mess, my breasts bumped the topsy table, spilling the remainder of her glass all over her lap. This was a new low. My breasts had destroyed my equilibrium.

"Oh dear, if they're that big now what'll happen when she reaches our age?" Abigail asked, in a too-loud-for-a-whisper voice.

That question hadn't occurred to me. I was still too young to consider old age. I pushed that image away, along with my mounting anxiety, and went back to the bar and poured her another glass of wine. At that moment, a Christmas song came roaring from the jukebox: Baby it's Cold Outside, featuring Louis Armstrong and Ella Fitzgerald.

"Ooh, I love this song!"

"My Pappa used to know Louis Armstrong."

"Yeah right. He probably knew Neil Armstrong as well."

"Yup, him too!"

Although it was her day off, Kate arrived to fill out some paperwork. She came flying over and hugged me and kissed me and asked how everything was. She looked concerned. I told her everything was fine.

I made up a lie and she pretended to believe it, but her look of concern never wavered. She handed me a Christmas card, signed by her family. When I opened it, a Dunkin' gift card fell out.

"From my parents," she said, without impertinence. She said she was stoked to see the Nashville Runaways perform on New Year's Eve; and how she would love to sing Baby it's Cold Outside with the band, with Gordon Lester as the special guest. This sounded better-than-good to me.

"You'll have to check with Susie. She's the boss. I'm merely the bass player."

"Oh, I already asked her," she said, blushing. "She just rolled her eyes and walked away."

That didn't surprise me. Susie may be one of the most incredible performers in the Hub, but she could be pretty darn cruel when she wants to be, especially to amateurs, and even more so to busty, young redheads.

"Don't worry, I'll talk to her. Besides, Gordon's a legend around here. If he says it's cool. It's cool."

Kate, clearly relieved, sat down at the bar and ate her grinder (or what normies call a submarine sandwich). I poured her a fresh pint; I was about to check up on another table, when she sprang a loaded question on me. One I was getting used to by now.

"Um, Nora, your boobs are fabulous, don't get me wrong— but—um—tell me: what's the deal? Are they actually real? Oh gosh, I can't believe I just asked you that."

"Real as rain," I said, rolling my eyes.

I lumbered over to a table where a man in a brown suit was giving me a hearty look. I took his order: a bottle of Bud light and a plate of calamari with garlic bread. Yikes, I'd hate to be his partner.

A smattering of Boxing Day shoppers peppered into the pub; one fine gentleman, sporting a beard worthy of ZZ Top, ordered a pint of Sam Addams for himself and a glass of white wine for his partner. He paid with a $50 bill and told me to keep the change. You gotta love the holidays.

When I returned to Mrs. Connelly's table, they were arguing about the Midnight Rambler.

"He's a dirty old man who can't get it up without a hundred-dollar pill," Linda shouted, to a chorus of agreement.

"Nuh uh," Roger piped in. "He's young and sprout. Has to be. To do all that creeping about."

"Maybe he's a cop."

"I heard the Boston Strangler was a cop."

"Nuh uh. You're thinking of Jack the Ripper."

"Nonsense!"

They stopped arguing when I arrived with the bill. They stared at me as if I had the answer. Maybe I did. As I was asking whether they needed anything else, the temperature in the room dropped. Someone, or something, was rustling in the back of my mind:

BIGGER IS BETTER, DEARY?

My face went numb. I turned. There he was, peering through one of the big bay windows from outside. The old man in the hat. A square patch of fog bordered his carved-up face, which was pressed against the frosted glass. His lips pursed into a snarl. His eyes were venomous. When he raised his hand, electricity coursed through me.

ZAP. My body buckled. I would have collapsed, if not for the table. Another glass of wine spilled. My nose was dripping blood. For a moment, time stood still; I was lost in the void.

When I regained my composure and looked up, the old man glowered, tipped his hat, then vanished.

"You keep clear of him." Mrs. Connelly said, tugging on my sweater. "He's no good. No suh. He's no good for anyone. Believe you me."

She knew more than she was letting on. I wanted to ask her some questions, but there was no time. Besides, I had to clean up the mess. Also, I was trying my best not to cry. The old man hurt me good. My innards were nuked. I needed to sit down and rest, but couldn't. There's no rest for a bartender.

I wiped the blood from my nose, while they gathered their purses and coats and hats and scarves and mittens.

Mrs. Connelly asked me again about meeting her for church this coming Sunday.

"It's the first mass in 2020," she boasted.

I agreed, but under one condition, she would have coffee with me afterwards. My treat.

"You have yourself a deal, Miss Murphy."

She placed a furrowed hand on my arm and squeezed. Her eyes were as blue as an open sky. She let go. I ordered them an Uber. Within minutes the driver poked his head into the pub, and they left, but not without wishing me a Merry Christmas.

An attractive young woman, dressed as though it was a sunny afternoon on the beach, entered as they left, and went on to order bangers and mash, which Steve burned to a crisp. She left without tipping; and would go on to leave an appalling review on Tripadvisor, which included the size of my—and I quote— knockers.

The rest of my evening consisted of chopping limes, wiping counter tops, clearing tables, pouring pints, changing kegs, taking orders, laughing at jokes (some actually quite funny), wishing others a Merry Christmas and/or Happy Holidays, ignoring lewd comments, returning uncooked fish (apparently Steve was having a bad day, even for him), serving hot food and cold drinks, making money.

At the end of the night, after counting my tips, managing the inventory, balancing the till, restocking the bar, cleaning the glasses, organizing the cutlery and enjoying a couple pints of Sam Addams, I closed up and called for an Uber for myself this time.

I was eager to get home. My back and feet were throbbing.

Worse, I couldn't get the old man out of my head. I worried about the cancer I would surely acquire, being zapped by that miserly old tramp. I hate it when he does that to me. I'm like a hotdog in a microwave, cooked too long. How he does it, I don't know.

Somewhere, Kate called out to me, pulling me away from my disparaging thoughts.

"Nora."

She must have snuck in through the back door. She rushed over and hugged me and kissed my cheeks. We were standing next to the immemorial phone booth, underneath the mistletoe.

She looked me squarely in the eyes. "I'm worried about you. We need to get together soon. Just the two of us. We can go to Dunks. I'll help you spend that gift card."

"How about New Year's Day? We'll hit up Washington Street. One of the Dunks should be open."

"Yes! And we're both off."

"It's a date."

We shook hands, making it official.

"Just the two of us," she reiterated.

"The Boobsy Twins."

She stuck out her tongue, gave me the peace sign, then left.

Those were the last words Kate ever spoke to me.

17

The Nashville Runaways were set to perform until 3 a.m., counting in the new year with over a hundred of our favorite townies.

Behind the kit was Danny Boy Gallagher, arguably the finest drummer in all of Massachusetts. Danny is the most normal musician I've ever known. He is happily married to a gorgeous Asian woman named Lauren; with two bouncing babies, twins: Rayden and Rhianna. If only I was attracted to men like Danny.

My plan of coaxing Billy Swanker into a late-night confession proved futile. I should've expected this. We barely spoke. The pub was packed like sardines. People were coming and going all night. In fact, the entire Back Bay district was swarming with partygoers and pub crawlers jumping from pub to pub, doing God knows what else. Kate was expected to join us on stage, but it never happened. I never even got a chance to speak with her. I was sidetracked the entire night.

The band played incredibly tight, diving into deep jams of musical exploration. Susie was electric. On top of her game. In fact, Susie St. Pierre had them all on their feet and dancing on tables, whooping and hollering and singing along to almost every song. Naughty Taughty Trisha was as sensational as one would expect from such a talented guitarist.

It was a joyous gig. The Nashville Rejects rang in 2020 Boston style, we even got Gordon Lester to join us for a few numbers, which was fabulous! He stole the show. The afterparty ended up back at Lesley's, and it was a rippah. It all seemed innocent enough.

It wasn't, as we would soon find out. The world doesn't move on the straight and narrow. The world has teeth, and when it's hungry, it feeds.

Right away, I knew something was wrong. We all did. Since her infamous first day at the Cock & Fiddle, Kate has never been late for work, nor has she ever called in sick or left early. She was a pro. Her worried-sick parents were phoning every hour on the hour asking if we'd heard from her. We hadn't. Apparently, Kate never made it home on New Year's Eve. No one's heard from her since.

That was two days ago. Still no sign of Kate. Not good. Lesley, who was the last known person to have spoken to Kate, was on the phone with Kate's parents, who were trying to discern any useful information she might have. This is what Lesley knew:

Kate and Lesley were working the day shift, while Maggie tended bar. The pub was enjoying a matinee show from the Brian Washington Band. Kate was as bubbly as Champagne, showing no signs of distress. To the contrary, she was wearing a strapless dress with white faux fur trim, black buttoned belt with matching Santa hat, as well as long white stockings and black high-heeled boots. By all accounts, she was a smokeshow.

Kate finished work at 7 p.m., only to return around 11 p.m., dressed to the nines. Everyone was ramping up into the new year. The pub was shoulder-to-shoulder packed. Billy Swanker bumped his way into the darts room, where Kate was drinking with friends. Not long later, Kate was seen slapping Billy. Lesley rushed over, only to find Kate bouncing on Billy's knees, asking if she's been naughty or nice. Apparently, she'd been naughty. Extra naughty. Lesley's tiny head shrivelled in disgust. Shortly after midnight – after the streamers and champagne and hugging and kissing and posing for pictures – Lesley watched Kate vacating the premises with Billy Swanker, presumably to share a smoke. Kate was expected to join Gordon Lester on stage for Baby, It's Cold Outside, but sadly, that never happened. She never made it back to the pub.

I locked myself in the restroom stall and started crying. Lesley came in and hauled me out.

"What do you know?" she asked.

I wiped my face, unable to respond. Lesley picked me up and pushed me against the stall door.

"What do you know, goddammit?"

"It was him."

"Who? Gordon?"

"No. Billy. Billy Swanker. It was him. I'm sure of it."

Lesley dragged me into Blaze's office, and called the police. Within a heartbeat, a six-foot cop carrying an eight-foot notepad was interrogating me. His name was Officer Dale Lionheart. He wanted to know where Billy Swanker lived; where he hung out; who were his friends; his social media.

I told him everything I knew about Billy Swanker, which was surprisingly little. After all was said and done, I went back behind the bar feeling worse than ever. After working the dinner rush, I cleaned up, clocked out, scarfed down a burger and fries, drank two pints, smoked three cigarettes, peed four times, chatted with Gordon Lester until he ran out of things to talk about; then with a heavy heart, I walked home thinking only of Kate.

She must be alright, I told myself, again and again. I was absolutely sure of it. People don't die when they're twenty-one. That's prime-time baby.

I was awakened by the police. Officer Lionheart called, leaving a long and detailed message. As was to be expected, I spent the worst morning of my life at the police station, answering questions no woman should ever be asked.

"How long have you known Kate?"

Apparently, Kate's corpse was found tossed behind a dumpster, two blocks from the Cock & Fiddle.

"Since July, when she started working at the Cock & Fiddle."

"Can you describe your relationship with her?" Officer Lionheart sat at his desk, arms crossed, looking like he hadn't slept in a month.

"You know, we were friends. Not besties, but friendly enough. We were—"

I started crying. Being cramped inside a cubicle with three police officers towering over me, regarding me with blatant accusation, after hearing the news of Kate, was dreading on me.

"—We were becoming much closer."

"Did she have any enemies? Did you hear her say anything concerning? Anything at all?"

"It was him!" I shouted, startling the four of us. "Billy Swanker."

The officers straightened up immediately. The woman officer, stout with blonde hair twisted tightly into a bun, started taking notes, as did the other officer, a bulky black man with a classic cop mustache and gorgeous gray eyes.

Officer Lionheart, clearly in charge, was typing furiously on his desktop computer, which was as old as a Nintendo. His desk sat in the middle of the stuffy office, taking up most of the room. Next to his computer, was a coffee cup filled with pens and pencils and yellow and orange highlighters; a mountain of papers threatened to collapse at any moment. On the wall, underneath last year's swimsuit calendar, was a picture of a small boy wearing a batter's helmet, swinging a baseball bat. The resemblance to Officer Lionheart was uncanny.

I shifted in my seat. This was my first time inside a police station; and it was exactly how I expected it, right down to the smell of stale farts and fresh gunpowder, shitty coffee in

Styrofoam cups, and the perpetual chattering which permeated from every crevasse of this airtight building.

"Yes, yes," he said. "You'd mentioned this guy already. Tell me more about Mr. Swanker. We can't locate a permanent address for the guy, nor a phone number or social media. He's like a ghost."

I repeated what I had told them during our previous meeting, leaving out our 'special' relationship, although I'm sure they could read through the lines.

"Do you know the whereabouts of Mr. Swanker's family, Miss Murphy?"

"No."

Clearly, Officer Lionheart didn't believe me.

"We tried the number you gave us. It was out of order."

I didn't know what else to say. I wanted to be left alone. Most of all, I wanted Kate back.

"Listen, officers," I said, using my friendly-yet-professional voice. "I've told you everything I know. If I hear from Billy Swanker, I'll call you."

The cop with the mustache slammed his meaty fist on the desk. The stack of papers fell. He swore, then he bent down to clean up the mess, hitting his head on his way back up.

"Yes. Yes you will." Officer Lionheart said.

He handed me another card, then he escorted me out of the office. Tremendous bouts of weeping and moaning greeted us from a nearby cubicle; Kate's bereaved parents, I presumed. The tension in the building was as thick as a porterhouse steak. I wanted to leave as fast as my feet would allow me, curl up in bed, fall asleep and never wake up.

Out of respect for Kate, her family and the staff, Blaze closed the Cock & Fiddle the following day. A bouquet of red roses was stapled to the front door. No one knows who put them there, but I suspect Randy. As expected, the story was sensationalized. The media had a field day with it.

Kate's fresh, young face was plastered all over social media. Testimonials were pouring in. It was all so tragic. The city of Boston was entering full crisis mode. Another march was planned for this coming Sunday. I didn't go. Marching was the last thing I wanted to do.

While online, I stumbled upon Barbara Swanker's obituary. I was taken back. So, Billy Swanker wasn't lying. His mother's funeral was taking place at that very moment, which I found disconcerting and slightly morbid. Surely, the police would be scoping out the service, looking for Billy. Unless they were totally incompetent, and didn't read obituaries.

Meanwhile, the public was calling for the police chief's head. I tried watching the press conference, where he came out and resigned, but quickly turned it off. Instead, I stared out my window, and worried. A blanket of snow had fallen overnight, the snow continued to fall. I closed my eyes, and took a deep breath. All I could do was think of poor Kate. An image sprang to my mind: Billy's knife. Fear came fast. I took another breath. I must remain calm. Billy must pay for what he did to Kate, and how he used me to get to her.

I must be cursed. There are over four million people in the Greater Boston area; how is it that I end up having an affair with a serial rapist?

It can't be true. But if it was, I needed to find out. I needed redemption.

18

It was a closed coffin wake.

Atop the casket was a gorgeous picture of Kate wearing her navy-blue Catholic school uniform with a poignant heart-shaped necklace reaching down her freckled neck. She was young and carefree. If only she knew that in three years, she would be raped and murdered and discarded unceremoniously behind a rat-infested dumpster, just a few blocks from where she worked.

Standing next to her casket was Kate's father, a bald, paunchy man with a sympathetic face and beady eyes; he was clinging to his sobbing wife, who was the spitting image of Kate. It was heart-breaking to witness such sorrow. I sat alone in the corner, doing my best to stay composed. Behind me, a heated conversation was taking place. A hefty, red-headed man with a round face and muddled beard was talking to a woman wearing a burgundy suit. They were discussing the gory details that had been kept from the public.

I listened in.

"It must've been him. I know it, you know it. I mean, she was all cut up and—" He stopped to blow his nose. "—She was raped and brutalized then tossed into the trash. By a monster. And what are the cops doing? Nothing!"

Cut up.

Those words sent a shockwave through my body. I felt nauseous. I decided to leave, but not before saying goodbye to Kate, one last time. So, with my eyes pointed to the floor and my mind full of misery, I slumped through the room toward Kate's casket, which smelled of gentle lilies, sweet roses and pale yellow chrysanthemums. I could feel her warm presence in the room. We all could. Wherever our spirit goes in the afterlife, surely it hangs around long enough to whisper goodbye, before drifting off into the great unknown.

I touched her framed picture and told her how sorry I was, and that I loved her dearly. It took every ounce of strength not to fall apart. I considered comforting her parents, but they were surrounded by loved ones; they certainly didn't need me to intervene. A group of girls Kate's age were huddled together, chewing bubble gum and fidgeting with their smartphones, looking dazed and confused, awkward and sad. They were pale-faced and morose, their troubled minds riddled with grief. It never occurred to me that Kate had a life outside of work. I never bothered to ask. Too late now.

I pushed aside my guilt as best I could. This was not the time for self-pity. I found Lesley, Randy, Blaze and Steve, hugged and kissed them with everything I had, then I dragged my feet towards the exit. I didn't look back.

Kate's funeral service was held at the Church of the Holy Cross, which I took as either a sign from God or the devil, or both. Only time would tell.

The church was filled well over capacity. Teams of people were standing in the aisles, some with their backs against the wall, others staring at their shoes; the upper level was brimming with bodies moving languidly to and fro, whispering, hugging, kissing and crying. Friends, family, distant cousins, acquaintances, schoolmates, coworkers—you name it—were all gathered in the church. Everyone except poor old Maggie Cunningham, who was back at the pub, tending bar.

I sat with Lesley, Randy, Steve and Blaze, who was wearing a sharp black suit, crimson tie and dress shoes so finely polished, he could use them to peek under women's skirts. I'd never seen him look so handsome before. His face told another story. His eyes were glassy and bloodshot, the bags under his eyes were threatening to devour him entirely. He looked like David Crosby circa 1979.

Father McCleary delivered a wonderful eulogy, but it was lost on me. My mind insisted that Kate would come bursting into the church, and yell, "Surprise!" and we'd all share a heartfelt laugh, and life would return to normal again.

That didn't happen, of course; and by the end of the service, we all stood and sang Blest Are They, then we slowly and listlessly vacated the church, and went our separate ways.

When I got home, I called Mrs. Connelly to apologize for missing our church date. According to the receptionist, she was sick with the flu, but was expecting a speedy recovery. I asked for more details, but was denied any. The receptionist said I could visit tomorrow afternoon, as long as Mrs. Connelly's health improves. Feeling unsatisfied, I sat by the window, Mr. Jimmy on my lap, reading a paperback under the waning light of the January moon. A siren soared; a dog was barking. A lady with a heavy Boston accent (even for Boston) was swearing at her boyfriend, using colorful language (even for Boston), somewhere close by. Eventually, I dozed off, and my mind was bombarded with an endless cycle of nightmares.

I awoke in the middle of the night, needing to pee, and immediately felt the presence of pure, unadulterated evil. Although I could not see him, I could feel him: The old man in the hat. He was inside my apartment. I knew this. I could feel his mind sneaking into mine, repeating his dirty mantra. His breath whisked my lonely lips. His smell was everywhere; a mixture of pipe tobacco and decomposition.

Then I saw him flickering above my bed like an unholy hologram. He was grinning. When his hand brushed against the nape of my neck, I leapt from my bed, screaming. Too scared to pee, I jumped back into bed, rolled over onto my side and pretended to fall back asleep, hoping the old man would go back to whatever hell he came from.

For the following hour, I laid in bed, stiff as a corpse, until the early light of dawn cracked through my one and only window. Just a dream I told myself. Just a dream.

Mrs. Connelly looked withered and frail. She seemed confused at first, not recognizing me as I stood beside her bed at the Anderson nursing home. Soon enough, however, the color returned to her furrowed face, and her weary eyes found mine. "Nora? Nora Murphy? Well, I'll be. How are you?" Her voice was just above a whisper.

I was nervous, unable to form the appropriate response, so I simply sat there with her, in an unbelievably uncomfortable chair, holding her cold and craggy hands, feeling the weight of a life long-lived within them. When I spoke, I told her my story, leaving nothing out. She listened with remarkable curiosity. By the end of my rant, she was in tears, we both were.

Soon after we were blubbering like lifelong chums. She wanted me to describe Kate with unspoiled clarity. I tried my best, resenting each tear as it fell from my water-bucket eyes.

"Death gets more familiar with each passing year," Mrs. Connelly said. "But it never gets any easier. Life is cruel that way. I'm an old woman, Nora. I've known many wonderful people over the years, most of whom are long gone, like rain after it falls. We all wash away in the end, you know. But you must always keep a pure heart, you here? Always. As best you can."

She started coughing; a nurse came over to take her temperature, then left without saying a word. Soon, Mrs. Connelly regained her strength, and began telling stories. Wonderful stories. It was her turn to talk, and to my delight, she had plenty to say.

"Believe it or not, Nora dear, but I was once a young girl. Life was different then. Simpler. In fact, the church, the same church where we first met, was the center of the universe. We would congregate there every Sunday. Every Sunday."

Her eyes, cerulean and wet, flooded with memories. "I can still remember the preacher; Father O'Leary. Curious fella. Strong, fearless. Especially after the War. We had a peculiar summer following the end of that dreadful war. Yes suh, we did."

"Can you tell me about the old man in the hat?"

Her eyes became fierce. Her grip on my hand tightened. "You stay clear of him, Miss Murphy. You hear? He's a bad man."

"Bad? How?"

"Never mind that! You best be mindful when you're around him. That's all. He's quite clever. That old man's done terrible, terrible deeds to countless poor souls over the years. You hear me? He's a huckster. Plain and simple."

Mrs. Connelly fell silent for a moment. Her wrinkled face wrapped in worry; but only for a moment, before her mind brought her back to a happier time. She pointed to her bedside drawer, where I found a stunning antique pocket watch.

"Would you be a doll and open it for me?" she asked. "Oh, how I'd love to see Pappa again. And pass me my glasses while you're at it."

I did. The gold pocket watch exuded an awesome energy; its weightiness alone commanded respect. It was ravaged with age. When I opened it, the most extraordinary thing happened: it played music. The most incredible music I'd ever heard. I couldn't believe it. Tucked inside the gold-plated lid was a black and white portrait of a ruggedly handsome young man. A soldier from the looks of him.

Mrs. Connelly's face brightened.

"Look here," she held the treasure with both hands. "This here is my Pappa. Yes suh. I only remember him through this picture, though I still hear him speaking to me from time to time. But only in my dreams. Oh, how I wish I could see him again. Although, I suppose I will be seeing him soon. After all these years."

It was a faded black and white headshot, but I could make out the man in the photograph, who looked to be my age, if not younger. He wore his U.S Army garrison cap; he had a long, pointed nose, a sharp face and stern, unwavering eyes. He looked braver than he ought to be.

Mrs. Connelly motioned to the bedside table, where a black and white family portrait rested in a stunning vintage frame. Beside it, the portrait of a young man.

"This is me, as a young girl. I'm with my family. But without Pappa of course. He never did come back from the War. I don't know how Mother raised us on her own, but she did. Yes suh, she did. Mother never complained. Not once."

I let the portrait lie in my hand, regarding it with awe. It looked impossibly old. I felt I was holding a piece of history.

"That there is Mother in her favorite dress, which she made herself, by the way. That's me, looking off to the side, also in Mother's handmade dress. I don't remember why I wouldn't look at the camera that day. Oh, I was quite the spitfire back then, yes suh. You know, just getting a photographer must have cost everything we had.

"That there is my brother Barry. He was so young in this picture, not more than three or four. He looks so handsome in his little brown suit. Chubby, too, back then. Standing in the middle of us was our older brother Mathew. Mathew died in the Korean War. He wanted to be a soldier, just like his father."

She paused, wiped the corner of her eyes, then continued. "Mathew was quite the fiddle player, you know, although Mother would torture him about it. She'd holler, 'Play proper violin music, not that Devil's music!' Poor Mathew. He couldn't help himself. He was always sneaking off to play his music."

She motioned to the other photograph, this one in color. A young man in a dark suit; short, curly brown hair, a pleasant face and Buddy Holly glasses.

"This here is my husband. Oh, I was married to the most wonderful man. But I never could conceive any children, sadly. No suh. That's why I'm all alone."

"What was your husband's name?"

"Harold, Harold Connelly. Oh, he was a good man. He loved the Pats, yes suh. He kept season tickets. I bet I know more about football than any person in this building. Even you!"

She coughed, took a deep breath, continued. "Harold passed away, some fifteen years ago, maybe more. The Big C finally got the best of him. All that's left is me and Barry. He's off somewhere up in Canada. Barry used to run his own construction company out in Halifax before he retired. He always loved Halifax."

She placed her hands over her heart, and closed her eyes. Then she opened them and looked at me.

"Do you know that they plant a Christmas tree at the Common every year, commemorating the Halifax explosion?" she asked. "Have been for many years. Barry would help deliver the tree, then he'd come and visit me. He did this until he got too old. Maybe he can tell you about it sometime."

A nurse interrupted us. She handed Mrs. Connelly a small container of blue pills and a plastic cup filled with water; she watched her swallow the pills, then left. Soon thereafter, Mrs. Connelly drifted off to sleep, but not before giving me one final piece of advice.

"Remember Nora. You're in control of your own destiny. You and nobody else."

I held her words in my heart as I walked to the bus stop. Mary Connelly died peacefully in her sleep later that night.

NASHVILLE RUNAWAYS SETLIST: NEW YEARS EVE

SET 1:

New Year's Resolution (Cover)

I heard Bells on Christmas Day (Cover)

Oh, Pretty Woman (Cover)

Sometimes, I Don't Feel Like Coming Home (Original)

Nashville Can Kiss My Malarky (Original)

Christmas isn't Christmas Time (Cover)

Country Christmas (Cover)

Single Woman's Blues (Original)

Santa Baby (Cover)

SET 2:

Gimme One Reason (Cover)

Run Run Rudolph (Cover)

In the Midnight Hour ***(Countdown song)

Whiskey in a Jar (Cover)

Redneck Mother (Cover)

Hard Candy Christmas (Cover)

Don't Push Me Over (Original)

Crimson and Clover (Cover)

Grandma Got Runover by a Reindeer

SET 3:

Jingle Bell Rock (Cover)

Mustang Sally (With Gordon Lester)

Maybellene (With Gordon Lester)

Blue Moon of Kentucky (With Gordon Lewis)

The State of Massachusetts (Cover)

You Will Listen Love and Learn (Original)

Ain't That Lovin' You Baby (Cover)

Lady Bird Lullaby (Original)

Train Kept a Rollin' (Cover)

ENCORE:

Fight for Your Right to Party

Let's Start the New Year Right

19

The call came while I was asleep.

It was from the Anderson Nursing Home, but I didn't get the message until much later; after I'd washed up and made myself halfway presentable, and fed the cat, of course. When I called back, they told me that Mrs. Connelly's brother would be flying in tomorrow to take care of the funeral arrangements.

Turns out, I was the only visitor she'd had in years. How sad. After a lengthy chat with the receptionist, I discovered that Mrs. Connelly had only been strong enough to attend church once last year: the very day we'd met.

Was this a coincidence? I mean, what were the odds? My mind was jumping to many conclusions. Once thing was certain: I was a pawn in a game that I had little control over; and although the cards were stacked against me, the game was far from over. If only I knew what the rules were. Maybe then I'd have a fighting chance. I'll have to go back to the church and search for the old man in the hat, that much seemed obvious. But then what? I had no idea what to say to him, nor did I know how to convince him to put an end to this wretched curse. None whatsoever.

Maybe I could bribe him? If so, with what? That's a question I could do without answering. This only added to my sense of doom and gloom. Although I was discouraged and overwhelmed and dog-tired, I forced myself to face the day with dignity. No more tears, I told myself. Tears will get me nowhere.

I was outgrowing bras like a teenager goes through trends. My feet were swelling up, and my breasts were abolishing my back. They were growing more and more each day. Worse, they were no longer sexy. In fact, people were showing signs of alarm at the very sight of them. I certainly was. The rest of me was small; still that tiny-framed woman I was last year, except now I've got Mount Breastmore growing from my chest.

I looked absolutely ridiculous. I was a freak. I needed to conceal Bonnie and Clyde as best I could. But how? I could only wear bulky sweaters for so long. Then what? I was at a loss. At least I could have new bras delivered to my door each week; for that, I was grateful. As for now, my work remained the centre of my existence. Drinks needed to be served, money needed to be made, people needed to be cut off.

My first day back to work after Kate's death was subpar to say the least. Lesley greeted me the moment I entered the pub, with a frown. She was quite shaken, looking as though she hadn't slept in days. Randy had flowers delivered to the pub, in Kate's honor, every day that week. The smell of the place certainly improved. The framed picture of Kate placed behind the bar became the topic of many conversations; sadly, but not surprisingly, alcohol added fuel to the fire.

A fistfight broke out between two life-long friends who were arguing over Kate's killer; one guy declared her killer to be someone new and unrelated, the other stating the more obvious conclusion: it was the Midnight Rambler. The pair argued for quite some time, before resorting to fisticuffs. Lesley managed to stop them, but not before landing herself a fine-looking shiner. The police were called again, which caused the pub to clear out. I hardly made any tips after that. I can't recall ever working a more wretched shift in my life. When I got home, I checked my voicemail. There was a message from Barry Fitzpatrick, Mrs. Connelly's younger brother. He wanted to get together for coffee. I called him back the next morning, and we made arrangements to meet up. Looks like I'd be putting Kate's coffee card to good use, after all.

The afternoon was as dreary as a bad soap opera. We met at Dunks. I was reminded of Kate, as I produced the gift card her family bought for me only weeks prior. No more tears, I reminded myself. Barry arrived first, and was already halfway through his coffee by the time I sat next to him and introduced myself. He didn't mince his words. He spoke with a wonderful accent, reminding me of my Maritime friends back home. He was tall and hefty, with thinning hair and navy-blue eyes. He had a square jaw, considerable nose and enormous hands; he sat with impeccable posture, and he wore thick-lensed glasses that made his eyes seem larger than life. His resemblance to Mrs. Connelly was unquestionable. I guessed his age to be eighty, but he seemed reasonably healthy and strong as an ox.

I told him how sorry I was for his loss, and asked if there was anything I could do to help.

"Oh, you know Mary," he said, in a gruff-yet-pleasant voice. "She wouldn't want us to make a fuss. In fact, she made me promise not to hold a funeral for her. She was quite adamant about this. No, she wanted her ashes to be scattered along the Common, and that's that. I haven't been to that park in years."

He took a sip of coffee, then paused to reflect. "I'm happy that Mary had a friend to talk to in her final days," he said, at last.

I didn't have the heart to tell him we'd only just met, so I smiled politely, trying not to say anything inappropriate. As he spoke, I was picturing the small boy inside that furrowed black and white photograph. I wondered again how old he really was.

"You must've made quite the impression on her," Barry said, looking me up and down. "Because before she'd passed, she had set aside this on her bedside table, with your name attached."

He reached into his briefcase, which had a faded Halifax is Home sticker, and a pink lobster wearing sunglasses, holding a knife and fork. He pulled out a folder and handed it to me. It was surprisingly heavy. "I'm not sure I should be showing you this, but—" he trailed off. "But why the heck not, eh?"

Although I both liked and trusted this man, I wasn't prepared for any of this. To prove this point, my legs wouldn't stop shaking. They were stuck at high speed, as though I were treading water in a lake. All the while, Barry Fitzpatrick was studying me. I wasn't sure if he, in fact, trusted me. "Go on," he said. "Open it. You may be surprised at what you'll find."

I was surprised. Inside the folder, scraps of newspaper clippings, articles and photographs, color and black and white spilled out. The photo that caught my attention and raised the hairs on the back of my neck, was a close-up of the old man in the hat. But he looked much younger in this picture. His suit was dazzling. The scar on his chin was missing. He was leaning against an old Ford, smoking a hand-rolled cigarette; his deadpan eyes staring monstrously into the camera. I could feel his eyes penetrating mine. I looked away. I was afraid to touch the photo; just looking at it shook me. I wondered how Mrs. Connelly came to acquire this picture; and why did she keep it so many years?

Barry shifted in his chair.

"Ahh, yes. You know of him, eh? You do, I can tell."

He was doing everything he could not to stare at my chest.

I blurted out, "Can you tell me who he is?"

Barry paused before answering this. He glanced nervously over my shoulder, scanning the vicinity of the coffee shop, looking for any eavesdroppers. The tables closest to us were empty, only a murmur of voices could be detected.

Barry Fitzpatrick remained quiet for quite some time; then, as I thought he would simply ignore my question or change the subject, his eyes found mine.

"Oh him? He's the Devil."

I dumped the contents of the folder onto my futon as soon as I was home. There were plenty of old newspaper clippings, some laminated, others faded and illegible. I found what may have been the oldest clipping, dated Saturday December 14, 1946:

FRIDAY THE 13th PROVES MAGIC IS REAL

Local magician wows crowd with 'out of this world' card tricks, according to locals. Abaddon Beelzebub, or simply Beelzebub, typically seen decked out in fine Italian trousers, pin-striped suit and pork pie hat, has been under intense scrutiny for performing ostensibly impossible card tricks every Sunday for much of this year.

Many Boston folks simply adore Beelzebub. "He's an ace magician," Margarette Fisher said. "And a dreamboat." Residents often frequent his outdoor events, even during the winter. But is his magic real or an illusion? Another resident, who asked to remain anonymous, claims: "That man is pure evil. That is, if he's even a man at all. The good people of Massachusetts should beware."

It seems that many residents are in distress, and some are taking him to court, charging him with fraud and public nuisance. "It's time we rid the city of its trash," said Kenneth Blake, a local fireman. "All he does is talk gobbledygook, then take our money."

Police Chief Joseph Sweeney refused to comment on this story. The trial for Abaddon Beelzebub will be held January 6, 1947 at the Courthouse. He will be representing himself.

Another newspaper clipping was paperclipped to this. This one from the Boston Globe, dated January 10, 1947:

LOCAL MAGICIAN VANISHES IN THIN AIR

In what appears to be the ultimate disappearing act, Abaddon Beelzebub performed his grand finale in court yesterday. "It was the swellest magic trick I've ever seen," an onlooker proclaimed. "It was impossible. But I saw with my very own peepers."

Prosecuting lawyer Dick Vandermark had this to say: "The man vanished into thin air."

Abaddon Beelzebub was on trial yesterday for fraud and public nuisance. Beelzebub, a local magician, has been dazzling locals ever since he arrived unceremoniously in the spring of 1945. He has since earned a reputation as one of America's greatest hucksters. "He's a grifter. That's all he is," says police Chief Joseph Sweeney. "I don't know how he did it, but we'll have him behind bars the very second we catch the scoundrel. I promise you this: his scheming days have gone belly up."

The Boston police are advising residents to avoid any contact with this malignant magician; and are asking for any person with information of his whereabouts to please come forward.

Below the article was a small black and white photo of the old man. I pushed the article aside, and rubbed my temples. I needed to think. Who or what was he anyway? I did the math. If he was thirty years old in the picture, back in 1947, that would make him one hundred and three today.

Impossible. I remembered what Mrs. Connelly said about him: "You best be mindful when you're around him." What was I doing the moment I bumped into him last spring? That's easy: I was wishing for bigger breasts. In fact, if I were to be honest here, I was pining for them. Oh, sweet irony.

The old man gave me what I wanted. Yes, be careful what you wish for indeed. Thus, my life. I needed a drink. I checked the time: two more hours before work; I'd better make it a coffee. After brewing a fresh pot, I glanced at the pile of clippings and decided to read through some more. I searched by date and found an article from the Boston Herald dated August 5, 1947:

MORE CHILDREN GO MISSING

Another child has gone missing, raising the total number of disappearing children to seven. Arthur McElroy was last seen playing at Magazine Beach in Cambridge on Sunday at 3:30 p.m. His mother had been watching him play with other children that fateful afternoon; until suddenly, Arthur was gone. No one saw the boy leave, or heard any commotion, or saw a disturbance.

As summer begins, countless children are kept busy playing jump-rope, hopscotch, riding bicycles, playing on teeter-totters and tossing the old pig-skin around; or as in the case of Arthur, building sandcastles on the beach.

Unfortunately, the summer of 1947 has not been safe for children in the Boston/Cambridge area; and while the number of missing children continues to rise, Boston police still don't have any leads. Therefore, families are being advised to keep their children well-supervised during this time of crisis; and to stay alert and cautious at all times, until the perpetrator has been captured and arrested. Police are asking for anyone with information to contact them immediately.

Missing children? The plot thickens. But what does it mean? Better keep looking. I lit a cigarette, coughed, then put it out. Maybe I'll quit smoking today. My lungs would certainly thank me, not to mention my bank account. I scrambled through Mrs. Connelly's folder and found a stack of newspaper clippings held together with rusted paper clip. The words 'Boston Strangler' caught my attention.

I was reminded of my father, who would drink Glenfiddich and tell me tall tales about famous serial killers, including the infamous Boston Strangler, until I was too scared to fall asleep. He was enthralled with these types of stories. Apparently, so was Mrs. Connelly. But why?

One headline I spotted, dated January 5, 1964 read: BOSTON STRANGLER CLAIMS 13TH VICTIM. I continued to read through others. Mrs. Connelly had kept articles discussing each victim by highlighting key words and dates. It was fascinating, but I still couldn't decipher what it all meant. Maybe it means nothing. Maybe this was her hobby and she thought I'd enjoy it. I read another article, dated August 26, 1964:

CONMAN CAUGHT AND ARRESTED

Mysterious conman nabbed this weekend after grifting an undercover policeman. The officer, whose name has not been disclosed, had set up a sting operation earlier this summer looking to catch the hustler. Locals have been complaining of a grifter who steals large amounts of money by performing seemingly impossible card tricks to people passing by on the street.

The swindler is currently in custody, and is expected to appear in court later this week. As it stands, the perpetrator has no clear identification, and is going by the name Rafael Black. Police are asking for any information about this man (picture below).

It was the old man alright. This was the face of a madman. His haircut was razor-sharp. The scar just below his chin had returned, which I hadn't noticed in the previous photo. His ears were like turnips, his eyes jumped out of the picture. Stapled to this article was another clipping dated two weeks later:

VANISHING MAN THWARTS POLICE

The grifter known as Rafael Black has vanished, seemingly into thin air, whilst waiting in a solitary jail cell this past weekend. Police reported that sometime after 10 p.m. the suspect escaped.

"We have little to go on yet," Police chief Liam O'Toole stated. "This man is a professional conman. One of the best."

Locals have dubbed this conman 'the Vanisher', as rumours mount about his true identity. Older locals claim this man had been running scams after WW2, before disappearing for almost twenty years. O'Toole claims that this man has no connection to the murders which have been plaguing the Boston area all year, but insists residents should keep clear of the man if spotted. Any whereabouts of this man must be reported to the authorities instantly.

Was there a connection? Mrs. Connelly had thought so. Why did she go and pass away on me? Oh, how I'd love to have her with me, telling me her theories, while we searched for clues. There was one hour before I had to leave for work.

I continued reading, this time from a stack of clippings dated from 1987:

MURDERS SOAR AS POLICE FAIL

The 21st homicide this year has been reported over the weekend leaving Bostonians fearful of their lives. Murder? Yes please. That is the latest slogan heard throughout Boston. It is unknown how many of these homicides are related, but Police Chief Darrel McNeal isn't ruling anything out.

"We're seeing patterns at work here," McNeal said. "The victims tend to be male, and between the ages of twenty-one and thirty." Homicide rates have been steadily increasing throughout the year. Police are advising residents to stay alert for any suspicious activity.

There was a pile of similar reports dating from 1987-1988. The article attached to the top of the pile, with a yellow highlighter circling the story, showed the old man in the hat. He was dressed in a purple suit with a long, peacock-blue feather pinned to his fedora. He looked like a good old-fashioned American pimp. Except his eyes, which were clearly not human.

VAGRANT INCITES VIOLENCE

A local vagrant sparked a riot outside a church during the weekend. As churchgoers left the mass, a tottering man began speaking through a megaphone, inciting chaos and confusion. There are disparaging reports about the incident, but what remains certain is what ensued: violence.

Twenty-three people were injured during a brawl which took place outside the church. Two men and one woman remain in critical condition. Father McCleary, the newly appointed resident pastor, says he's seen this type of behavior before. "This is the mark of the beast. I am most certain of it."

I held another stack of clippings; I read some headlines: **MARATHON TERROR, 28 CHILDREN MURDERED, BOMBER CAPTURED, SUMMER OF DEVISTATION, BODIES PILE UP AS HORRIFIC SUMMER RAGES ON.**

The article that most caught my attention was dated Dec. 6, 2013:

HOMELESS MAN DEFIES ODDS

A local food bank recipient has caused quite a stir by apparently starting a fire without any tools. According to several eyewitnesses, Hannibal Addams, 66 (seen below), was standing outside the Church of the Holy Cross, when he became irate, and caused quite a disturbance. This incident occurred last Saturday morning. During the disturbance, the bushes outside the church burst into flames.

Local firefighters responded, and quickly put out the fire. Fire Chief Bradley King said, "As of yet, the cause of the fire has yet to be determined."

According to one eyewitness, "This was the work of Satan. I know it. I saw it. I saw Him." The Church of the Holy Cross has provides food for the needy every Saturday morning for over sixty years. It plans on continuing to do so this coming weekend.

These articles were all from 2013. Interestingly, I remember that year. It was the year I moved to Boston and started dating Tyson. I had recently started my job at the Cock & Fiddle, only back then I was still a waitress, and I was too young and naïve to pay close attention to what was happening throughout the city. Instead, I was preoccupied with increasing my tolerance to alcohol, learning how to be someone's girlfriend, and trying to figure out what language these people of Boston were speaking. They were a far cry from the Steel City folks back home.

Sifting through these stories, I was reminded of my father's number-one favorite Hamilton murder mystery: the infamous case of Evelyn Dick, who narrowly avoided hanging in 1946, after being charged with dismembering her late husband, John Dick. Evelyn Dick was a dazzling young woman whom the Canadian press adored; and why not? She was sexy and provocative. Her trial went national. Soon thereafter, Evelyn Dick was immortalized by a popular nursery rhyme heard coast to coast:

You cut off his legs

You cut off his arms

You cut off his head

How could you Mrs. Dick?

How could you Mrs. Dick?

It wasn't until my first year of college that I discovered its double entendre, having seen The Forgotten Rebels perform the song at the Legendary Corktown Tavern. The brassy band of punk rockers not-so-elegantly put those lyrics into song. Classic. Now, I'm left wondering if that despicable old man had something to do with Hamilton's Evelyn Dick case as well?

Time for work. I brushed my hair, slapped on some lipstick and eyeliner, put on my yoga pants and a turtleneck sweater (a beige one this time), grabbed my smokes and my lighter (just in case), found my purse, grabbed my coat and struggled out the door. If I hurried, I'd make it on time.

I did. Those newspaper articles danced around my mind all night. What did they mean? Why would Mrs. Connelly want me to have them? I sifted through these questions while I poured drinks, opened wine bottles, listened to this one woman's problems all night (she had plenty), ignored comments regarding my chest size, and cut off two gentlemen (the second not so gently); all the while keeping a close eye on their tabs and their levels of intoxication. My workplace was becoming more and more unruly. Men were afraid of me; women resented me. Their eyes gave this away. My tips reflect this flagging fact. This is how my shift went:

Me: What ya having today?

Customer: I'll have… OH MY GOD!

Me: Would you like that in a glass?

Customer: Oh, sorry Miss, but… (stares alarmingly at my chest). Oh, for the love of anything holy.

Me: Would you like fries with that?

Customer: Um, well, I dunno.

Hey, at least the music was tight. The Brian Washington Band was brilliant; they even called me up to perform These Boots are Made for Walking—always a crowd favorite—and we slayed it. There's me, thumping on those flatwound strings, thick and muddy, growling that descending bassline; next to me, Brian doing what he does best, which is wailing on that cherry red Gibson 335. Now, I'm no Susie St. Marie (I mean, who is, right?), but I can certainly carry a tune. I also sang, by request, the Alanis Morissette classic, Ironic. Throwing in a little CanCon.

It's amazing what these moments can do to a girl with a broken heart, you know? Brian is a true gentleman. At some point during my performance, however, I noticed something troubling. People in the audience were mocking me. Their words were scissor-sharp, their scornful eyes beating on me like a dirty rug. A drunk woman started heckling me, talking during my entire performance: "Those tits are as fake as a three-dollar bill!" she proclaimed, in her ratty voice. "And twice as ugly."

It took all my willpower not to put the bass down, hurry over, and unapologetically dump her low-calorie, fruit-filled hipster beer over her head. But I digress.

When I returned home, all I wanted was to pour myself a glass of red wine, light scented candles, grab a paperback and have a hot and steamy bath; unfortunately, my train of thought was derailed the moment I flicked on my apartment lights. The back door was left open, snow was drifting in. One large boot print lay at the foot of the door like evidence, taunting me.

I slammed the door shut and locked it. How the hell was Billy Swanker getting into my apartment? I wasn't as surprised as I should've been when I saw the report on the news the following day: MIDNIGHT RAMBLER SLAYS AGAIN.

What I was surprised at, however, was the latest victim's name: Stephanie Cockburn.

NORA'S CURSE

By: Nora Murphy

I wrote a letter to myself this morning

Reminding me what I'll have to say

I wrote a letter to myself this morning

Sordid teardrops fell like rain

I wrote a letter to myself this morning

Reminding me what I'll have to say

But I'll never heed this warning

Honey, please don't look at me that way

I need to leave this stormy weather

My head and heart are oh so blue

If I could leave this stormy weather

Book a flight to nowhere, soon

I'll need to keep my mind together

A bit of love can see me through

To heal these open wounds

But Honey, I best be over you

My heart is like a glass of water

Once so clean and pure and true

Your heart is like a bath full of water

I cannot wash myself of you

What I need is a worried father

To come to help me see things through

You cursed my broken heart

So, I wrote this lonesome tune

I wrote a letter to myself this morning

Words on page that sound sincere

I wrote a letter to myself this morning

Wicked words, I once feared

I wrote a letter to myself this morning

Gentle poem, held so dear

You cursed this heart of mine

You cursed me every time you're near

This curse, my heart preserves.

This heart of mine, Nora's Curse

20

I was in my PJs getting ready for bed when my phone started doing the freaky dance.

Billy Swanker.

I checked the time: 3:05 a.m. He's late. Timorously, I reached for my phone, expecting the usual rhetoric from Billy, but was surprised to see a familiar phone number instead. It was Tyson. This could only mean trouble.

It could not believe Tyson was here with me, inside my apartment, in the wee hours of the morning, but alas, here he was. There was something about his text: **I NEED U NOW**, followed by **PLEEEEASE**, that I simply could not ignore. I had to push aside my own personal feelings and let him in.

He smelled as I remembered: rugged, earthy, masculine; a hint of sweet cologne, but not enough to induce a seizure. My heart melted the moment he entered my home. I was actually nervous. He removed his boots, hat and scarf, and placed them neatly by the front door. I took his coat, then I went to my turntable and put on my B.B. King - Live at the Regal record, his favorite album, then I grabbed us some beers.

We sat awkwardly across from each other in my living room, wondering who should speak first. He was morose, quiet. His hands, trembling. I didn't know what to say. I was still hurt from being broken up with; and as tragic as it was about Stephanie Cockburn, I still didn't like her.

What was the first thing she said to me? Oh yeah: Go fuck yourself. Classy. But I still loved Tyson very much, and deep down he still loved me. We had a history together, a life; and then one day, it ended.

I spoke first. "I'm sorry for your loss, Tyson. I'm shocked. I'm sure you are too."

He sat stone-faced with his hands together folded between his knees, rocking back and forth. I could tell he'd been crying; something I'd only seen him do once, when he accidentally dropped a grand piano on his big toe; and even then, it was only for a minute. He just stared at his beer.

"The police will catch the guy soon enough," I said, without conviction. "I know it. They must. I mean, he got Kate too."

I burst into tears. I couldn't help it. They'd been building for some time. Tyson moved next to me, put his arm around me. We just sat, hearing our hearts beat in unison, yet somehow separate. There was no need for words. Words have no weight sometimes. They simply float away.

Tyson sighed., "I don't know what to do."

I handed him a Kleenex. Every time I was about to say something, I stopped myself. There was nothing more to say. His dead girlfriend's killer had most likely been sitting on this very couch less than twenty-four hours ago. My conscience felt like a sack of weighted stones, dragging me to the bottom of a lake of fire.

"I know what happened," he said, reaching for cigarettes. "First, he coaxed her, got her talking. Then he beat her, gagged her, then carved her up. Then, after doing God knows what else, he slit her throat." He paused to light his cigarette. "He ejaculated all over her. I was the one who found her."

He told me his story. Every wretched word of it.

Tyson was working for the Buddy Guy Band that night. Stephanie, who had the night off, was supposed to meet up with him at 11 p.m. She was late. She didn't respond to any of his texts. He figured he'd done something wrong, or said something stupid (I could attest to that). He went out for a smoke sometime after midnight.

By this point, she was over an hour late. He started freaking out. First, he tried reaching out to her friends; and when that failed, he tracked her phone. She was close. She was probably getting high with Buddy Guy's keyboard player (you know how them keyboard players are, right?) So, he went out to look for her. Except he didn't find her smoking pot with Buddy's keyboard player. He found her raped and mutilated body lying next to the dumpster behind the Tasty Burger, four blocks from where he worked.

"Just as they'd found Kate," I said, holding my breath.

Mr. Jimmy was rubbing up against Tyson, purring and stretching. Tyson scratched under Mr. Jimmy's chin, who then found a spot next to him on the couch. Tyson looked up at me with the saddest eyes I've ever seen on a man. I was worried about him. Nonetheless, I couldn't shake the feeling that the worst was yet to come, and that I played a big part in all of this. I pushed aside my own grief and tried my best to comfort him. We talked and cried and smoked and drank and listened to blues records all night. Somewhere along the line, we must've fallen asleep.

I dreamed I was at the altar. Tyson was standing next to me, wearing his polka dot boxers and a T-shirt disguised as a tuxedo. He was grinning ear to ear. I wore a lavish, traditional wedding dress, my hair was pristine, my breasts perky and slight. The sweet scent of roses lingered like a memory. The church organ stopped playing. Then came heavy silence. Father McCleary was standing over us. "Do you Nora Murphy take Tyson Miller to be your lawfully wedded husband, for richer or for poorer, in sickness and in health, until death do you part?" I tried to speak, but couldn't, so I nodded. Father McCleary turned to Tyson, ignoring his ridiculous attire., "You may kiss the bride." Tyson turned, opened my veil. We shared a long and mouthwatering kiss that lasted forever. His mouth was warm and solicitous. There was applause; the organ erupted into song, but I hardly noticed. I wanted this moment to never end. I was happy. Then I felt him edging away from me.

What's happening? Tyson's grip was loosening; his face full of horror. He wasn't Tyson anymore; he was one of the old man's minions. Without warning, my breasts started growing like a beanstalk, stretching halfway across the church. I heard scandalous cries and a flurry of footsteps vacating the church. Soon, all that was left was Father McCleary. "Nora," he said, shaking me until he had my full attention. "Nora, you must resist. While there's still time. Resist. And repent. For the Devil Himself is working within you. You must resist. While there's still time."

At that moment I felt another presence, a much darker presence: the old man in the hat. I ran toward the exit, carrying my bouquet of roses. The pedals were withering away. My breasts were sweeping the floor as I ran.

When I reached the door, the old man was waiting for me. Only now, he was young and handsome, save for his hideous teeth which were sharp as swords and the color of mud. His suit was creaseless; his shoes made of the finest Italian leather. His eyes were piercing into mine; his face carved into a crooked smile. BIGGER IS BETTER, DEARY? He produced a knife. Billy Swanker's knife. His long and crooked fingers dazzled the smooth handle. He stuck the blade deep into his wrist, then started licking the blood that came gushing out of him. He drank his own blood with glee. The crimson waterfall which flowed down his face was making him stronger. He grew ten feet tall. YES, BIGGER IS BETTER!

My eyes snapped open. I was crying.

It was morning. Tyson was passed out on the couch, peacefully snoring. A string of drool was dangling from his gaping mouth, threatening to let go at any given moment. Mr. Jimmy was lying next to him, purring gently. After washing up, I rushed to the store for some bacon and eggs, and was back before you could say over-easy.

The bacon sizzled and snapped, the eggs like golden yolks. I piled the toast a mile high on the plate, then poured two tall glasses of OJ. The coffee maker groaned as it brewed a fresh pot. I had to pinch myself to make sure this was real.

I'd also bought some treats for Mr. Jimmy; who, once he heard the rattling of the bag, leapt off the couch, raced to his dish, chowed down, then retreated back to his spot next to Tyson.

"You little traitor."

I missed cooking breakfast. I hadn't cooked a decent breakfast since Tyson ran off with Stephanie, nearly a year ago. Has it been that long? Funny how time flies. Tyson stirred in his sleep, farted, scratched his balls, then accidentally kicked poor Mr. Jimmy, who scooted off to the safety of the window sill.

"Wakey wakey," I said.

"What the—"

Tyson opened his puffy eyes, fell face first off the couch, then ran into the bathroom and peed with the door open.

Just like old times.

He came out of the washroom rubbing his belly.

"Mmm, bacon."

I served up a wonderful breakfast, which Tyson ate voraciously.

"Listen, Nora," he said, after cleaning his plate. "I need to thank you for taking me in last night. I hope I wasn't much of a burden. I didn't know who else to turn to. Man, what a shitty week this is going to be. As if talking to the cops isn't bad enough, Steph's parents are harassing me as well. They think I had something to do with it."

He showed me a lengthy text from her parents. It was gross.

"What? Do they think I'm the Rambler?"

"That's awful," I said.

"Oh Nora, what the hell is going on around here? With cameras everywhere, how do they not catch the bastard?"

"They will. Soon." *Unless I catch him first.*

"I know, but…"

We sat in silence, drank coffee, and smoked cigarettes. I'll quit tomorrow. Or maybe another day. I considered telling him about Billy Swanker, but decided against it. I still needed hard proof. Besides, there is no way I could tell Tyson my story. No way. Not happening. Ever.

Tyson washed and dried the dishes. Then before he left, he asked the million-dollar question.

"So, like, I gotta ask. Um, is everything OK? I mean, what's the deal with your boobs? Sorry for asking again, but—"

I'd been expecting this question, as I've been getting asked this daily, but I've yet to come up with a suitable answer.

"Oh these? They started growing—"

"Right after we—um"

"After you dumped me? Yes. That is correct."

He was standing at the foot of the door, fidgeting with his phone, looking dumbfounded and embarrassed.

"They're real?" The surprise in his voice was alarming.

I sighed. We shook hands, awkwardly at first, then he pulled me close and we embraced for what seemed to be an eternity. He kissed me on the cheek, said goodbye, and left.

I curled up beside Mr. Jimmy and had a cat nap on the couch. I could still smell Tyson on my pillow as I slept.

From that moment on, work was deplorable. The city of Boston was fully terrorized, and the best (or worst) was yet to come. It takes quite a lot to knock a city like Boston off its feet. This city has seen its share of crises: explosions, devasting fires, pandemics (more to come!), floods, hurricanes, tornadoes, nautical disasters, plane crashes, ice storms, blizzards, serial killers, bombings, terrorist attacks; you name it, Boston's had it. And yet, it always finds a way to bounce back.

The city was facing its worst crises in a decade. All everyone talked about was the Midnight Rambler. Who he might be, when he'll strike next, and the six-million-dollar question: when will he be captured? And here I was worrying about my ridiculous curse.

Except, it wasn't ridiculous. The strain on my back was unyielding. I was in constant fear of developing Kyphosis, or something worse. I knew if I didn't put an end to this madness, my back would snap like a breadstick. That is, if the Rambler didn't kill me first. Either way, I'll end up dead. Dead, like Kate and Stephanie and Mrs. Connelly. My panic was turning to despair. Time was running out.

Reluctantly, I texted Amanda, who came over with cupcakes. She recommended a plastic surgeon who specializes in breast reduction surgery; and, after chowing down three delicious desserts, I asked for his number.

Could a simple surgery solve my dilemma? Or, would my breasts simply grow back? This is a question no woman should ever have to ask herself, but alas, welcome to Nora's World, or dare I say, Nora's Curse?

We let Switchblade Symphony be our soundtrack as we sleuthed through Mrs. Connelly's newspaper clippings. We imagined ourselves as sexy young detectives in a crime novel; Mr. Jimmy was, of course, our furry sidekick. After an hour of detective work, he meowed in protest, then hobbled towards his food dish.

"Maybe I'll bring you in for a tummy tuck. Would you like that?" I asked him.

He ignored me. Instead, he ate his dinner, found a pile of laundry next to the window and slept.

Amanda and I continued our investigation, looking for the obvious connection: why did Mrs. Connelly save these articles, and moreover, why did she want me to have them? What did they mean?

These questions continued to pester me until, after my fourth cup of coffee and fifth cigarette, I finally made the connection: the old man in the hat seems to show up whenever there's a crisis. He causes havoc, then he disappears. But where does he go? My guess would be he visits other cities, either in America, or possibly (and more likely) around the world. But who is he?

We decided to find out. Amanda was stoked. It was obvious she needed a distraction from her flailing love life; or dare I say, her online dating disasters?

Besides, she's always up for an adventure, and I was grateful to have her here with me. There was no one else in the world I trusted more than her.

Although it was nice having her here helping me, I was scared. I mean, what if we can't stop the curse?

What then?

21

Lesley dragged me into Blaze's office the moment I arrived at work. "What's going on?"

She had on a plaid shirt with a red bandana wrapped around her neck, jet-black spikey hair and no makeup. She looked as tough as Chuck Norris, and twice as serious. Her fists were clenched; her eyes as cold as a gunslinger's heart.

"Wake up, Hamilton! Tell me what's going on. I'm not taking any more bullshit from you. I want the truth."

Apparently, I'd been ambushed. "What do you mean?"

"No. No. No. You don't get to play dumb with me, sister." She grabbed my chest with both her hands. "Where did these come from?"

"Oh, you know?" I asked. What more could I say? It was one thing to roll your eyes at a drunk customer and say silly catchphrases like, 'Oh these things?' Or, 'Do you like them?' Wink, wink, flirt, flirt. This wouldn't help me now.

"Honestly," I said, reluctantly, "I don't know. Something strange happened to me in the summer. Now I've got these on my chest and they won't stop growing. I wish they would."

Lesley frowned, stuffed her fists into her pockets, then shook her head. "I don't buy it. Not for a second. But I can't for the life of me think of what could've caused this. Besides a curse."

"A curse?" I nearly spat out the word.

"Yes. It's possible. I have an uncle who still looks twenty-one, except, he's pushing seventy. That racist asshole's gonna outlive us all, too. I know it, and he knows it too. What a prick. Rumor has it, he sold his soul to the devil when he was, well, twenty-one I presume. That's how he's managed to stay so young.

"It got to the point where he had to leave Boston. People started asking questions around the time he turned forty. Now he's somewhere up in Canada living in a cottage. Probably hunting moose and eating donuts like a friggin' hoser. Um, no offence."

I was flabbergasted. It was one thing to think I'd been cursed, but for her to say it aloud was something entirely different. I sat down, put my head in my hands and closed my eyes. The idea of disappearing up north was indeed tempting.

"Honestly, Les, I don't know what's happening to my body. And I don't know how to stop it."

Lesley gave me a stern look.

"You're lying." She took a long breath, composed herself, then turned away. As she was leaving the office, she asked, "You really think Billy Swanker is the Rambler?"

"Yes."

"I know people," she said, through gritted teeth. "Dangerous people. I'll be putting the call out, since the coppers aren't doing nothing. My people will find Swanker. And when they do, he'll wish the coppers found him first. Do you have a picture of him?"

I didn't.

"He's a slippery little shit, isn't he? Well, I'm on it. I promise you this: you won't have to worry about that son-of-a-bitch anymore." She laughed. "Poor bugger won't know what hit him." She paused midway out the door, then added, "I'd get those things checked out if I were you. Something ain't right."

I was alone in Blaze's office, wondering what my next move should be. With Lesley and her friends looking for Billy, that left me with only one problem: finding the old man in the hat, and making him undo this curse. How hard can that be? Sigh. With all the strength I could muster, I forced myself up, then meandered toward the bar, trying not to fall over.

Maggie was busy counting the money in the till, getting ready to go home. She moved effortlessly behind the bar. She was born to bartend. It was her calling. The ease in which she can strike up a conversation with the customers was astounding. She'd been a bartender for as long as I'd been alive. Soon she would retire and have the greatest retirement party in the history of Boston held in her honor.

That said, even Maggie was prone to taking shots at my current predicament; when she saw me, she took a long look at my chest and rolled her eyes. "Careful not to poke an eye out with those things, why don't you."3 She gave me a friendly swat on the bum with a dish rag.

Gordon Lester chimed in. "I bet you can stand a full pint on each titty! Let's see for ourselves!" Apparently, Gordon was getting warmed up. "What does an eighty-year-old woman have between her breasts that a twenty-year-old doesn't?" The barflies leaned closer. "Her bellybutton!"

The barflies roared as though it were the funniest joke they'd ever heard. I joined in. I would not let them see my embarrassment. Never show weakness, that's what my father would say before my ballerina competitions. Smile, he said, and the whole world smiles with you.

Ten sets of rear-ends were positioned at the bar; all eyes and ears were pointed at Gordon Lester, who turned his attention back to the Midnight Rambler, whom the media was referring to as The Killer.

Gordon, the only person I know who still prefers an old-fashioned newspaper, held up today's paper.

"Check this out, Nora."

His glass was almost empty.

"Another beer, Gordon?"

"Yes, of course," he said. "He's close, you know. The Killer. This igit could be in this room right now, you know. He could be any one of us."

The barflies gasped. I poured him a pint, while he worked his audience. Gordon was a natural. He had It. As long as he kept talking, these people would listen. Before he could say another word, a young couple stepped into the pub; they pounded the slushy snow from their boots, then sat at the table next to the phone booth. Once they'd removed their coats and scarves, they looked up toward the bar, hoping to grab my attention.

Gordon pointed to them and shouted, "Look. It could be that guy right there. He could be The Killer! He certainly looks like one!" The poor fella looked devastated. Once he realized everybody was staring at him, he whispered something to the woman he was with, then they stood up and left.

Gordon's laughter was laconic. As the young couple was leaving, he shouted, "Goodbye Killer. I'll see you in hell!"

The door slammed shut. I never saw them again.

By 6:30 p.m., every table in the pub was full. Meanwhile at the bar, Gordon Lester was still ranting. He pointed to the picture of Kate behind the bar.

"Boy, that redhead could sure light up a room."

"Yeah. What a tragedy," a barfly said.

"The Killer should be strung up by his balls."

"Hear, hear!"

"What I would do to him…"

A chorus of agreement.

Two hours later, as the dinner rush was waning, a couple of college students strolled through the front door carrying instruments. They seemed eager for the Wednesday night jazz jam. As they passed the bar, the shorter student with the pimply face and long, wavy hair, waved hello to me. His eyes were so fixated on my chest, that he tripped over his feet and dropped his guitar case, and consequently, fell on top of it. The other student, showcasing a nifty handlebar mustache and plug earrings that stretched his earlobes down to his chin, tried to help him up. The two halfwits giggled like school chums, as they found a spot next to the fireplace in the music room.

Lesley took their orders: tall glass of ice water and a coke (surprise surprise). She approached the bar, grumbling at me with her usual look of scorn, then placed their order. Unlike Lesley, I actually dig those jazz cats, even when they can't keep their penetrating little eyes off me. They may be lousy tippers, but they sure can swing.

Around this time, an assembly of well-dressed middle-aged women gathered in the dining room. They had the entire back room reserved for their annual work party. They ordered twenty-five bottles of our finest wine; and by the time they left, there were no steaks left in the freezer. A ravenous bunch, they were.

Unfortunately, they hated the band. Apparently, jazz was not their bag, you dig? One woman, dressed in a tacky red suit that one would expect on a park bench ad next to a realtor's name, insisted that I go up and tell them to start playing rock music.

I glanced at the upright bass player standing next to the kid blowing on a French horn and chuckled. The lady in red, on the other hand, scowled. As the band was performing Fly Me to the Moon, this lady, who's lipstick matched her high heels, approached the French horn player, mid solo and requested Nickelback. I could hear her from the bar. The jazzcat smiled behind his horn, blew a Bb into her schnoz, then carried on as if nothing had happened. The lady in red slammed her heels down, huffed and puffed, then dropped the most incredible F-bomb in this pub's long and defamatory history. Then, with inebriated determination, she retreated back to her table with folded arms, bawling: "Why won't they play Nickelback?" over and over.

After racking up a bill of over a grand, this table left a tip smaller than the space between the Lady in Red's ears.

By 11 p.m., there were enough jazz musicians on stage to fill Carnegie Hall. They were really swinging. As I was changing a keg, lost in my thoughts, I felt a dark presence wash over me.

The old man in the hat. He was outside, peeking in through one of the big bay windows. He made big-breast gestures, while laughing hysterically. Without warning, his voice slithered inside of me: BIGGER STILL BETTER, DEARY?

"Oh no you don't," I muttered. "Not this time."

Against my better judgement, I left the bar and rushed outside. It was colder than a brass toilet seat on the shady side of an iceberg. Snowflakes fell like bombs from the furious sky, painting the streets with its fine white brush. The howling wind was blowing hard against my brittle face.

The old man was gone. I couldn't believe it. Then I noticed something peculiar: there were no footprints or track marks on the sidewalk, leading to the spot by the big bay window; nor were there any breath marks on the glass, where his face had been. Nothing. I shook my head. Was he really there at all, or did I imagine it? A terrible question to ask yourself. I had no answer, nor any way of explaining what just went down, so I hurried inside the pub and tried to warm up.

"You chasing ghosts?" Lesley asked, the moment I stepped back into the pub. She was regarding me with both pity and suspicion.

"Oh, I just needed some fresh air," I said, trying not to make eye contact.

"You're lying again. I'm gonna get to the bottom of this, you know. I promise. Nobody lies to Lesley McGuire. Nobody." She stormed away.

A sickly feeling was stirring inside me. I stole a sideways glance toward the big bay window, just in case. My body felt strange and out of place; my tongue too big for its mouth, my hands full of pins and needles. My breasts were burning up. They felt diseased. I needed to stop and rest for a moment, but that was not feasible. To prove this point, someone approached the bar, looking to order another bottle of Blue Moon. I sighed. Then I bounced behind the bar and went back to work, while the jazz cats improvised under the not-so-subtle spell of Witchcraft.

22

My appointment at the Back Bay Plastic Surgery Clinic was a calamity. After an hour of filling out paperwork, answering more questions about my lifestyle choices than I thought necessary, and disclosing immeasurable personal information regarding my body size, I finally met with Dr. Jefferey Palmer, who did a double take the moment I removed my jacket. He took a lengthy look at me, licked his lips, then began typing on his desktop computer, which was placed in the middle of his expensive-looking executive desk.

Dr. Palmer was extremely tall, over forty, and dressed in a buttoned-up Hawaiian shirt with the top four buttons undone. His face was agreeable, his hair partially gray.

His office was cluttered; random certificates and awards were displayed on flowery walls, as was a taxidermied steelhead fish, whose eyes seemed to follow my every move. Beside his computer was a family portrait boasting a beautiful wife and two smiling young daughters clad in pink and yellow dresses. Next to this picture was a portrait of a golden retriever carrying a beaten-to-death frisbee in its mouth. I sat on a comfy leather high-back chair, waiting for the plastic surgeon to speak.

Eventually, he looked up from his computer, removed his reading glasses and smiled automatically. "Tell me, Miss Murphy, why the breast reduction surgery?"

I stuck out my chest.

"Um, yes," he said. "Can you tell me how long your breasts have been—well—so large?"

"Well, that's just it. At some point last summer, they just showed up."

He rolled his eyes, repeated the question.

I gave the same answer.

"I'm not getting you, Miss Murphy. You are," he checked his notes, "twenty-eight years old, correct?"

I nodded.

"And you're claiming that up until last year, you, what?"

"Here. Look for yourself." I pulled up some older pics of me on social media. Nostalgia swept over me like an old Disney movie. Most pics were either of me performing with the Nashville Rejects, looking cool as can be with my glorious Fender Jazz bass, or with Tyson. I handed him my phone. He put on his glasses, then studied the pics for an uncomfortable length of time, running his hands through his thinning hair.

"Hmm. Interesting. I've heard of this once before."

He began typing furiously on his computer. He stopped, having come to some conclusion, then reached for the phone on this desk. "Liliana, would you please postpone my next appointment? Thank you."

He folded his glasses and put them into his shirt pocket. His eyes were big, wide, full of excitement. "Are they, still growing?"

"Yes."

"Have you been documenting their growth?" A good question.

"No. Sorry. There's so much going on at work and stuff."

"Okay, okay, no worries. Um, my dilemma is this: if we go ahead with the surgery, and your breasts somehow grow back, then what? That could ruin the integrity of my practice. You understand?"

I did.

"And there's the question about insurance, of course. You have insurance?"

"Well, no. I'm actually Canadian." I blushed. "But I've got money set aside." But did I want to spend my life savings on my breasts?

"Alright. We'll worry about that part later. Do you mind if I have a peak?" He read my face, then added, "Let me remind you, Miss Murphy, I'm a professional."

Yes, of course you are, I thought, as I forced off my sweater and bra. My breasts sprung like a pair of pogo sticks.

"Jumping jellyfish!"

I rolled my eyes.

Dr. Palmer took all my measurements, recorded them, then continued asking questions. He wanted me to see a psychologist— just in case—then come back in a month. There was no point, he said, in going ahead with surgery if those darned things were to grow back.

As I got dressed, he poured himself a scotch and offered me one, which I gladly accepted. We drank. He pulled up the Guinness World Records and showed me a picture of the woman with the biggest breasts in the world. She was quite the lady.

What worried Dr. Palmer the most, he said, was my tiny frame. This woman, he pointed out, has a body that can support itself. Her body was proportional. She was, in fact, big-boned, as well as big-breasted.

I on the other hand, was not. I'm a toothpick trying to support two Big Macs. He advised me to eat more red meat, drink plenty of milk and start exercising regularly. I needed more body strength to support the excessive weight.

I could have killed him. As our appointment concluded, he asked me if I had any further questions.

I did.

"What did you mean when you said you'd seen this once before? Seen what?"

Dr. Palmer sat back in his chair, deep in thought. He started tapping his pen on the armrest of his chair. Once I noticed, I couldn't un-notice—tap—tap—tap. Eventually, he spoke. "Tell you what, Miss Murphy, when you come back in a month, we can discuss it at length. I need to do some more inquiring." Then he added, more to himself than to me, "I honestly thought it was a joke. Now—" he took another innocuous look at my chest. "—Now, I do not."

We shook hands. I had to strain my head to look him in the eye. I glanced again at his family portrait, focusing on his picturesque wife. I'd hate to be the wife of a plastic surgeon. Talk about pressure. I left.

The following morning, I was bombarded with texts, from Lesley: **FOUND HIM!!!! Get 2 wrk urly MUST TALK!!!!**

I chose not to respond. Coffee comes first. But I did manage to get to work early. I could only imagine what she had to say. Needless to say, I was not disappointed.

Typically, the Cock & Fiddle is quiet at 4 p.m. on weekdays. It's the 'in between' time: the arduous lunch rush is over; the impending dinner rush an hour away.

However, you do get a few shift workers stopping in for a drink or three before they go home and retire for the evening; and you'll always find a handful of musicians sipping pints around the bar, chatting about their next big gig.

On this particular afternoon, the pub was dead. Lesley was folding cutlery when I arrived. Her demeanor changed the moment she noticed me. She grabbed her coat and hat and dragged me outside for a smoke. This is Lesley's story:

Swanker was spotted at a nightclub late last night. Word is, he was drunk out of his mind, dancing with a sexy Latino lady. The club was hot and sweaty; the music was so loud the bass could knock out a filling. One of Lesley's friends—we'll call him Biff—followed Billy into the men's restroom. Once inside, Biff's partner—we'll call him Tony—was waiting outside the restroom, preventing anyone else from entering. Biff cornered Billy and started asking questions: Who are you? Where do you live? Where were you the night Kate Campbell was murdered? Billy claims he was home alone watching Netflix. Tough alibi. Where was he the night Stephanie was murdered? Billy said he was with his girlfriend. The sexy Latino lady waiting for him on the dance floor? No. She was an acquaintance. Okay, then give me the number for this girlfriend so I can confirm. Billy told Biff to go to hell. Not a good idea. Swanker had been standing at the urinal, peeing during this exchange, (oh, to be a boy, and pee standing up). Biff reached down and grabbed Billy by his member, and started squeezing until Billy collapsed onto the urine-soaked floor. Biff kicked Billy in the head repeatedly, before dragging him to his feet. Billy's cock, still exposed, was flaming red and swollen.

Biff, being a professional bodyguard and tougher than a two-dollar steak, was a foot taller than Billy. Pull up your pants, then empty your pockets, Biff ordered. Reluctantly, Billy complied. Biff ransacked Billy's wallet; there was over $200 in there. Planning on having a good night tonight? he asked. Billy ignored the question. Answer me! Billy didn't. Instead, Billy kicked him in the balls. Definitely not a good idea.

Billy raced for the exit, only to find Tony waiting there for him. Oh no you don't. Tony punched Billy square in the nose. Billy folded like a cheap suit. Buckets of blood came billowing from his broken nose, cascading down his once handsome face, ruining his white collared shirt. Strange, garbled sounds came from his mouth, as the blood leaked out of him. Outside the restroom, a lineup was forming. People needed to pee. Someone peeked inside, pointed at Billy, and cried for help. Soon a gathering had formed outside the men's restroom, watching the showdown. The ear-splitting music made talking impossible. Biff bent down on one knee and spoke directly into Billy's bloodied face. Listen here you dirtbag, we're watching you. We know who you are and what you've been up to. And once we catch you doing anything inappropriate—anything—you'll wish the police had found you instead of us. Capiche? Billy spat in his face. Oh, that's it. Biff dragged Billy to his feet, then roundhouse kicked him in the head, knocking him out cold. A security guard came hustling over. Biff handed the security guard a wad of cash, gave him a wink and a nudge; then the three of them dumped Billy behind the dumpster in the back alley, leaving him for the crows.

I tossed my cigarette carcass into the snow, pondering what I'd just heard. I shivered. It was the coldest day of the year. The traffic noise was raucous. Commuters were slogging through the icy streets, inching their way home; pedestrians struggled along the snow plowed sidewalks, wrapped in warm clothing, trying not to freeze to death.

I thanked Lesley for her help; but if I were to be honest, part of me was worried for Billy Swanker, although I'd never confess this to her. I could only imagine her reaction. Besides, I still needed proof that he was, in fact, the infamous Midnight Rambler, aka: The Killer. Deep down in my heart of hearts, I knew I was avoiding the truth about Billy. The fact was: I've been sleeping with Boston's most notorious serial killer. What are the friggin odds? There are over four million people in the Greater Boston area, how is it that I ended up with a friggin serial rapist? Jeez. I mean, I liked Billy Swanker. There, I said it. *Liked him.* Did I love him? No, not even close. Could he change? It's possible. I've always liked dangerous men. Show me a badass with a heart of gold, and I'll show you a proper suitor. There's no accounting for taste, I suppose.

Lesley finished her cigarette; then, with the beast of burden resting on my shoulders, I followed her inside the toasty-warm pub and ordered myself a bacon double cheeseburger and fries. Time to build up my tiny frame.

That was the day I first heard of the virus. Gordon Lester made damn sure every person in the pub knew about this new Coronavirus circulating the globe. People were beside themselves. They'd already been through a lot. Now this?

As usual, work was hectic. Unfortunately, I was having trouble moving behind the bar. I had zero balance. Everything was now a struggle. I kept bumping into things. My feet were imperceptible. I couldn't bear this much longer. I was tired and sore all over. Nobody knew what to say to me at this point. Every joke's been made, again and again. So, that's why I paid little-to-no notice of the virus. There was only one thing on my mind. Getting rid of this damned curse. Before it's too late.

23

The impending lockdown was all anyone would talk about, which was fine with me; I'd had enough of them yammering on about the Midnight Rambler—and don't get me started on the size of my you-know-what's—that said, the idea of a lockdown caught me completely by surprise.

I'd been so preoccupied with my own problems that I'd failed to see any of the warning signs. Apparently, I wasn't the only one. Gordon Lester, with his loyal band of debauchees, was sitting in his usual barstool, ranting.

"They're gonna close this pub for good, wait and see," he said in between generous gulps from his tottering glass. He slammed his empty glass down. "Be a doll and pour me another, would ya?"

It was 5:15 p.m. and he was already slurring his words. Not a good sign. I poured him his pint. Gordon took the beer, stood on top of his wobbly barstool, held the glass up high and ordered everyone in the pub to be quiet. They obliged.

"Good people of Boston," he said magnanimously. "Fellow patrons of the Cock & Fiddle. Let us have a toast. A toast to ourselves. We've already been through a lot, and our journey has just begun. I'd like to wish you all the best in the coming weeks and months. May you all be kind to one another. Never show fear. Only love. And now I'll quote the Lizard King: 'This is the end. My only friend. The end.' So, let us drink and be merry, shall we?"

The barflies raised their glasses, drank.

Despite his usual gusto, Gordon had a melancholic look about him that troubled me. This pub was his life; moreover, music was his life, without it, he had nothing. On the surface, Gordon Lester was an aging rockstar living out his remaining years as a local guitar hero, drinking at his favorite pub, telling tall tales to his loyal listeners, but there was more to him than that. He was an artist in every sense of the word: passionate, creative, dynamic, exciting. He was totally dependent on his craft.

He was also inebriated.

My last shift as a bartender at the Cock & Fiddle was full of not-so-subtle reflection. I recalled what Mrs. Connelly said to me: "Remember Nora. You're in control of your own destiny. You and nobody else." Those were her final words to me. I reflected on this while I chopped, wiped, poured, refilled, cleared, tallied, flirted, cut-off and counselled. I thought about how selfish I'd become. Self-realization is a bitch. I glanced at Kate's picture behind the bar and wiped the tears from my eyes. She once asked me if I had any tattoos. I'd told her no. She said, "Well, I do." She showed me her one and only tattoo. It was a simple red rose placed neatly below her shoulder blade. "My grandmother's name was Rose," she said, then she tooted off to take an order.

I missed Kate more and more with each passing day. Everywhere I look I see something that reminds me of her. Work hasn't been the same since. She was young and smart and gorgeous and an all-around good person; and deep down, I begrudged her for it. Now look at me. I'm gross. What I wouldn't give to have my old body back. I miss the way people used to look at me. What's that old saying? Hindsight's 20/20. Touché.

Gordon Lester drank four more pints before joining Sean Sinnicks, a local Celtic songster who performed regularly at the Cock, for his final set. The pair went off like the 4th of July. Sean Sinnicks, who stands a whopping six-foot seven, is a force to be reckoned with. His long, drawn-out stories, told in his exaggerated Irish/Boston accent, has made him another local favorite.

During their final song, I witnessed a woman burst into tears, as Sean, in his usual countenance, stepped up to the mic and declared, "The city of Boston will be officially closed for business. Thank you for your patronage, please come again." He closed the show, appropriately, with It's The End Of The World As We Know It (And I Feel Fine).

A sense of despondency wafted through the pub that night; maybe it was the stench of puke permeating from the men's restroom (which I had to clean), but the patrons spent most of their time staring solemnly into their half-empty glasses, not knowing what to do or say. Unfortunately, that didn't prevent me from receiving grotesque looks from customers, which added mountains to my misery. By now, my breasts had reached Olympian proportions. They were impossible to ignore. One guy walked in, approached the bar, was about to speak, then stopped and stared at my chest. He tripped over his tongue, scratched his head, then turned and walked out the door.

Lesley showed up at the end of the night, heavily intoxicated. She'd been drinking at a neighboring bar all night, and had that don't-fuck-with-me look about her.

"So, how's life in Nora's world?" she slurred.

I was stunned. She never says my name. I'd been counting the till. I looked up from the cash register, trying not to forget the number that was in my head, but of course, I did. She was dressed in military-style khakis, a camouflage jacket and a bandanna tied loosely around her neck.

"Oh, you know, getting by."

"Well, we did it," she said. "We actually did it. Billy Swanker's face is all over social media. It's now official. He's the leading suspect. You were right all along. They'll lock up that bastard any day now for sure. And when they do—" She punched her right fist into her left.

I nodded, then finished recounting the cash in the till. At that moment, I really wanted to get off my feet and rest. Lesley staggered behind the bar and started getting saucy.

"What's the matter with you? I told you: Swanker's going down, down, down."

She slid down onto her knees as she said this. She looked up at me with bibulous eyes. I forced a smile. It was after 2 a.m., I was too exhausted to be having this conversation, but Lesley didn't pick up on this.

"Hey, come hang out tonight, will ya? We're having a party back at my place. Whatcha say?"

"Twist my arm."

The party, as usual, was a rippah. People of every shape, size, color, creed, gender—you name it—stayed up all night, dancing and partying under a smoky haze that would make Willie Nelson proud.

At some point, and not surprisingly, my breasts became the topic of conversation. One woman, with brittle hair, strong cheekbones and fingernails that would make Freddy Krueger cringe, kept poking and prodding them. She wanted pics, and nothing would stop her. Now, to be fair, most of the partiers at this point were at least partially naked. But I wasn't having any of it. It wasn't difficult to imagine my breasts becoming the punchline for a plethora of online jokes, GIFs and memes.

Meanwhile, Lesley's friends continued to speak of my breasts as if they were the most miraculous site they'd seen. At some point, everyone was topless. Total debauchery ensued. Eventually, when no one was looking, I sneaked away and left the party. That breast reduction operation couldn't come soon enough, let me tell you.

I collapsed onto my futon upon entering my home, but not before putting on my favorite Tedeschi Trucks Band record on the turntable. The music soared. I checked my phone. There was a message from Amanda. Apparently, she'd made a date for us to visit the old church first thing in the morning. She had a hunch the old man would be there. Her cards told her so. And the cards are never wrong. Amanda, now fully consumed in my personal life, had taken matters into her own hands. She even texted a link to the church's webpage. They were serving a pancake breakfast tomorrow morning at 9 a.m.

9 a.m.? Gross. Amanda is a day person. She works the morning shift. What she doesn't understand is that us night people don't do 9 a.m.

Sorry, I replied, you're gonna have to wait until noon. Noon, I reminded her, is my 9 a.m.

Mr. Jimmy curled up beside me as I choked on my cigarette.

"I really need to quit these cancer-causing machines," I told him.

Mr. Jimmy blinked. I stroked his long orange fur and listened to his gentle purring, while he looked up at me with love and affection. "That's it," I told him. "I'm done with these cancer sticks. This time I mean it."

I butted out my cigarette. I needed to do something positive in my life, quitting smoking was a start. Just think of the money I'll save.

I was getting closer to my goal of saving for a down payment on a home; not too shabby on a bartender's budget, especially considering I don't live with my parents, like Amanda does. She too is saving for a house, but I believe (although she'd never confess to this) that she's clinging to the idea of falling in love and getting married and having babies and living happily ever after. Unfortunately, she's looking for love in all the wrong places, as the song goes. Being single these days isn't easy, by any stretch of the imagination.

I decided against setting my alarm. I'll wake up when I wake up. Sorry Amanda, a woman needs her beauty sleep. I fell asleep sometime after 5 a.m., and was exasperated when my phone started ringing three hours later. I went on a warpath once I heard the rapping on my door twenty minutes after that.

It was Amanda; it was 8:45 a.m., and she was ready to roll.

24

At least Amanda brought coffee, albeit coffee as weak as dishwater, but it did the trick.

Amanda dragged me out of bed, forced a brush through my hair, cleaned me up, dressed me, marvelled at my sweater-stretchers (her words, not mine), then shooed me out the door by 9:35 a.m. "Better late than never," she said.

It was a frigid February morning. The snow-trampled sidewalks were bustling with busybodies, the wind was unsympathetic. I squinted, straining to see through the ice pellets pounding my half-covered face as we trudged towards the church. Why didn't we call an Uber? My brain hurt and I was exhausted to the point of stupidity. I watched with wonder as people scooted their way through the frenetic, silvered streets, going wherever they needed to go at this ungodly hour. So, this is what the day people do. How neutral.

We arrived at the church just before 10 a.m. Amanda gabbed the entire time about her latest boy toy. He's tall, dark and handsome (do they even come like that anymore?). His name is Chuck Roberts; he's thirty-five, has two kids with two separate partners, lives in his mother's basement and plays keyboards in a band called Skull the Pamper. I thought she was kidding me. She wasn't.

As we approached the stone church, I became increasingly disheartened. Even more so, when I reached into my coat pocket, searching for my cigarettes, then remembered I'd quit. I begged Amanda to let us turn around and head home. I mean, what were we doing here in the first place? We certainly couldn't take food from the needy. Surely, we'd rot in hell for that. Amanda, who's as stubborn as a bad idea, journeyed on, and I was too tired to argue the point any further. Instead, I slurped the final sips of coffee from my Styrofoam cup, celebrating the caffeine as it came to the aid of my slogging brain.

A congregation had formed outside the old church. It saddened me to see so many impoverished people gathered together; mostly older men in scabby clothes with unkempt beards and hardened faces, and single mothers clinging to their child's tiny, sordid hands. Despite this, the mood was jovial. A woman with wild purple hair and a homemade sweater that was too large for her meatless body greeted us with a pamphlet.

"Christ the Lord is always on your side," she declared, then she walked to the next person.

We were standing along the sidewalk, on the outer parameters of the church, when Amanda elbowed me in the ribs.

"There he is! That's him, right?"

He was crouched behind his minions, with a cigarette dangling from his lips, shuffling a deck of cards.

"What do we do now?" Amanda whispered.

How should I know? I should be sleeping, my mind complained. As I was about to give my snippy response, I was started by a familiar voice.

"Miss Murphy?"

I looked up to see Father McCleary heading down the steep set of stairs, smiling from ear to holy ear. He was wearing a long trench coat and a winter hat. He put his arms around me, and introduced himself to Amanda, who then bowed. I could have killed her at that moment.

The priest laughed.

"I must say, I'm surprised to see you here Miss Murphy," he said. "But not as surprised as I was to hear of Mrs. Connelly's passing. How sad. She was a remarkable woman. I'd known her for many years." A plume of steam wafted from his face as he spoke. "You know, we can certainly use more volunteers around here on Saturdays. We'd love to have a couple energetic young women, such as the yourselves, on our team. If you're interested, feel free to contact me any time. We'd really appreciate it, as would our Lord and Saviour."

Team God, I thought, cynically.

Amanda grabbed a stack of pamphlets and started handing them to the folks entering the church. The priest seemed delighted by this. I wasn't. Something felt wrong. A cool breeze was sifting down my spine. At first, I passed it off as nothing, but soon everything changed. It was him.

The old man was leering at me. I could feel his horrid gaze scratching through my bones. His dastardly voice was prying into my mind, BIGGER IS BETTER, DEARY? I forced my mind shut, trying to keep him out, but it didn't work. YES! BIGGER IS BETTER!

His cronies were causing a disturbance. To my dismay, one of them started shouting at me. Meanwhile, the people in the line inched nervously towards the entrance.

The priest, now at the top of the stairs, looked concerned. At that moment he seemed to know exactly why I was here. He pointed to the old man. A gasp fell over the crowd.

"You!" he shouted. "I thought I told you to stop badgering people around here."

The old man snarled. Beside him, his cronies were shifting back and forth on sodden feet, egging him on.

"She wanted it, Father," he said, in a slithery voice. "She did this all on her own. I've done nothing wrong. Besides, I've kept my part of our bargain, although I can't say the same for you Father. You negligent, narcissistic fool-of-a-priest!"

"Lies!" the priest cried out.

The old man turned toward me; his eyes drenched in malice. He stretched out his gangly arms; his face twisted and evil. A bolt of lightning ripped through my body. I collapsed. Everything went dark, like I was dead. My body was twitching, desperate for air. I gripped the handrail, using whatever strength I had left to remain conscious.

The scene outside the church turned hectic. The old man's henchmen scattered like the breeze. People rushed inside the church, panicking. One woman shoved aside a small child, as she hurried through the church doors. A man declared this the end times, as he pushed himself to the front of the line. Once everyone was safely inside, the tremendous doors groaned, as the priest slammed them shut.

The old man advanced, seemingly floating up the stairs, spoiling for a fight. At that moment, I knew he wasn't human. He was something far worse. Amanda was clenching my hand. Her eyes were sparkling with anticipation, the devil's grin stamped across her chubby face.

The old man in the hat, now two steps below us, started taunting. "What are you going to do, Father? Kill me? You don't have the nerve! You're weak and pathetic!"

He turned toward me and hissed.

Amanda was pulling me down the stairs. Or at least, she was trying to. But it was no use. I was stuck. My boots were frozen to the stairs.

The old man sneered.

"Now, now. Where do you think you're going, Miss Murphy?"

Hearing him speak my name was absolutely revolting.

The priest rushed over and stood between us. "Don't you dare talk to her that way, Raphael, or whatever it is you're calling yourself these days. We have an agreement. So, if you know what's best for you, you'll leave."

The old man pursed his lips. "Or what? What will you do, Father? You've been a thorn in my side for far too long. It's time I teach you a lesson. Just as I did for Miss Murphy here." He winked. "What? You don't like those changes to your body, Deary? Bigger *isn't* better?"

Amanda rushed the old man and kicked him in the shins. "Fuck you, you withered old-man-piece-of-shit!"

"How dare you!" He shoved Amanda with unearthly force.

She flew to the top of the stairs, striking her head on the handrail. She collapsed.

"Amanda!" I cried out.

The priest leapt in front of the old man. The old man scoffed, tossing him aside like an empty pack of smokes. The priest tumbled to the bottom of the stairs. The old man turned to me, licking his lizardly lips. I tried to move, but couldn't. He was holding me prisoner with his mind.

Using as much bravado as I could muster, I said, "Who are you anyway? And what have you done to me?"

"Not me," he croaked. "You. You did this to yourself."

"Bullshit."

The old man let out an exultant laugh. The ground below him trembled. He approached me with alarming speed. I tried to move, but couldn't, so I looked around for help. Amanda was finding her footing at the top of the stairs, forcing herself to her feet. The priest, clearly shaken, was looking up from the bottom of the stairs.

It was just the four of us. The steady stream of pedestrians beyond the church were oblivious to our plight. We were inside a glass dome, invisible to the outside world. No one seemed to hear or see us. An ice rink had formed under my nose, my skin was pale blue and my body limp. My toes were frostbitten, as were the tips of my fingers. My breath was sputtering. Death was fast approaching, but hey, at least I would die at church. Maybe my soul would be saved after all.

Amanda grabbed my arms and started pulling me with extraordinary strength. I thought she would rip my arms from their sockets. "C'mon girl, you can do it!" she said. "C'mon, c'mon c'mon!"

I wouldn't budge. Father McCleary sprinted towards the old man, who was looming over Amanda and me. The priest reached into his coat and produced a flask.

"Holy water," he said with a simper.

"You imbecile," the old man retracted. "Look at what you've become. A mere priest. A peasant. You could've been so much more. Like me."

"You always were evil, Raphael. You just couldn't help yourself, could you? Is that why you always return here? Because you're restless and unfulfilled? Or are you just bored?"

"You lie!"

The old man's feet were no longer touching the stairs. He hovered toward the priest, reciting ancient-sounding words that shook the ground below us: "WAYLORD KRANDIS O'LAUFREY, NATASS CALLETH COMETH BLIZZODORFF..."

As he spoke, the church started quavering. Its exterior walls were collapsing. I could hear wailing and screaming, as the people trapped inside started pounding on the doors, desperate to escape their gruesome fate. Above us, the sky turned frantic; the wind raged onward as the temperature continued to plummet.

Father McCleary, standing toe to toe with Raphael, started preaching: "BUT YOU, O BETHLEHEM EPHRATHAH, WHO ARE TOO LITTLE TO BE AMONG THE CLANS OF JUDAH, FROM YOU SHALL COME FORTH FOR ME ONE WHO IS TO BE RULER IN ISRAEL, WHOSE COMING FORTH IS FROM OF OLD, FROM ANCIENT DAYS."

The priest made a sign of the cross, then started dousing Raphael with holy water.

"MOREOVER, AS FOR ME, FAR BE IT FROM ME THAT I SHOULD SIN AGAINST THE LORD BY CEASING

TO PRAY FOR YOU, AND I WILL INSTRUCT YOU IN THE GOOD AND THE RIGHT WAY."

The old man's eyes rolled into the back of his head. He started convulsing. The holy water was burning trenches into his translucent skin. When his eyes snapped open, they were as black as night. He pointed a long and gnarly finger at the priest, and started his retaliation.

"THE TOMB OF ENITH-SUTRA, CAULOUSE TENNAMENT, GALUG OF CITHOG WRELTCHIT TURF…"

The bushes in front of the church went ablaze. The priest shielded himself with his coat and continued preaching. Raphael, clearly delighted, fought the priest tooth and nail, all the while chanting inside my head: BIGGER IS BETTER DEARY? YES! BIGGER IS BETTER. I put my hands over my ears and screamed.

Father McCleary slipped and fell. Raphael grabbed the priest by the throat and started choking him. The priest struggled; purple veins were bulging from his neck, his tongue protruded. Despite this, he continued his sermon.

"EVEN THOUGH I WALK THROUGH THE VALLEY OF THE SHADOW OF DEATH, I WILL FEAR NO EVIL, FOR YOU ARE WITH ME; YOUR ROD AND YOUR STAFF, THEY COMFORT ME."

"Shut up, you wretched old fool!"

The priest escaped the old man's grip. They fought their way up the stairs, with only the handrail separating them. One preaching to the Lord, the other preaching to the Devil. It was a showdown: good versus evil.

The old man advanced.

"No!" Amanda cried, rushing toward them.

"Amanda, don't!" I shouted, but my voice was drowned out by the burning bushes and the howling wind.

The old man's face stretched into a snarl. He turned to Amanda, and thrusted his hands at her. Rays of brilliant blue light blasted through her, hitting her square in the chest. She flew to the bottom of the stairs, cracking her head on the pavement, as she came to a halt.

"Amanda!"

The priest regained his balance.

"Oh no you don't."

He threw the old man to the ground. The ground crackled and groaned, as if to protest. The old man stood up, dusted the snow off his suit, tilted his hat, then regained his composure. He scowled at me.

"You did this to yourself, Mrs. Murphy. Not me. *You.*"

I was about to speak, when he made a go-away gesture, knocking the wind out of me. I sat on the frozen step, clutching the handrail, unable to move. The old man, with a sneer that made my skin crawl, looked up at the priest, stretched out both his arms, sending him a series of lightning bolts. The priest leapt out of the way, just in time. The lightning struck the church instead, and it caught fire.

"No!"

The priest dashed down the stairs, grabbed the old man by his collar, cracked him in the jaw. Then with one large hand, he clenched the old man's throat; "Open up!" and started pouring the contents of the flask down his throat.

The old man garbled and coughed and fought back vehemently. His hands and feet flailing, his face steeped with rage. The priest labored on, shaking him back and forth, blocking his windpipe from receiving any trace of air. The old man grappled. He let out one final gasp. A stray bolt of lightning struck the church steeple, which erupted in flames. Then he went still. His body, fully transpicuous, started dissolving into nothing, until it was gone. Only his pork-pie hat remained.

"Wicked pissah," Amanda said.

We laughed.

Amanda struggled towards me. I could move my feet again. We hugged and embraced and cried for an eternity. Then I took a moment to enjoy the simple act of breathing. I was pretty shook-up.

The streets beyond the church vicinity were littered with pedestrians and motorists and even the occasional cyclist, all unaware of our quandary. To them we were invisible, non-existent.

Inside the church came a gargantuan roar. The priest hustled up the stairs and opened the tremendous church doors. Clusters of people came dashing down the stairs, holding hands, covering their faces. All the while, the nefarious flames grew taller. The smoke coming from inside the church was harrowing. The heat was threatening to burn off my otherwise frost-bitten flesh. Off in the distance, sirens sprang to life, as the Boston Fire Department raced to the rescue.

Amanda was holding my arm, as we descended the slippery steps. On the sidewalk, I found myself standing on a mound of sickly green mucus, where the old man had just evaporated. My boots caught fire. I stamped in freshly fallen snow, creating a vile, rank-smelling cloud of steam in the process. Amanda, reached down and picked up the old man's hat, placing it neatly on her head. It fit like a dream. She smiled and gave a two-thumbs-up.

Meanwhile, the church continued to burn. Father McCleary managed to rescue everyone inside; soon a congregation had formed at the base of the church, edging along the sidewalk. All eyes were pointed at the priest, who was crouched over, breathing shallow. He looked frazzled.

Amanda said, "You sir, are one hell of a priest."

He smiled, put an arm around her and squeezed. Amanda lit up like a Christmas tree. I was about to bring up the elephant in the room, but he beat me to it.

"We won't be seeing Raphael for awhile," he said, while adjusting his spectacles. "He's gone back to his special place in hell, it would seem. So, all's well that ends well, as they say."

The crowd roared its approval, then began chatting amongst themselves. They dispersed once the firefighters arrived, who spent day and night trying to manage the raging fire. When I turned to thank the priest, he was gone. The entire street was now blocked off, as teams of firefighters and first-responders continued to arrive.

Weariness and hunger won over curiosity, so Amanda and I ventured off to Chuck's Diner, where we gobbled bacon and eggs and fried badadoes, all the while discussing whether or not we should go to the hospital.

"No way," said Amanda, in between bites of bacon. "I spend enough time there as it is, with work and all."

That settled it. Besides, how would we explain what really happened? If only we'd thought to pull out our phones and capture some of the craziness on video, maybe then people would believe our story. Life is funny that way, when you're face-to-face with death, your phone is the furthest thing from your mind.

After eating and chatting and licking our wounds, we hugged and said our goodbyes.

I went home. My body felt like a dump truck. If I wasn't so exhausted, I might be worried about my current state of health.

All things considered, I slept twelve hours straight that night, then woke up feeling fresh as a daisy. I hadn't had a cigarette in over two days. Maybe things were starting to perk up.

The church was burned beyond recognition.

25

The following week everything changed.

The pandemic forced the Cock & Fiddle to close, leaving me unemployed, and all alone in my hapless apartment with Mr. Jimmy, who couldn't have been any happier. He finally had me all to himself. If I were honest, a terrible part of me was happy for the lockdown. It gave me an excuse to hide away, while my breasts continued their languid journey across the state of Massachusetts.

Sadly, I spent my birthday alone and in lockdown. But hey, who's complaining? Next year will be my Dirty-30. WOOT. I'll make up for it then. On top of everything else, my appointment with Dr. Palmer had been postponed indefinitely. This added to my anguish. Time was running out. Soon my breasts would prevent me from being able to walk. What then?

There was no sign of Billy Swanker. It was as though he'd disappeared off the face of the earth. Correspondingly, the press had turned their attention to the pandemic, and the Midnight Rambler, aka: the Killer, was no longer front-page news. It's amazing how quickly the public forgets. But I didn't forget. Deep down, I knew Mr. Swanker would show his smug face again. It was only a matter of when.

Everything in the world was changing. Lesley disappeared for a month, only to pop up on social media, protesting the lockdown with a group called the Freedom Fighters. This made her the target of constant online hate, something I never would have dreamed possible, but this was a new world. Blaze Temmerman, in all his glory, ended up being busted in a drugs scandal; and ultimately, the Cock & Fiddle perished, as did the Boston Manners. No one batted an eye.

The months of March and April were not kind to Amanda, who worked tirelessly as a receptionist at Mass General Hospital, which meant she had to deal with the panicking public. This made her a superhero in my mind.

Amanda's love life became the center of my existence. We'd drink wine and scroll through her list of potential suitors on Plenty of Fish, rating them one by one. Apparently, Chuck Roberts wasn't all he was cracked up to be. Amanda decided to go with bachelor number nine: a rugged-looking biker named Waylon Bent, who owned his own tattoo parlor (now in lockdown, of course). Waylon was a perfect gentleman, she told me, once you got past the wall of ink covering his entire body. She did stress *entire* body.

Sometime in May, Amanda forwarded me some articles she'd recently dug up. Her tenacity amazes me. Even while working a strenuous job and seeking single men online, she still found time for sleuthing. The first article was dated 1886:

ARSON SUSPECTED IN CHURCH FIRE

A devastating fire has decimated the Church of the Holy Cross. Frank Cosentino, a local firefighter, perished trying to save it. The fire occurred early Saturday morning; and although no cause has been found, foul play is suspected.

Since opening its doors in 1843 the Church of the Holy Cross has seen its fair share of unusual activity. As it stands, the church is unsure whether or not it will ever open its doors to the public again.

The next article was dated 1889:

CHURCH PROVES MIRACLES DO EXIST

Three years ago, a local catholic church burned to the ground. Although the arsonist has never been found, foul-play is still suspected. Yet in what can only be described as a modern-day miracle, the Church of the Holy Cross stands once again, taller and more beautiful than ever.

"It's a miracle," says Mildred Frank, who was baptized at the church over twenty years ago. "This church rests on sacred land." Others claim the reason for the church's quick recovery is simply due to the blood sweat and tears of the men who worked tirelessly on its restoration.

Whether it's magic or sheer man-power, the Church of the Holy Cross proves that nothing can stand in the way of delivering its message to its people. The church will open its doors again this Sunday. Mass services begin at 9 a.m., 12 p.m. and 3 p.m. respectively.

The last article was from June 9, 1947:

CHURCH UNDER FIRE AGAIN

Tragedy struck this weekend as the Church of the Holy Cross was ravished by fire. A local family has since come forward with a remarkable story. According to Gertrude Fitzpatrick, her daughter Mary, 9, and her siblings arrived early Saturday morning to help the church serve breakfast to the public, as they've done many times. According to Mary Fitzpatrick, a magician was loitering close by, hawking goods and performing card tricks. She claims it was the magician who caused the fire.

"He did it with his mind," Mary told the authorities, in a startling claim. "I watched him do it."

The incident is still under investigation. Anyone with information regarding this incident is asked to contact the authorities immediately. The cause of the fire remains speculative.

She followed this up with a text: what does this mean?????
I responded with a GIF of Buddy Christ, from our favorite Jay and
Silent Bob movie, Dogma.

In truth, I had no idea what any of this meant. There was
something peculiar about the church, the priest, and of course, the
old man in the hat. It would be foolish to think otherwise at this
point. But we still had little to go on.

Wearily, I filled the tub with foamy water and lit a scented
candle. Then I dusted off a bottle of Chardonnay, uncorked it and
filled my glass. A Gentle Rain playlist sifted through my
Bluetooth speaker, while I lay naked in the tub, regarding my
mess of a body. Maybe this curse will last forever. Maybe this is
my fate. Maybe this is Nora's Curse. Holding back a sea of tears, I
allowed myself to revel in the warmth of the water; and with the
help of the soothing playlist, I closed my eyes and let the darkness
wash over me.

I slept.

I was inside the church basement. The smell of fresh coffee
and hotcakes was pungent. There was a murmur, as the lineup of
people congregated toward the food. At the head of the line was a
corpulent black woman with frizzy hair, generous lips and arms
that could strangle a python. She was standing behind a folding
table, fulminating as she handed the people their plates of food.
Her voice was both sonorous and foreboding.

I joined the line. Slowly and without order, the lineup
lingered, until I found myself standing directly in front of her. She
snickered as she handed me a food plate. I took the offering, then I
looked around for Amanda, who was calling out in distress. I
followed the sound of her voice. As I neared the stairwell leading
to the main level of the church, her voice grew steadily louder.
She was screaming for help. I rushed up the stairs, pancakes and
all, to see what was the matter.

Then I saw him.

Raphael was standing at the altar. A beam of blue light spilled from the stained-glass window high above his head, giving him the appearance of a fallen angel. He wore an outlandish lavender tuxedo, a black bowtie and a Gentleman's silk top hat with a bright purple feather tucked neatly in its side. His hands were clenched tightly around Amanda's throat. She was on her knees, struggling futilely to escape. I watched in horror as her face turned salmon-red. Her tongue protruded like a thirsty dog. She thrusted both her arms out in one final attempt to free herself. Then she went still.

"Get away from her!" I cried, tossing aside my food.

"Well, well, well," said the old man, looking up at me. "Look what the cat dragged in. Why, it's little Miss Murphy. How's it hanging? Or should I ask, how are *they* hanging?" His laughter filled the church like a bad dream, and echoed for an eternity.

His minions—vile, despicable creatures with beady eyes and rotting faces—were crawling toward me. Their bodies scraped across the linoleum floors as they slithered. Without hesitating, I took a deep breath, made the sign on the cross, then lunged toward the old man in a sudden dash. He tossed Amanda's lifeless body aside. It made a THUNK. He smiled at me and said, "Do you like magic, Miss Murphy? Because there's plenty to go around!" His hat was twirling; his bow tie spinning like a wheel, much to the delight of his minions.

"Go to hell, Raphael, or whatever your name is. I'm not afraid of you."

"No?"

His hat stopped turning; he took it off, then he reached inside and produced a beating human heart.

"But you should be."

He bit into the heart like an apple. His face went crimson red, as blood leaked from his gruesome teeth, covering his face in gore. Without warning, the church steeple lifted off, and a heavy storm swept in. Great gusts of wind came at me in every direction, sweeping me off my feet. I flew to the back of the church, latched onto a pew and held on as tightly as possible, watching as the flash flood carried Amanda's lifeless body into the endless sky. Raphael's voice hijacked my mind, whispering, taunting, provoking.

"I'm not afraid, you wicked old crank!" I shouted, but my voice was drowned out by the torrential downpour. The old man advanced. Meanwhile, my grip on the pew was loosening; my fingers threatening to let go at any second. My feet were flailing high above my head. The force of the wind was relentless. If I let go, I'll die.

Just then I heard the voice of my father, beautiful and solicitous, somewhere deep in my soul, telling me everything will be alright. At that moment I became lucid. I realized I was dreaming, and found incredible strength and resilience.

I let go.

My body fell to the floor. The old man attacked. He reached out to grab me, but I turned and shoved him with indescribable force. He was the one who went fluttering away, spinning into the menacing tornado. The storm devoured him whole. As he disappeared, my father called out one last time: "Ha, ha, ha. Well done, Princess. You're almost home."

Everything went quiet. The church was still. At the center of the altar lay Amanda's lifeless body. I heard footsteps coming up behind me. I turned to see Father McCleary. He was looking kindly at Amanda's corpse. He knelt down beside her, placed his hand over her forehead and prayed. Within seconds, her eyes popped open. He turned to me and said, "We're almost at the finish line, Miss Murphy. It's up to you now. But remember, I'm just a click away."

I woke up in frigid bathwater, the priest's words ringing in my mind. The bathroom was pitch black. How long had I been asleep? I lit the candle and relished in its light. My unfinished glass of wine was waiting faithfully beside me at the edge of the tub, so I gulped it down. 'I'm just a click away,' the priest said. Was that an invitation? I thought it was. I was wide awake and equally restless. After unplugging the drain and waiting for the bath bubbles to dissolve, I found three towels; one for my hair, one for my lower body, one for my chest. I was at a loss. What's it going to take to lift this dreadful curse, once and for all? What I needed was a plan, so got dressed and made a list:

NORA'S LIST:

Email Father McCleary

Contact Dr. Palmer ASAP

Text Amanda to come over for some Wine Time (it's always Wine Time)

Quit smoking (I mean it this time)

Avoid 'B.S.' at ALL COSTS!!!

Try to relax. Life's too short for stress

Record a solo album.

END THIS CURSE

I spent the night feeling guilty while scrolling through Kate's Instagram account. I viewed her final post. It was the silly pic Randy had taken during our staff Christmas party: the Boobsy Twins stuffed inside the shiny red booth with our arms wrapped around each other.

My heart sank. She was so animated in this picture. Her whole life was ahead of her. That is, until she met the likes of Mr. Swanker. You don't know how precious life is, until it's gone. Mrs. Connelly said, "Death gets more familiar with each passing year, but it never gets any easier. Life is cruel that way." How tragic. My guilt was like a sledgehammer to my soul. I knew who was to blame for this: me.

Billy was my responsibility, and he killed Kate. I could not deny this. I deserved what was happening to my body. It's my karma. What did the old man say to me, right before the priest kicked his ass? "You did this to yourself, Mrs. Murphy. Not me. You." I sighed as I poured myself another glass of wine.

I checked to see if the church had a Facebook page. It did. I searched through its many pictures, stopping at my favorite one. In it, Father McCleary was preaching from his pulpit; a sliver of omniscient light sprinkled over his congregation, making the mass divine.

The urge to contact this priest was irrefutable. Maybe it was because of my dream. Maybe it was because he'd saved me from that demon-thing not so long ago. Maybe it was because I was running out of options.

I sent him a formal email, trying not to screw it up too much.

Good day Father,

I write to you because I cannot get those final moments we spent together at the church out of my mind. What a day it was! I'd like to express a heartfelt thank you for saving my life from that 'thing'. I'd also like to express my deepest sympathies for your church having been so badly damaged. What a tragedy.

As you may imagine, I have numerous questions that I would like to discuss with you, too many to send via email. So, if you can find it in your heart of hearts to meet with me sometime, please do so. These are wicked times indeed. What a world we live in.

Best,

Nora Murphy

After a long and arduous pause, I clicked send. Then I slipped into my PJs, poured the remainder of the wine into my glass, and reached for a cigarette. I stopped myself before lighting it. There was no way I was going to light that death-stick. This lockdown is giving me the chance to rid myself of that dreadful nicotine habit, without being held accountable for any bad behaviour that might otherwise ensue. I snapped the cigarette in two, then tossed it in the trash, along with the rest of the pack.

I felt better. I've gone this long without a cigarette, no point starting back up again. I flipped through my records until I found 'Heart Shaped World'. I closed my eyes, and got lost inside the music.

What a wicked game you play, to make me feel this way

What a wicked thing to do, to let me dream of you

What a wicked thing to say, you never felt this way

What a wicked thing to do, to make me dream of you

And I don't wanna fall in love (this world is only gonna break your heart)

No, I don't wanna fall in love (this world is only gonna break your heart)

With you

My father loved this song. In fact, this twelve-inch piece of wonder was playing as I was being conceived. I pushed aside that icky thought, and let my mind drift towards my mother.

I wondered how she was doing during this lockdown. We've only spoken once since she came back from the Bahamas; and as usual, she spent most of the conversation criticizing me for becoming a bartender.

Here's the tragic part: my defence for becoming a career bartender was that the world would always need bartenders, even during times of crises (especially during times of crises), so I would never be without a job.

Apparently, I was wrong. My mother was the first to point this out. To be honest, I think she resents me for moving so far away.

Yet, despite her constant disapproval over everything I do, I still love her. She is my mother after all, for better or for worse.

Sleep came instantly, but it didn't last. At some point during the night,

I was startled awake by my blasted phone. I didn't need a fortune-teller telling me who was on the other end. It was Billy Swanker.

I answered the call.

26

"What do you want?"

No response. "Hello? That you Swanker? Or should I call you Midnight Rambler? Or how about the Killer? Yeah, I like that. The Killer. Has a nice ring to it. Wouldn't you agree?"

Heavy breathing.

"Listen, you little shit. You better stay away from me. Or, if you know what's best, you'll turn yourself in to the police."

More silence.

I was about to hang up, when I heard one puny sob, followed by a sniffle. Billy was crying. I couldn't believe it. Both my hands were shaking, my mind full of rage. I was no longer afraid of Billy Swanker, I realized. He's got nothing on the old man in the hat. Yet, I hated him for how he used me. For keeping me at the edge of a cliff.

Well, not anymore. Not this time. Before my heart could interfere, I hung up on him, then I put my phone on silent mode, and went back to sleep. That was the last time Billy phoned me.

The following morning, Father McCleary returned my message. His reply was short and concise:

Greetings, Miss Murphy, how do you do? I would be delighted to answer any of your questions (to the best of my ability). Shall we meet at the Commons? If so, how does tomorrow morning at 11 sound? Look for me on the bench closest to the pond, by the big rock.

God bless,

Father McCleary

And with that, I set out to meet a priest. The air was crisp, the sun was warm on my face. That, plus the steadfast sound of birds chirping and dogs barking certainly improved my mood. I felt energized for the first time since being forced into lockdown. Moreover, I was eager to talk to someone other than Amanda. Even if it was a priest. Yes, my nicotine cravings were egregious, my nerves were shot, my hands as steady as an agnostic's view on world religion, but I hadn't gone out or seen anybody besides Amanda in over two months. I needed this.

There was a problem: I was hunchbacked. Walking was damn near impossible. I could pour a proper pint of Guinness faster than it took to cross Beacon Street. But hey, it was nice to get out of my stuffy little apartment. Small victories, right?

The Boston Common is stunning during springtime. With the snow having melted and the sun peaking through the coffee-colored clouds, and the green returning to the freshly-cut grass, it was heaven on earth. I passed the bandstand where I once stood with Kate and Lesley and thousands of other women; except now, the bandstand was boarded off with police tape. Only a handful of people passed me as I slogged through the ghost park, each person staring at their shoes, avoiding me like the plague. Not a single person made eye contact. It was like watching a zombie apocalypse movie, and I was the lead character.

I spotted the priest standing awkwardly beside a bench covered in police tape. He wore brown corduroy pants, leather boots and a tight-fitting cardigan sweater with his clerical collar poking out. He waved me over.

We shared an awkward exchange, then he suggested we find a proper place to sit, one without police tape. We moved to a large, smooth rock next to the pond, where we stayed for the better part of an hour, discussing the events which had taken place back in February.

The priest, who had a lot to say, spoke first. "The Church of the Holy Cross was built on sacred ground, you know. It's unclear whether this was done intentionally, but I think it was. The church was meant to be a cathedral. It was to be the greatest church in all of Massachusetts; that is, until a string of peculiar events took place during its construction. Workers were falling off scaffolds, or getting poisoned; some reported burning bushes, others reporting a foul stench permeating from the bowels of the church basement."

He removed his spectacles, wiped them on his sweater.

"Meanwhile, workers were also reporting miracles. For instance, in the late 1880's, during the church's reconstruction, a young mother had brought her newborn son to the church, visiting her husband during his lunch break. This baby had a serious illness, and was expected to die very soon.

"That baby's name was Charles O'Leary. To her amazement, after spending an afternoon at the church, the boy's health steadily improved. In fact, he lived a long and healthy life, devoting his entire adult life to that church."

"Yes, I'd read about him," I said.

The priest raised an eyebrow and gave me a curious look, before turning his attention to the freshwater pond. A gaggle of geese was resting under the sweeping branches of a weeping willow; its silver-tinged catkins kissing the passive pond, eager to flourish for another season. I was reminded of back home. As a child, my father and I would go hiking through Confederation Park. Father would discuss the latest Bruins' draft picks, while I gave secret names to each of the willows we passed. My favorite was Alice.

"You read about him, did you? What did you read?"

I snapped myself away from memory lane.

"Oh, not much. Something about burning bushes and the church being forced to close. It happened twice, I believe. A young girl spotted the second fire."

As soon as those words spilled from my lips, it hit me: this was the 'something' that had been tickling the back of my brain for quite some time. The little girl from that article was Mrs. Connelly. It was her family. They were the kids at the church.

"Ah, yes. The Fitzpatricks," he said, shifting uncomfortably on the rock. "The church has many secrets, Miss Murphy, and keeping them under wraps has been a daunting task, indeed. I guess you're wondering who Raphael really is. This is going to sound crazy, but I know I can trust you. Raphael—although this is merely one of the names he goes by, he has others—is just a crotchety old man. Yes, he is very old, but he is in fact human. Um, or at least he was human. It's hard to say now."

"Barry called him the Devil."

"What?" He seemed startled.

I pictured Barry sprinkling her ashes throughout this park, and wondered if Mrs. Connelly was watching over us. I hoped she was. "Um, Barry. Mary's brother. I met him shortly after she died. He gave me some old newspaper clippings she'd been saving."

The priest chuckled. "I haven't seen Barry in, oh, too many years to count. But, no, Raphael is not the Devil, although he likes to think of himself as such. He's just a sorry old sod with delusions of grandeur. You must forgive me, Nora," he said, wiping the tears behind his spectacles. "I haven't spoken of this to anyone in a very long time."

Just then, a mother duck bobbled her way toward us, her brood of ducklings close behind. She hobbled toward Father McCleary, stretched out her elongated beak, then honked. He produced a chunk of bread from his pocket. The ducks gobbled up the bread, then tottered toward the pond and swam away.

"Where does his magic come from?" I asked.

"Good question. There's a lot at stake here. I'm unsure how much I should tell you. I've spent the last few weeks praying, asking for guidance, but the Lord works in mysterious ways. Elliot Blues said that."

"The Blues Brothers."

"The sequel," he said, proudly, "Quite possibly the most underrated sequel in movie history, I might add."

I smiled. Anyone who references the Blues Brothers 2000 movie is more-than-okay in my eyes. It was Tyson's go-to play-along movie; I've seen it more times than I've announced 'last call'.

The priest, who was becoming flustered, continued. "So, I've decided to tell you this. Just in case something was to happen to me. Besides, you saw with your own eyes. And, forgive me for saying this, but it looks as though you've been touched by one of his spells."

The jig was up. We were back to my breasts.

"Raphael was once a regular man, back when the church was first being built. In fact, he was one of the men who worked on its construction. I believe he stumbled upon its power by accident. How, exactly? I do not know. But he's found a way to harness its power to keep himself alive. All these years he's drifted in and out of people's lives, causing havoc everywhere he goes. He feeds off people's misfortunes. Or negative energy, if you will. And these days, there's plenty to go around."

"Of course!" I blurted. "That's what Mrs. Connelly was getting at. That's why she'd kept all those clippings. She was monitoring him. Keeping tabs. You said you and him have an agreement."

He scratched his head. I hadn't noticed the clumps of gray in his hair, nor the deep lines cutting into his face, until now.

"Yes. And we did. But he rarely, if ever, keeps to our agreements. You see, he passes himself off as a grifter, or sometimes as a magician. He takes small amounts of money from passerbyers, while they're being dazzled by his flair. But every so often, he needs to power up. That's when, pardon the expression, all hell breaks loose. I believe that is happening now."

"Do you think his spells are reversible? I mean, look at me." I burst into tears.

The priest gently touched my shoulder. "Yes. Absolutely. His spells dissipate in due time. In fact, I have a theory about this, which I'm willing to share with you. If you're interested in hearing it, of course."

I nodded.

"He picks up on people's weaknesses, then exploits them. Which I believe happened to you. So, if my theory is correct, your curse can only last as long as it holds merit."

"Which means," I said, trying to find the proper words. "If and when I learn my lesson, my curse will be lifted?"

"Precisely."

I asked him another question; one that's been troubling me. "Where do you think he is right now? If he's not dead, of course."

"Well, Nora, I've been tracking him for quite some time. This is what I've concluded: he goes wherever the next big thing is about to go down. He looks for tragedy. He senses it. Could be New York, could be Montreal, could be Paris or even somewhere in Australia. The old kook sure gets around. But he always comes back to the church. It's the true source of his power."

"Do you think he's responsible for the Rambler?"

"Yes, of course. I'm certain of it. That's the reason why he showed up again. I knew trouble was brewing. I braced myself."

I reached for my non-existent pack of cigarettes, swore in silence, then made a silent prayer for this nicotine craving to cease. Then I stood and stretched my legs. Laughter was coming from the grassy field to our left. Two ridiculously good-looking guys were tossing around a frisbee in the middle of the otherwise empty field. One wore jean shorts and a Phish T-shirt; the other guy was topless, displaying wonderfully crafted chest muscles.

The priest glanced at his wristwatch and coughed. "Well, Nora, I must return home. But this was nice. Thank you for listening to my silly stories. We should do it again soon."

"Tomorrow?" I blurted out, surprising both of us.

"Yes. I would like that. Same bat time?"

"Same bat channel."

On the walk home, I passed the Cock & Fiddle. A For Sale sign was taped to the main doors. This saddened me. I peaked in through one of the big bay windows. The pub was dead and stark. I spotted the picture of Kate atop the bar. What would she think of the current state of the world? She would have a positive outlook. She always did. I don't recall ever hearing her complain. I certainly cannot say the same for myself.

The rest of the walk home was spent pondering what the priest had told me, putting together the final pieces of the puzzle, wondering what he was hiding. There was more to the priest than he was letting on. I was sure of it.

My mother called. She was insistent that I move back to Hamilton. After a lengthy discussion (if you call getting reamed out for an hour a discussion), I hung up and called Dr. Palmer, ready to book my follow-up appointment.

While on hold, listening to jazz so smooth, Michael Bublé would shudder, trepidation crept in. I recalled what the priest said: "Your curse can only last as long as it holds merit."

Was it really that simple? If I repent, would I wake up one morning to my rightful body? Or maybe my breasts would start shrinking while I was out in public; and if so, how would I explain this? Maybe I do need a psychiatrist after all. How ironic. Over the past seven years, I've been Listen Lady to countless lost souls spilling their guts to me, while I poured them their next drink. I've heard more problems than a priest during confession. Oftentimes, simply lending an ear is all that's required. People tend to solve their own problems, once they've got everything off their chest.

In the summer of 2017, a man entered the bar and ordered himself a scotch. The good stuff. I'd never seen him before. He was new. He smiled as he paid for his drink, but his eyes were brooding. It was a Wednesday, I remember, Jazz Night, and this gentleman, who was dressed in a paisley suit, started chatting me up; and seeing how he was tipping me $5 on every drink, I took notice. He told me, several shots later, that he'd caught his wife cheating with his best friend. Now he was going to kill the bastard. I didn't judge, nor did I take him on his word. I simply listened. Just as he was leaving, he concluded that the best thing to do was to end the marriage and move on. One year later, almost to the day, this gentleman entered the bar and ordered a scotch. I did a double-take. He'd shaved his beard, cut his hair and dropped ten pounds, but I recognized him straight away. It would be impossible to forget those eyes. He paid me $50, shot me a wink, then split, never to set foot in the pub again.

I was miserable. I missed my job. I missed playing music. I missed seeing people face to face. But I missed my body the most. I wanted it back more than anything else. My anxiety was skyrocketing. My situation was dire. I couldn't see a way out of this mess. With a mind full of razor blades, I cranked up my father's classic Aerosmith record and spent the night scrolling through pictures of me online, watching my breasts grow larger and larger. This didn't help, but some of the comments were great. My favorite being a GIF showing a sad looking dude staring down into his T-shirt with a hopeless expression on his face. The caption read: when you drop food down your boobs but then you can't find it. Zing! If I didn't have my father's sense of humor, Swanker wouldn't be the only one wanted for murder.

Those pictures were a not-so-subtle reminder that I should be careful what I wish for. Things can always get worse. And usually do. I'm living proof. Sigh. I went offline, absconding the callousness of the digital world; and as I transitioned from the waking state to the dream state, I let Steven Tyler have the final word:

Dream on

Dream on

Dream on

Dream until your dreams come true

27

The following afternoon was overcast, the air basement-damp, the wind relentless; in stark contrast to the day before.

I wore my soft suede jacket (a recent purchase), a turtleneck sweater (stretched to the max), my favorite pair of Levi's (blue, of course) and my best walking shoes. I pushed aside my anxiety and allowed myself to enjoy the simpler things in life, like being outdoors. Two days in a row. A miracle.

I took a different route this time, passing the church on my way to the park. It's stone skeleton still stood; its guts under a pile of rubble; a shell of its former glory. A team of strong men were busy clearing out the debris. I was expecting to bump into the old man and his cronies. Constantly, I checked over my shoulders, sure he would spring out and surprise me. He didn't. I soldiered on, finally reaching the beautiful Boston Public Garden.

The priest was standing by the pond, with two piping hot coffees. He handed me one. We said cheers, then we sat on our rock, waiting for our coffees to cool. Behind us, a raft of ducklings swam languidly in the blue-green pond, under the umbrella of the weeping willow. The scene was breathtaking. I took some pics, then I put my phone back in my purse before it could steal any more of my attention. The coffee had cooled enough for my first tentative taste.

"Mmm, I just love a hot coffee on a cool day," I said, breaking the silence.

"Indeed. Dunks does it right, don't they?" The priest took a cautious sip, then added, "I hope you like double-double."

I did.

We sipped our coffees in silence. I cherished it. It's not every day you find someone who you can sit quietly with and not have it feel uncomfortable. This was nice. When the priest spoke, he spoke cautiously, but his confidence grew as the words came spilling out of him. "I thought some more about this curse of yours, Miss Murphy. And, um, I hope you don't mind, but I did a little research. You may or may not be surprised to know this, but Mrs. Connelly wasn't the only one keeping tabs on Raphael. There were stories that the newspapers wouldn't cover. The stranger ones. Back in the nineties, for example, there was a girl of seventeen who'd had the misfortune of crossing Raphael's path. It's unclear as to what their exchange was about, but soon after, this girl had become pregnant, which was impossible, of course, because she was still a virgin, although nobody would believe her. Especially not once her belly started swelling up like a beach ball. That's when she came to see me for confession."

I leaned closer until our shoulders met. Bunches of gray hairs were sprinkled on his head, and his crow's feet now seemed exaggerated. Although the man looked fatally exhausted, his enthusiasm never wavered.

After making the sign of the cross, he said, "Lord forgive me for what I'm about to say. This young woman had just come from mass, like every other Sunday, but on this particular day she was full of questions regarding sex. She'd recently watched a movie—I can't recall which one—where a teenage girl had become pregnant. After watching this movie, this girl became obsessed with the idea of having a baby. Seems silly now, but maybe you can understand. She then became fascinated with the story of Mary, the Mother of the Immaculate Conception. Believe me when I say this: I was stunned. At this point, I was convinced that the church had become irrelevant, especially to young people. So, in a way this young woman rejuvenated my faith. Anyhow, this was going through her mind when she bumped into Raphael, who was panhandling on the sidewalk outside the church. She reached into her purse but when she went to hand a couple dollars to the old kook, she claims something happened. A spark. She heard his menacing voice echo inside the chambers of her mind. The shrubs outside the church burst into flames. People started panicking. Her parents pulled her away. They got into their car and drove off. The following week something was stirring inside her belly. Oh, how I remember her tears."

I gasped. "So, what happened to her?"

His face hardened, making him look extremely old. He removed his spectacles and gave them a wipe. "Well, she hid this as best she could, fortunately winter was coming, so she could wear heavy sweaters and multiple layers of clothing to hide her belly."

I laughed. I couldn't help myself.

"It was a scandal. Her parents, both devout Christians, were furious and wanted to send her away to stay with her grandparents. Sadly, when she went for her final ultrasound, the doctors reported that her baby had no heartbeat. Let me tell you, Nora, it was devastating."

I wiped fresh tears from my face, then considered asking another question, but couldn't decide which of the twelve to ask.

"Now get this," he said. "When it was time to deliver the stillborn baby—arguably the most inconsolable thing a woman can do—the doctors told her the baby was gone. Vanished. There was no baby in her belly. Within a month she was back to her normal size. Except, as one can imagine, she herself never returned to normal. How does one get over something like that?"

"But, that's impossible."

The priest shrugged. "She's since devoted herself to the church. She's become a nun. And what an incredible nun she's made of herself."

I'd never known a nun. In fact, up until that very moment, I'd forgotten they even existed, but I smartly kept this to myself. It struck me how odd this must seem. Here I was, a career bartender, sitting next to a Catholic priest, chatting like long lost friends, when I myself know nothing of church or religion. I was a fraud. But I didn't mind. I liked the priest. There was something special about him. Maybe some of his omniscience would rub off on me. Lord knows I could use it.

"This woman," he continued. "Rarely speaks of this incident, as one could imagine. She closed that chapter and has never looked back." He closed his eyes and rubbed his temples. Whatever was happening to him was accelerating. I wanted to ask if he was okay, but my curiosity over what he was telling me was tenacious. "Do you think it was a trick?" I asked. "What the old man—Raphael—did to her? It must've been a trick, right?"

"Yes and no. But mostly yes," he laughed. "He's an illusionist. What some refer to as dark magic. But it's all an illusion. Trickery, if you will. But then, look what he did outside the church. He's never acted this way before. His powers are increasing."

"Can he be stopped?"

The priest mulled this over. He seemed lost in thought, entangled in memories. Finally, when I thought he'd forgotten my question or simply was refusing to comment, he spoke. Honestly? I do not know. I've done the best I could, trying to keep him at bay, but he's gotten out of control. He's a wicked man, that's for certain. But when it's all said and done, he's just flesh and bone like the rest of us. I don't think you'll be seeing the likes of Raphael any time soon."

At risk of having an anxiety attack or drowning in the pond, I changed the subject.   "Tell me more about Mrs. Connelly."

"Ahh yes, Mary Connelly." He smiled. "She was always special. Even as a girl. So full of questions, always curious. She worked as a dental assistant. Did you know? She married a wonderful man, who worked as a millwright, right up until he passed away. Cancer got him. He was a heavy smoker, I remember. Mrs. Connelly spent her remaining years as a widow, helping out around the church. She was always in positive spirits. So very helpful."

"According to the newspaper article," I said. "She'd seen a burning bush outside the church."

"Ahh, yes. Raphael has done it many times over the years. I don't believe it's intentional. It's as though whatever dark energy he's channeling has consequences."

"The spark that lights the fire," I said, quoting some forgotten lyrics.

"Precisely."

"There's so much I want to ask you, Father. I hope I'm not boring you."

"Oh no, quite the contrary. I hadn't realized how much I needed to get these stories off my chest until you came along. You know, Nora, the past is like a ghost whispering in the wind. You can hear it—*feel it*—when the winds blow in the right direction. Sometimes, the winds blow strong."

He sat sullenly, looking exhausted, then stood, stretching. "Sorry, I must leave," he said. "I've got plenty of work to do. And very little time to do it. There's more to being a priest than simply giving a mass once a week, you know." He winked.

Without thinking, I hugged him as tightly as I could, and with everything I had. I wanted this moment to last forever, but forever never comes. He pretended not to notice the armful of breasts digging into his chest, separating us considerably. Instead, he graced my cheek and said goodbye.

I watched his silhouette fade under the newly fallen rain. Something in me changed. What just happened?

I shook my head and cursed myself for not bringing an umbrella, although I didn't need one when I left home; then I slogged my way down the wormy sidewalks, with sorry feet and a tortured vertebra.

My mind kept returning to the priest. There's no way he's an ordinary man. He wasn't telling me everything. He's got secrets.

I made a promise to myself right then: I was going to find out who he really was. Once and for all.

THE BURDEN OF YOU

By: Nora Murphy

I got myself a man who ain't no good
He done give me the blues
Yes, I got myself a man who don't do what he should
He done give me the blues
What's a lonely girl to do?
But bear the burden of you

Did you hear about the Midnight Creeper?
There's talk all over town
Yes, I heard about some midnight peepin'
Bad deals going down
If I were the Devil
You'd be six feet in the ground

I know that you're a late-night stalker
And Honey that ain't all
I know that you're a real nice talker
I always answer your call
That's why I'm broken, beaten and blue
I bare the burden of you

You're always sneaking out the back door
With your switchblade knife
Always getting what you're after
Gonna steal someone's life
You're always sneaking out the back door
At least you turn out the lights

So, what's a lonely girl to do?
I bare the burden of you
Come and save me from these blues
I bare the burden of you
And now you're front-page news

28

Billy Swanker's name and face was smeared all over the news.

Amanda sent me a link to the chilling front-page story. The caption read: The KILLER HAS A NAME: BILLY SWANKER. The article recapped the carnage committed by Billy throughhout the past year, including the names and ages of his victims.

After reading Kate's name, I scurried to the bathroom and regurgitated my breakfast, flushing the remainder of my eggs Benedict down the toilet. Then I sat at my kitchen table, head in hands, longing for my morning cigarette.

With more effort than should be required, I placed a teaspoon into my coffee cup and began mixing the cream and sugar until they properly dissolved, all the while contemplating the bleakness of my future.

I was running out of money, my savings depleting faster than a student acquires debt. The threat of moving back home seemed inevitable.

While watching a report on CNN which showed the Chief of Police resigning, and introducing his replacement, something startled me back to reality. Someone was banging on my front door. Suddenly, I felt cold all over, my mouth was dry, my hands were trembling. I crept to the door and scanned the spyhole, surprised at what I saw.

It was the police. Cautiously, and with my heart beating even louder than my conscience, I opened the door.

"Good afternoon, Miss Murphy, sorry for bothering you. May we come in?" Officer Lionheart asked. I let the two officers enter.

Officer Lionheart looked worried, in contrast to the six-foot-four cop standing next to him, who seemed overzealous and short-tempered. Both officers were in uniform, their firearms serving as a friendly reminder of who was in charge here.

I offered them both a coffee, which to my surprise, they accepted. We sat around my kitchen table, drank coffee and chatted about Billy Swanker.

The larger officer, whom I recognized from the CNN report, introduced himself as newly appointed Police Chief Booker Brown. Oh my God, I thought, the actual Chief of Police here inside my apartment. This could only mean one of three things: they're desperate; they think I'm an accomplice; or both.

"Miss Murphy," Officer Lionheart said, with a tinge of annoyance. "Have you been in contact with Mr. Swanker since we last spoke?"

"Nope. Haven't seen or heard from him."

"Are you sure?" Chief Brown's voice was as deep as an ocean, his eyes full of accusation. "Has Mr. Swanker tried calling you. Has he reached out in any way?"

They've been tapping my phone, I realized. Spying on me. I should have known.

"Nope." I said, trying to remain calm, which was taxing considering these two men sitting at my kitchen table were both clearly perturbed and armed to the teeth. "I barely even know the guy."

"So, you don't know where he's staying?" the police chief asked; his irritation was palpable.

I shook my head.

"Social media? He must be using Facebook or Instagram or something."

Again, I shrugged.

The frustration of these officers was borderline comical. Billy Swanker had made a mockery of the Boston Police Department and they were seriously pissed off about it.

Chief Brown stood up abrasively, causing my coffee to spill, then tossed his business card on the table.

"Well, the moment you hear from him or learn of his whereabouts, be sure to contact me. Right away. Day or night. Got it?"

I agreed.

He stormed out of my apartment. Officer Lionheart stopped to give me and my place one final inspection, then left without a word.

My mind was off to the races. I considered running to the store to buy cigarettes, but resisted the urge. Instead, I brewed a fresh pot of coffee, put on Fearless—my 'secret-favorite' Taylor Swift record—and considered yet again, where Billy Swanker might be hiding out, and more importantly, when he was going to show his murderous face around here again.

After drowning myself in Taylor Swift, I started watching my Buffy the Vampire collection, starting with season one. "When all else fails in life," I told Mr. Jimmy, who was purring softly on my lap. "We can always find solace in the Buff."

Who needs Netflix or the Disney channel? I've kept all my DVDs, and my father's. I made it halfway through season one before dozing off.

My phone woke me up. I tossed it across the room, in a fit of weary vexation. It slid under the stove and disappeared. "Stupid phone," I said in a groggy voice. "Must sleep."

Sleep didn't return, so I peed. As I stepped out of the bathroom, Mr. Jimmy started hissing. He scurried to the closet and hid.

"What is it, Jim Jim?"

The door banged. I resisted the urge to scream. The clock on the wall said 2:47 a.m.

Billy Swanker.

Alas, the moment has come. Not surprisingly, I was completely unprepared. I cursed my own stupidity.

KNOCK KNOCK KNOCK.

I stuffed the Police Chief's business card inside a drawer.

KNOCK KNOCK KNOCK.

"C'mon Nora, let me in. I know you're in there."

Billy Swanker sounded completely deranged.

KNOCK KNOCK KNOCK.

"Okay, okay, keep your pants on."

I peeked into the spyhole. Billy Swanker was standing at the foot of the door, where only a few hours ago the new Police Chief had stood.

I was afraid. My heart was pounding like a bass drum at a hip-hop concert. I inhaled deeply, counted to five, then slowly released the lock on the door. If this was to be my last night on earth, so be it. I'll see Billy Swanker in Hell.

I opened my front door. Billy Swanker entered my home for the very last time.

29

Billy stank of cigarettes and alcohol.

His black hoodie matched his tired-looking sweatpants. His head was shaved and he'd grown a beard. Not a good look. I would be hard pressed recognizing this version of Billy Swanker in a crowd. Except, of course, for his crystal-blue eyes, which looked as crazy as a bedbug.

He kicked off his sneakers and went for the refrigerator.

"Whatcha got to drink around here? Got any smokes?"

"What does this look like, a restaurant?"

There was blood on his laces. Lots of it. I reached for my phone, but it was under the stove. I could have killed myself at that moment.

"Oh Nora, how I've missed you."

Billy's voice was as lonesome as a Hank Williams record. After raiding my fridge, he retreated to the couch, and patted the spot next to him. I went. He reached over and grabbed my breasts with all the arrogance in the world.

"Oh my god!" he gasped. "What happened to them? They were big before. But never like this." The surprise in his voice was genuine.

"Shut up Billy," I joked.

He slapped me firmly in the face.

"Don't you ever talk to me like that again. You understand? Ever!"

I brushed my bangs aside, and rubbed my swollen cheek.

"Oh, I'm sorry babe," he sulked.

He caressed my hands, while kissing the nape of my neck, then up to my earlobes, then working his way to my mouth. The moisture of his lips touching mine gave me goosebumps, and I hated myself for it.

I noticed the knife.

"Hold on, hold on, Mr. Horny Pants," I said flirtatiously. "We need some music."

I pried myself off the couch and went searching through my stack of records, until I found the one that I was looking for. I dusted the record off, then waited as the needle found its groove. The warm and familiar sound of popping coming from this old record brought back a flood of memories. 'This album was old when I was your age,' I remember my father telling me, more than once. My father loved The Rolling Stones, especially their live version of Midnight Rambler. It was his favorite song.

I smiled with bad intentions. I knew what needed to be done. I only hoped I had the audacity to pull it off.

We moved to the futon. I let Billy have his way with me. He was rough but I knew I could take it. He started kissing me all over, starting with my toes, then quickly and efficiently working his way toward my naughty places. The knife always in reach. Meanwhile the music, which he was completely oblivious of, came blasting through the speakers:

Did you hear about the Midnight Rambler

The one that shut the kitchen door

He don't give you a hoot of warning

Wrapped up in a black cat cloak

He don't go in the light of the morning

He split the time the cock'rel crows

Our clothes came off. He pulled me close, his skin was hot and sweaty. His penis was pressed against me, pulsating like a warrior preparing for battle. Using his knife, he removed my bra. My breasts smacked him in the head. He cried out in surprise; then he shoved his face in between them and started motorboating. Judging from the concupiscent grin plastered across his face, Billy Swanker was in titty heaven.

We moved to the futon, where I started massaging his hairless chest, inching my way south until I had him by the balls.

He reached for the knife.

"Not so fast, mister." I squeezed tenderly. "Turn around."

His erection wanted none of this; his knife prepared to prove this.

"Turn around," I repeated. "You've been a bad boy, mister. And now I'm going to punish you."

I cupped my hand and spanked his bare bottom, hard. The thwacking sound thrilled me, so I gave him another. Then another. I spanked again, this time with everything I had. THWACK. His bottom turned fire-engine red. I forced him onto his back, then blew out the final candle.

My apartment fell under the seduction of shadows. I eased myself on top of him. We groaned simultaneously. Meanwhile, the music soared:

Did you hear about the midnight rambler?

He'll leave footprints up and down your wall.

Billy, now smothered in breasts, was lapping them up like the dirty dog he was. "Oh my God, Nora," he garbled. "You're all boobs!"

"You like them, Mr. Rambler?"

He didn't reply. Instead, he shifted from side to side, lathering them up as they pounded his face. The sound was pure porno: SLAP, SLAP, SLAP, SLAP, SLAP.

"No, Mommy! No!" he cried out.

Ignore him. I kept rocking back and forth, up and down, taking my time, not wanting him to ejaculate too soon. All the while, my breasts continued pounding him with relentless force. He started wheezing. He grabbed my wrist and squeezed until the pain was unbearable. His grip was unyielding. He sprang for his knife and pressed it to my throat, the cold steel digging into my neck, ready to plunge.

I cried out suddenly. I was terrified. Then I thought of Kate, and what this monster had done to her. Oh no you don't. I continued pounding. SLAP, SLAP, SLAP, SLAP. His legs were pulsating, his knife edging into my throat. He couldn't see past my breasts, which made the knife even more dangerous. It could slice my head clean off. I bit down on my lip. This is for Kate. With everything I had, I forced Bonnie and Clyde directly over his mouth and started leaning in. He struggled. His arms flipped and flopped as he flailed. The knife went high. I ducked, losing a few locks in the process. Then he dropped his knife. It clanked as it hit the floor.

Now it's my turn, you bastard.

I rode him like a wild stallion, while he squirmed around, ready to climax. My breasts stealing his precious air. Billy was trapped. All the oxygen was cut off from his horny little brain.

Both his eyes were bruised, his legs twitching profusely. He made ugly noises. He punched me in the chest, but it bounced right off. His arm stretched out, reaching for his knife, but it was just out of reach.

As I continued, his face changed from scarlet red to deep purple. I pushed down with all my might. He let out one final gasp as he ejaculated. Then he went still. I leaned in further, keeping the pressure over his mouth, until I was certain he was dead.

I forced myself off of him, staring in disbelief. He was dead all right: puffy eyes, full erection, an idiotic grin stamped across his murderous face.

I was exhausted. Killing a man during sex is no easy feat. I needed a drink, fast. But first I had to figure out what to do with the body lying on my sex-stained mattress. As it turned out, I didn't have to do anything. There was a knock on my door.

It was the cops.

"What the hell is going on in here?"

Officer Lionheart pushed past me, as he entered my apartment. More cops barged in. My apartment was in disarray. The smell of sex was nauseating. The puzzled looks on their faces intensified as they stared at Billy's lascivious corpse.

Officer Lionheart called headquarters.

"This is Officer Lionheart; we are in Nora Murphy's apartment. We have captured the suspect—I repeat—we have captured the suspect. The suspect is deceased. That's correct. Deceased. Send paramedics right away."

He took a long and puzzled look at me, then shook his head. The officers were clearly upset. There they were, inside a young woman's apartment; the criminal they've been hunting the past year is right in front of their eyes, dead. Only then to realize this same woman, who's got the biggest you-know-what's they've ever seen, managed to do what they could not: capture and kill the Midnight Rambler. During intercourse, no less. Priceless.

Officer Lionheart put his gun away. He glanced at Billy's blackened face, then to me, back to Billy, then let out the longest and heartiest roar I'd ever heard. To my amazement, the other officers joined in. Soon they were laughing as though this were the funniest thing they'd ever seen. Alas, they rejoiced, the Midnight Rambler was dead.

I figured they would toss me in jail, and throw away the key. They didn't. When the EMTs arrived, my apartment became the scene from a crime novel: cramped and crowded, bodies coming and going, cops and first responders alike. The scene lasted long past sunrise.

Meanwhile, I sat like a lump at the kitchen table trying my best to remain composed. My nerves were shot, my body ached, and I was desperately craving a cigarette.

I was living in a dream world. Time slowed down. I was in shock. I spoke without contemplation, answering an endless array of questions. Billy's knife was of special interest. It was immediately confiscated. Finally, the first responders carried Billy Swanker out of my apartment in a body bag.

As the sun ascended over Boston's somnolent streets, the cops huddled outside my apartment door, discussing what to put on their report, and whether or not I should be arrested. I listened in as best I could.

After what seemed an eternity, Dale Lionheart re-entered my home.

"Miss Murphy, can I have a word with you?"

I shrugged.

"Um, we've decided to make this—um—easy, on all of us. If, of course, that's okay with you."

He was peeking at my chest, clearly visible underneath my nightgown.

"You told us your side of the story, and, um, surprisingly, we believe you. But we can't put what you said on our report. I'm sure you understand why. I'm terribly sorry for everything, Ma'am, it's been a rough year on all of us. Billy Swanker is—or um—was an elusive son-of-a-bitch. Hard to track down. We've confiscated his phone. I can't wait to crack it open. I'd like to know where he's been hiding out all this time. If it wasn't here."

He shook his head, more to himself than to me.

"So, if it's alright with you, Ma'am, let's keep this our little secret. We're going to mark the cause of death as self-defence. He attacked you, you clocked him good on the head, then you suffocated him with your—um—pillows. Short and sweet. We promise to leave your name and breasts out of the official report."

He was clearly enjoying himself. I'm glad one of us was.

"You've done good for yourself Miss Murphy. It took busts—um sorry—guts to do what you done. The people of Boston need a feelgood story. Having the Rambler captured and killed will put their minds at ease. Heck, they've got enough on their plates with this goddam pandemic and all. So, if you don't mind?"

Officer Lionheart went to the door. He was about to leave, when he turned around, looking to get something off his chest. "If you need anything—anything—don't hesitate to call."

He handed me his card, shot me a look, and left.

"C'mon boys," his scraggy voice echoed along the hallway. "We done the breast we can do. Um, best we can do."

The officers snickered as they trampled away.

Without haste, I found my phone and texted Amanda a short recap of what transpired.

Then I collapsed on my futon, ignoring the traces of blood and semen splattered across my otherwise pastel sheets.

I was about to close my eyes, just for a wee nap, when I noticed something peculiar stuffed under my futon. I had to get on all fours to retrieve it.

It was a little black book. It had no inscriptions or markings on either side of it. Just black. It must have fallen out of Billy's backpack.

I opened it. The contents of the book were shockingly horrible. Grotesque. The pages were full of lewd sketches, including various rape and sex acts, medieval torturing devices and modern weaponry. Mostly knives and guns and stuff. The attention to detail was uncanny. I started flipping through pages. The page I stopped at was staring back at me, ready to bite.

It was a full-page drawing of the old man in the hat. His features were illustrated with deliberate and precise determination. His pinstriped suit sketched slim and slender, his snap-brimmed hat shielding one side of his well-worn face, a cigarette dangling from his lips.

A cold feeling stirred inside my stomach. I became nauseous. Oh, how I hated this man.

Even after closing the book, I felt those empty eyes penetrating my soul.

This shouldn't come as much of a surprise. But it did. Was this why Billy had become so reckless and callous? Had he fallen prey to one of the old man's curses? And if so, how great a part had the old man played in all of this? How much of Billy was he controlling?

Mr. Jimmy came out of hiding and started bawling for breakfast. After feeding him,

I got dressed, then I went out and tossed Billy's black book into the dumpster where it belonged. Good riddance to bad rubbish.

Then, seeing how I was too tired to sleep, I finished watching season one of Buffy the Vampire Slayer. At some point, while the Buff was kicking some creepy vampire's ass, I closed my eyes and slept like the dead.

SWEET BOTTOM BOY

By: Nora Murphy

Be-boppin' booty, to pound on

Be-boppin' booty, throwin' down

Be-boppin' booty, if he says it's alright

We can be-bop that booty all night

He's my sweet bottom boy (he's my sweet bottom boy)

He's my sweet bottom boy (he's my sweet bottom boy)

He's my sweet bottom boy (he's my sweet bottom boy)

But I'll tell this now: he's for me to enjoy

He gonna rhythm n' blues me

He gonna keep me up last past dawn

We gonna wang dang doodle all night long

You know I'm spoilin' for my sweet bottom boy

He's my sweet bottom boy (he's my sweet bottom boy)

He's my sweet bottom boy (he's my sweet bottom boy)

He's my sweet bottom boy (he's my sweet bottom boy)

But I'll tell this now: he's for me to enjoy

We can be-bop, boogie-woogie, shake it real tight

We can shoop, shoop, alley-oop, feeling alright

We can rock and roll, like there's nothing to lose

Cuz my baby's got them sweet bottom blues

He's my sweet bottom boy (he's my sweet bottom boy)
He's my sweet bottom boy (he's my sweet bottom boy)
He's my sweet bottom boy (he's my sweet bottom boy)
But I'll tell you this now: he's for me to enjoy
He's my sweet bottom boy (he's my sweet bottom boy)
He's my sweet bottom boy (he's my sweet bottom boy)
He's my sweet bottom boy (he's my sweet bottom boy)
But I'll tell you this now: he's for me to enjoy
I'll tell you this now: he's for me to enjoy
I'll tell you now

30

Amanda arrived with cupcakes. She wore yoga pants with a Cannibal Corpse T-shirt; her hair was chestnut brown (its original color) and her face was makeup-free. This was not the same woman who did a Tarot reading here not so long ago. That's why I love Amanda: she has many layers, but inside, where it counts, she's always the same. She is, of course, my BFF. I made coffee and we enjoyed every last drop, as we read the news article:

THE MIDNIGHT RAMBLER IS DEAD

Police captured and killed the Midnight Rambler, AKA the Killer, early Thursday morning, bringing an end to a rein of terror inflicted on the city of Boston since the summer of 2021.

Billy Swanker, 24, has victimized at least eight women, killing two of them. Police have not released the latest victim's name, but claim that the woman was an acquaintance of Swanker's. The police were tipped off to Swanker's whereabouts. There was a struggle, which ultimately led to the killing of the perpetrator. The victim was unharmed.

According to Police Chief Booker Brown, "We'd been tracking Swanker's whereabouts for quite some time. His DNA matched that at the crime scenes. It was only a matter of time before we captured him. With the inevitable-yet-long-overdue end to the Rambler's reign of terror, the people of Boston can finally put this saga to rest. We did it. We killed the Midnight Rambler."

Much of Billy Swanker is still unknown. He avoided social media, he lived alone and was a recluse. Any person with information about him is asked to come forward. Here is the timeline of Billy Swanker's carnage:July 8, 2019, South End; July 19, 2019, South End; August 14, 2019, Mission Hill; September 23, 2019, Back Bay; October 26, 2019, Belmont; December 14, 2019, Brookline; January 1, 2020, Back Bay; January 13, 2020, Brookline; April 2, 2020, Back Bay

"Them lying sons of bitches," I said, but I was pleased they omitted my name. I could only wonder how long that would last.

Amanda was all fired-up. "I'll bet they'll make a movie about you. Or better yet, a Netflix series. You'll be famous. I can see it now: Nora's Curse: The Hunt for the Midnight Rambler."

"Or how about: Bigger is better?"

We had our coffee, and cupcakes, and let social media entertain us for the afternoon. Lesley had resurfaced, sharing an event on Facebook: LOCKDOWN PROTEST THIS SUNDAY AT STATE CAPITOL #loveovermasks. Her anti-lockdown stance reaction can be summed up by two comments: 'I used to like you Lesley, but not any more' and: 'You suck more than men do.'

If I hadn't known Lesley so many years, I'd be concerned for her safety. But let's face it, she's one tough cookie. She can take care of herself. I also came across a picture of me and Kate at Lesley's party, after the protest in November. Kate had her arm around me, we were both giving the peace sign. Kate looked fabulous. A beacon of positive energy. My heart fell to the floor.

"At least," Amanda said, in between nibbles from her cupcake. "She can finally rest in peace."

I nodded, then helped her finish the last cupcake: chocolate supreme with Oreo cookie crumbles. There was nothing I could do about Kate. That was the worst part. I'd have to learn to live with my guilt, otherwise it would rot away at my soul, killing me slowly. One day at a time, I suppose.

Amanda kissed me and wished me goodnight.

Father McCleary surprised me with an email: GREETINGS MISS MURPHY: PLEASE MEET ME TOMORROW AT THE COMMONS. NOON. NOT MUCH TIME LEFT. GOD BLESS.

I was about to respond with KK but immediately deleted it. This was a holy man for Christ's sake. Instead, I responded: You bet your holy buns ;-). Not much better, mind you, but neither was I. I was a murderer, after all. I'm gonna ride the Highway to Hell. Stairway denied. Nothing left to do but smile, smile, smile.

31

The day was hot and sticky and gross.

It took all my effort not to turn around and go home to my air-conditioned apartment, and curl up with a book. But I soldiered on. Yes, people were staring at me, taking pictures, pointing fingers. To them, I was a novelty. A punchline. A meme.

In truth, I'd become a hunchback. I was in constant agony. Soon, I'd be bedridden for good. Sigh. As I labored past what remained of the Church of the Holy Cross, a surge of catcalls was spat my way. One of the construction workers, sporting a pocket rocket that could fly me to the moon and back, started making jokes.

"Hey lady. Gravity apologizes to no one. Especially your tits!" Har-dee-har-har.

Unlike my previous two visits, the Commons was teeming with people. I spotted the priest. He waved me over to the bench closest to the pond. At his feet lay a brown, weatherworn briefcase.

"Good morning, Miss Murphy," he said, glancing at his watch. "Or shall I say, good afternoon?"

"Morning," I grumbled, feeling relief the moment my buttocks hit the bench.

The priest, sitting with impeccable posture, wiped the fog from his spectacles. "It certainly is a warm one today. God must be shining down on all of us."

Although my face produced a smile, my mind was heavy with burden. Should I tell him? Did he already know? Turns out, I didn't have to say a thing.

"It looks like they finally caught that Rambler bloke," he said, giving me a peculiar look. He reached into his briefcase and produced a Tupperware full of freshly baked brownies, and handed me one. "Nobody bakes better brownies than Sister De Luca. These brownies are simply divine."

Although he gave me a playful nudge, no amount of sugary goodness could make me ignore the jarring state he was in. Clearly, something was wrong. He looked tired and frail. His hair now fully gray, was dishevelled; his eyes were sunken, his face spongy.

He smiled. "Dare I say they're heavenly?"

I nodded, unable to speak due to my mouthful of fudge.

"Okay, okay," he said. "Enough with the cheap puns. I want you to have this."

He reached into his briefcase, and yielded a large yellow folder. He handed it to me, but my hands were covered in chocolate. I couldn't decide what to do, so I did nothing. The priest handed me a napkin, and waited patiently as I cleaned up.

After what felt like an eternity, I opened the folder and looked inside. There were articles and files dating back to the mid 1800's. He found an item of interest: a birth certificate from the Commonwealth of Massachusetts, dating back to 1884.

It was barely legible. I'd never seen such fancy cursive before. According to the name printed on the timeworn paper, it belonged to Charles O'Leary. He handed me a death certificate, dated 1960, with the same name on it. Before I could register the significance of this, he handed me another birth certificate, this one dated 1961. It had his name on it.

"This—this is impossible."

I said this, although I knew it to be true. Deep down, I'd known it along. He'd said Mrs. Connelly was special, even as a girl. I must be blind. The priest produced two bottles of chilled water and handed me one. He was eagerly waiting for a response.

My mouth was as dry as a musician's sense of humor. I didn't have the capacity for words. After drinking half the bottle, I said: "You're—you're him. You're the boy you told me about. The boy who was healed by the church."

He blushed.

"I should have known."

"You'd be surprised what the human mind will hide from itself. It's a defence mechanism. Believe me, Nora, I've seen it a thousand times. I'm quite old."

"But, how?"

"Look here," he said, and handed me an article. "Read the headline."

I did. It was dated 1890: THE HEALING POWER OF CHRIST RESIDES IN THE CHURCH OF THE HOLY CROSS. He showed me another; this one dated 1918: LOCAL CHURCH HEALS THE SICK.

After wiping a pool of sweat from his brow, he said, "I'm leaving you with this briefcase. There are many treasures inside which I hope you find of value. I was pleased to learn how much Mrs. Connelly figured out on her own, although I'm not surprised. She was a clever lady.

"The powers of this church have been known since its humble beginnings. But people refuse to remember. I've done my very best over the years to protect its secrets. And to protect this city from the likes of Raphael, who uses its power for malevolence and chaos. Sadly, yes, Raphael lives. Although I wish it weren't so. Two days ago, I met with him. And we made a deal. Oh, how many deals we've made over the years. I can assure you that your—um—affliction will soon cease. Raphael's powers are draining. He too must die. No one is permanent. Not in this world anyway."

He squeezed my hand, but only for a second.

"I must go," he said, straining each word. "Much work is needed before I—um—move on to the next world.'

My eyes swelled.

He forced a smile. "Yes, my time here on earth has passed. Heaven awaits me; Lord knows, I am ready."

He looked deep into my soul; I saw the universe inside him. I caught a glimpse of his boyhood self. Young Charles, skipping to school in hand-washed clothing; I saw him as a young man, tending to his mother after his father died in the war. This is a man who has outlived two world wars and countless other catastrophes; and here he was sitting next to me, on a glorious afternoon in the park, dying.

"No one should live forever in this world," he said. "Not even the Devil himself could stand such cruelty. But mark my words: I'll be looking out for you, Nora dear. Always."

He wiped fresh tears from my face, smiled benevolently, stood up and walked away.

As evening rolled around, the menacing clouds, which threatened rain became calm. Without warning, the clouds parted and a glorious multicolored rainbow hovered over the city. The most tremendous feeling of love swept over me; and for a brief moment, the entire world was at peace.

I knew in my heart what this meant: Father McCleary had passed away.

I slipped into the bath and let the warm, foamy water be my salvation. The contents of Father McLeary's briefcase could wait. Right now, it's Me Time. I was heartbroken. I missed Kate dearly, and my father; and yes, if I'm being honest, I still missed Tyson. Then there's the fact that I killed Boston's notorious Midnight Rambler, and I needn't remind you how.

But despite this, I was having some sort of an awakening. An epiphany. It came as quite a shock. My mind returned to Billy

Swanker. How could someone be so cruel? How could he have done that to Kate, and all the others?

My mind drifted to our love-making (if that's what you want to call it). Yes, he cared about me, in a twisted sort of way. But he had his demons; and ultimately, his demons got the best of him. He certainly had mommy issues. Yikes. And did I actually get away with murder? Was it really self-defence?

Yes, I suppose it was. He had every intention of killing me that night. No point in denying it. I wondered what he was thinking right before he bit the eternal dust? Happy thoughts, I presume. I mean, I can think of worse ways of dying. The Monty Python team couldn't create a more suitable death for the likes of Billy Swanker.

I was calm. Finding inner peace. Something inside of me was shifting. The curse was lifting. I knew this to be true. My breasts were tingling; tightening, contracting. I felt like rejoicing. Could this be the end of Nora's Curse? Had I done it myself? Or had I received help from the priest? Probably, both.

The priest certainly was special. I began to ponder his age. How old was he? He must have been well over one hundred years old. My entire view on reality had been shattered. Before draining the tub, I prayed. It was my one and only prayer, so I wanted to get it right. I prayed. Not to any god or government, not to any object of desire or celebrity; I prayed to the Universe, the truest and purest source of love imaginable. I begged her for forgiveness. Again, and again and again. Feeling satisfied, I pulled the plug and let the lukewarm water wash over me, cleansing me of my sins and transgressions.

Or at least, I hoped.

I dreamed I was a young girl at Gage Park with my father. It was a gorgeous day. We held hands, walking and talking under the soft light of the honeycomb sun. There was stillness in the air; nary a breeze nor chill; only the gentle sound of children's laughter dancing in the wind. Father loved Gage Park. We had a ritual. We would start with the slide, then progress to the swings—then, depending on whether or not I joined in on a game of Grounder—we would make our rounds throughout the park, stopping to pet random people's dogs along the way.

When my father spoke, I clung to his every word. I hugged him for as long as it would last, never wanting to let go. He looked at me, smiled as he ruffled my hair, called me his princess and told me everything was going to be alright.

Amanda arrived the following evening, and the two of us went to work rummaging through the treasures buried in Father McLeary's briefcase. The first, and most notorious item, was the bible. It had to be over two hundred years old. No wonder the briefcase was so heavy, this sucker was huge.

"Oh my friggin' God," Amanda gasped. "It's so big."

The bulky black bible depicted a large gold cross with Christ hanging from it. It took two hands to hold it. Amanda flipped it open and stopped at a picture of Pope Leo XIII.

"So, friggin' cool."

Watching her flip through a leatherbound nineteenth-century bible, flaunting a Slayer T-shirt with pentagrams stitched on it was brilliant. I snapped a pic and posted it on Instagram, #gothchicks.

"What else is in here?" Amanda asked, reaching for a sack of coins. "Oh my God. Look." She let a handful of coins slip through her fingers. They were old. Some depicted an Indian head and a buffalo; others were pure gold, some had the dates rubbed off. I held two coins under the lamp. One was dated 1924, another 1895. Amanda was taken aback.

"Woah," she said. "This one looks ancient. Oh my God. It's from 1838. It's a half dollar. And there's more!"

I smiled, but only to be polite. To me, this was merely someone's hobby. I saw no value in them, except in their aesthetics. Like something out of a Harry Potter novel.

Amanda, on the other hand, went frantically to her phone.

"My uncle is a jeweler," she said, while texting. "He'll know what these suckers are worth."

Within minutes, her phone rang. She answered it, then scooted off to the bathroom with the sack of coins. Inside the briefcase, I found a modest-sized leather pouch containing three rosaries. Being both ignorant of their purpose and function, I simply enjoyed their decor. They were from different eras. The oldest was the creepiest, with its olive pit beads, skull and crossbones at the feet of Jesus. Carefully, I put these items back into the pouch, and put the pouch back into the briefcase.

There was another folder buried at the bottom of the briefcase, it was smaller than the one with the newspaper clippings. Inside was a black and white family portrait; its edges frayed and the picture slightly blurred. It showed a husband and wife and a small boy. The boy, wearing tattered clothing and a dour face, was sitting on his mother's knee, staring directly into the camera. His cheeks were rosy, his eyes clear and sharp. I knew right away who the boy was. It was the priest. I closed my eyes and felt the roughness of the photograph, allowing myself to bask in its wonder. I could hear the little boy's cry as his mother tried to put him to bed. I saw his father working tirelessly day and night, building roads for future generations to enjoy. One afternoon, this family would visit the church with their dying boy wrapped in tired blankets. Did the mother know she was holding a miracle baby? Probably, she did.

Amanda came rushing into the kitchen, and sat across from me at the kitchen table. Her face suggested good news. She placed the sack of coins next to the briefcase, and pointed a finger at me. "You, Nora Murphy, are a rich woman."

I let her words linger through the air without trying to catch them. I simply let them be.

"My uncle says he can get you a cool half-mil for them. After, you know, he takes his cut." She blushed at the last part. Her hands were shaking, her eyes big and brown and full of anticipation.

"But do I really want to sell them?"

"Hell yes!"

Done. Easy money. I continued rummaging through outmoded photos, many of which were older than rock and roll, until I came upon one in particular. It was him: the old man in the hat. Carefully, as if the picture could cut me, kill me, or curse me, I held the picture to the light. It was him alright, in his prime. He was clean shaven, brutally handsome, exuding extraordinary confidence. He was wearing a clever suit with a striped tie tucked into his jacket, a feathered fedora tilted just so, with a hand rolled cigarette dangling nonchalantly from his lips. He was leaning against a classic Ford Model B Roadster. I'd seen this picture before. But where?

Billy's black book.

"Oh my friggin' God! Look at him!" Amanda said. "Wow. Hate to say it, but, damn. What a hunk. But..." She blinked. "How can he still be alive?"

Our silence answered that question. She knew as well as I did: he was no ordinary man. I made a quick mental note to burn this picture. If I never laid eyes on that wretched old man again, it would be too soon. We spent the remainder of the afternoon looting Father's McCleary's suitcase. When Amanda left, she took with her the coins; and after much negotiating, the old gothic bible. I spent the night singing songs on my acoustic guitar, pondering once again the idea of completing my solo album. Lord knows, I certainly had enough material.

Before going to bed, I noticed a missed call from Dr. Palmer's office. They left a voicemail reminding me of my appointment in the morning. The reminder was much appreciated. I'd completely forgotten about it; that, and my birthday, which was also tomorrow. I debated whether or not I should go to the appointment. On one hand, my curse was lifting. On the other hand, I was curious what the doctor had to say. This alone should make the trip worthwhile.

It did.

32

Dr. Jeffery Palmer was sitting behind his desk, showcasing his big-jawed, open-mouth grin.

His Hawaiian golf shirt made him look more like a 1980's talk show host than an actual doctor. He was taller than I'd remembered him to be. Wearily, I sat down, waiting for him to speak.

"So, Miss Murphy, a lot has changed since our last encounter. I hope you are safe and well."

I nodded.

"I'm sorry about the Cock," he said, tapping his ballpoint pen with one hand, putting his glasses on with his other. "It was a fine pub. My colleagues would go there on the weekends. They loved the music. Hmm, ah yes," he said, after reviewing my case. "The ever-growing breasts. Fascinating."

I couldn't speak. The words at my lips wouldn't progress to the next stage. How do I bring up the old man's curse? The simple answer is: I don't.

"Tell me, Miss Murphy, what are your intentions? Where do we go from here?" he asked, still tapping his pen—tap, tap, tappity tap.

"Well, honestly, I'm not sure. Um—I'm sorry I'm not as prepared as I should be. It's been a trying couple of months, to say the least."

"If memory serves," he said. "You claim—and I am not denying this in any way—that your breasts started growing spontaneously, and without end? Correct?"

"One year ago, I wore an A cup."

"Hmm. I'd mentioned previously that I'd heard of another situation similar to yours. I initially discredited it. But I began to wonder. Now, please give me a moment." He went searching on his computer. "Aha!" he shouted. "Well, I'll be a monkey's uncle." He stopped tapping his pen long enough to scribble down a name and contact, then handed me a pink piece of paper. This meeting seemed rather dodgy at best. I stared at him, mouth ajar, waiting for an explanation. Then I began questioning my motives as to why I was even here, on my birthday, no less.

"This young man may be of interest to you," he said. "Or not. I'll leave that up to you. You see, last summer, a colleague of mine—after a few cocktails—confided in me about a peculiar patient of hers. She never mentioned his name, just his—um—affliction. I thought she was exaggerating, or simply making it up. Honestly, I figured she was trying to impress me.

"So, I must confess, Miss Murphy, after our last meeting, I reached out to her and told her your story. I didn't use your name, of course. My colleague was fascinated.

"After a brief discussion, she sent me her client's files to compare. I cannot go into detail about it because, well, there are laws against that, but my colleague instructed me to pass along her client's email address to you. With his permission, of course. So, he knows of you, and is willing to meet with you. Maybe the two of you can—um—compare stories."

I was stunned. Why would I want to meet some stranger to talk about my breasts? I did enough of that at work, thank-you-very-much. Nope, not happening.

He read me well. "Listen, Miss Murphy. I've been at this for quite some time, and I've met with innumerable women, and quite a few men, I might add. Most breast-reduction surgeries are typical. Your situation is not typical. But that said, I am willing to perform your surgery. However," he paused. "There would be risks involved. And you'd have to sign a waiver that protects me from any liability. Because—well, you know—what if they grow back?"

He paused to consider this, then added, "Anyway, my colleague made me promise to give you her client's contact info. Believe me when I tell you, Ms. Murphy, this is highly unorthodox. But here we are."

I stuffed the paper into my purse. I was more than ready to leave. I stood up, smiled politely, and headed for the door, doing my best to ignore the taxidermied fish carcass following my every move. Dr. Palmer removed his glasses and tucked them neatly into his breast pocket. His pleasant face was unable to conceal its excitement.

"Go home and think about it," he said, tapping his pen. "There's no harm in sending this man an email. I've been more than assured he's safe. Otherwise, I would never have agreed to this. I could lose my licence."

On my way out the door, he wished me a happy birthday.

I hadn't even the slightest inkling to reach out to whoever's name was scribbled on that paltry pink paper. That is, until one year later, when curiosity finally got the best of me. His name was T-Bone Chappelle, which I found compelling. His email address: tboner69@gmail.com sealed the deal. Once my mind was made up, that's that. I reached out.

His reply was instantaneous: **LEZ MEET UP YO.**

GOING TO MUSCLE SHOALS

By: Nora Murphy

I'm going down to Muscle Shoals just as soon as I get money

I'm gonna buy me an old guitar, find me a honey

I'm going down to Muscle Shoals, that's where I belong

I'm gonna catch me an aeroplane, then I'll sing them all my songs

I'm gonna drive to New York City, getting lost in the lights

Find me the Big Apple, then I'll take me a slice

I'm gonna drive to New York City, that's where I gotta go

Next time you hear my voice, it'll be on the radio

Maybe I'll go to Mexico, where the sun meets the sand

Give up my possessions, try living off the land

Maybe I'll be that señorita, way down in Tijuana

Sipping Tequila, smoking marijuana

There's only one place left to go, my final destination

There's no one left to pray for me, there's no hesitation

I'll be standing at the crossroads, with this pain in my soul

But I'll let the devil take his due, when I'm six feet below

I'm going down to Muscle Shoals just as soon as I get money;

I'm gonna buy me an old guitar, maybe find a little honey

I'm going down to Muscle Shoals, that's where I do belong

I'm gonna catch me that aeroplane; I'm gonna sing them all my songs;

I'm gonna catch me that aeroplane; I'm gonna sing them all my songs;

33

2020 went down like a warm beer on a cold day.

As life tippy-toed back into a somewhat quasi version of normal, my curse slowly lifted. And I do stress: Slowly. It's taking its sweet time, and let me tell you folks, I'm okay with that. It's been a year since Billy Swanker's body was unceremoniously chucked into dirt, leaving behind nothing but his name.

I've been living the highlife ever since. Father McCleary's treasures sure paid off. My gratitude to him is unceasing. So much so, that I dragged my feet to church for Sunday service. Yes, the church was rebuilt. Some say it's a miracle. They'd be correct. The mass was held by a handsome young priest named Father Kelly. He was the spitting image of the boy in Father McCleary's black and white photo.

Yes, it's been a rip-roaring year, fraught with danger and disorder, lust and envy, deception and deceit; and lest we forget: murder. So, is it any wonder I find myself on this vomit-inducing city bus, meeting a wannabe gangster who goes by the handle T-Bone Chappelle?

I'd grown curious about Dr. Palmer's paltry pink piece of paper. You know, the one buried at the bottom of my purse. Irrevocably, I reached out. Let's just say my curiosity proved fruitful. I wasn't let down. Once I discovered T-Bone's 'affliction', it was only a matter of time before curiosity killed this kitty. I had to see first hand.

Consequently, I found myself sitting in discarded bubble gum (an omen, surely), on my way to T-Bone's home in the suburbs. My anxiety increased at each passing stop. Now don't get me wrong, I'd chatted with him several times before making this irreproachable decision; and although he's a douchebag, he seemed harmless enough. Although as memory serves, I'd made this mistake before, and paid dearly for it.

As I finished removing the cherry-flavored bubble gum from my high-rise shorts, my phone went on a rampage. Lesley, whom I hadn't spoken to or heard from all year, sent a platoon of messages:

lookit whos the proud owner of a new bar!

ME!!!!

in sunny fort myers beach

florida!

it could be OURS!

(cuz i need a biz partner come join me!!!)

do it NOW!!!!!!

CHECK OUT THE STAGE

Before I even could think of responding, another text arrived: a picture of a dimly-lit stage in a seedy dive bar. The stage showcased a single barstool on the filthiest Indian rug I've ever seen. The back of the stage was a rickety wooden wall boasting a plethora of band names and catch phrases. Ample room for drums, plenty of outlets. The stage certainly had mojo.

Next came an artillery of photos, showing different angles of the modest beach bar. Each pic more lovely than the last. It was a square room with solid oak floors, a bay window overlooking the sandy beach; a splash of tables and chairs pushed off to the corner, next to a mop bucket with a broken handle. A mahogany, triple arch bar proudly greeted its guests as they entered, with its two brass rails, and a barstool as sturdy as a unicycle. Most notable was the exquisite glass cabinet occupying the entire wall behind the bar—with enough shelf space to stock the British army—which added to the bar's distinctly vintage appeal.

I was awestruck. The acoustics would be top-notch. Getting that stage all rigged up would be a delightful chore. Plenty of work, but well worth it. The tobacco-stained walls needed refurbishing, and I could only imagine what sorry state the restrooms were in. I revelled in anticipation. All I needed was a one-way ticket to the Sunshine State.

Contemplating my small fortune, I strongly considered Lesley's offer. Deep down, I've always dreamed of owning my own bar, but never thought it feasible. Until now. The final pic Lesley sent sealed the deal. It was a real humdinger: a delectable patio surrounded by a sun-kissed beach. In the background, suntanned bodies with burnt faces pranced along the yellow sand.

My heart skipped a beat. I loved it. Was it time to leave Boston? Yes. That much was dreadfully clear. But should I go back to Ontario, or somewhere new?

The choice seemed obvious.

Smiling with anticipation, I replied: **HELL YESSS!!!!** Followed by: **SEE U SOON!!!!**

The bus, which was empty save for a woman reading a juicy romance novel and a teenage boy sitting at the back, fiddling with his Spiderman facemask. Suddenly it came to an abrupt halt, snapping my attention away from my phone.

As I sat in this sauna on wheels, wishing that the bus driver would turn up the air-conditioning, I received another text, this one from Amanda: **HAPPY BIRTHDAY NORA!!! WOOT WOOT! HAPPY DIRTY 30!!!** A naughty GIF followed, depicting a lewd-looking woman holding up a glass of wine, with the words: **MAY UR 30 BE EXTRA DIRTY!**

How could I have forgotten my own birthday? My Dirty 30, no less? That's two years in a row. Sigh. I shrugged, sent a cheeky reply, then pondered the ridiculousness of this trip. I considered catching the first bus back home, but it was too late. My stop arrived and I got off.

The bus dropped me off outside a McDonald's. The golden arches towering over me brought a smile to my lips. There's a joke in there somewhere. I texted T-Bone, if that was even his real name, telling him I was close. He instructed me to go around the house, and enter at the rear, followed by a wink emoji. He'd like that, I chuckled. His mother, he warned in a follow up text, was eagerly awaiting my arrival. This was all so bizarre.

The sky was Cambridge-blue; the neighborhood as quiet as Fenway Park at sunrise. The only sounds were the chattering birds and the occasional lawnmower whirling about its weekly business.

The houses were identical. I approached with caution. T-Bone's neighbor, a shirtless, middle-aged man with a sleeve of tattoos and biceps as big as a garbage truck, was washing his car. I stopped to take in the sites. He looked up and waved, and accidently sprayed soapy water all over his cut-off denim shorts. I didn't mind.

Gradually, but without judiciousness, I crept towards the Chappelle residence. The house seemed vacant. The blinds were drawn, the lights low; the front yard lacking any shrubs or trees or flowers of any sort. Just a patch of grass leading to a yellow door.

Under normal circumstances, I would be put off by this. But not today. I'd been through the lion's den. Been face-to-face with the old man in the hat, and survived his titillating curse. Not to mention Billy Swanker.

This was child's play.

I repeated this mantra, as I inched along the carless driveway. As per my instructions, I went around back, where I tripped over a sprinkler and swore. My profanity echoed throughout the picturesque neighborhood, announcing my presence like an unwelcome in-law. I knocked on the back door. A text came: **cum in**. I rolled my eyes, and entered.

The basement smelled of cat urine. It was semi-furnished, cluttered with various household appliances left to die in taped-up boxes. There was a loud *DING* as the dryer turned over one last time.

From upstairs, I heard a creaking voice say, "Dat you, Nora?" and was soon greeted by a short, stout black woman with curly white hair, thick glasses, loose-fitting tank top and casual pants. She came waddling over to me, extended her hand, then immediately retracted it. She remained six feet from me, hands on hips, waiting for my response.

Standing at the doorway, ready to escape, I said, "Yes, I'm Nora Murphy. Hope I'm not disturbing you."

"Oh, pish posh. We're so happy you finally stopped by. T-Bone don't get visitors these days. But he used to, that's for damn sure," she laughed. "Oh, where are my manners? My name is Odetta. Odetta Chapelle. I'd shake your hand but—you know—dat's not allowed these days. Would you like anything? Coffee? Soda? I've baked chocolate chip cookies."

"No thank you. I just ate," I lied.

"Oh, don't you be alarmed," she said, with a slight southern drawl, looking me up and down. "Dis here is a safe place. My T-Bone is in the next room. Please don't mind his, um, condition. The doctor says it's only temporary, but I don't know about dat. He been like dat for two years now. I tell you dis, he certainly don't take after his Pappa!"

She checked me up and down. "Maybe you two have something in common. Hard to say. Any who, you come right dis way, you can leave your shoes at the door there beside you. Please and thank you."

I slid off my shoes, then followed her past a red bicycle with two flat tires and a stack of magazines that reached the ceiling, until we reached the partition. From behind the curtain, I could hear him beating away on what I presumed was a video game controller.

This was high school all over again, the only thing missing was the sweet smell of pot wafting through the air and the self-conscious giggling of teenage girls.

Without warning, a black cat darted past me, knocking over a basket of neatly-folded laundry.

"Oh, knock it off Damion!" Odetta hissed, as the cat scurried off. "Damion is a stray we picked up last summer. He's the Devil incarnate. Any who, I best leave you two alone. Holler if you need anything."

Odetta disappeared upstairs.

My heart was beating faster than a high school boy's right hand. I couldn't believe any of this. I took a deep breath, trying to compose myself. Then, I peeked inside. Part of me was expecting my friends to jump out and shout: "HAPPY BIRTHDAY!"

Sadly, that's not what happened. Instead, I was accosted by a deep and frothy voice telling me to come closer.

When I did, I couldn't believe my eyes.

The room smelled of porn. The air was thick and somehow sticky. The walls were cluttered with posters of basketball players and hip-hop artists posing with big-breasted women. The tiny space could barely house the double-sized bed and plethora of electronic gadgets stuffed inside it. Food scraps were everywhere, including a half-eaten pizza crust, which I casually kicked under the bed.

T-Bone was on his bed, lying under Black Panther bed sheets, groping an Xbox controller. A large flatscreen TV sat at the foot of the bed, taking up the entire bedside table. His dreadlocks spilled out of his baseball cap, worn sideways. The rings on his fingers were as gold as the caps on his teeth. I pegged him at twenty-five, but he may be older, it was impossible to tell.

"Nora! Girl. Wow, look at you," he said, with a pasted-on grin. "Don't be afraid. Come closer. Lemme get a good look at you."

Immediately, I knew he was an idiot. The three movie cameras pointing at him were not encouraging. He shifted in his bed, causing the bedsheets to unravel. I glanced below his waist and gasped.

"Don't mind the Rock," he said. "He's my cock. Like, for reals. The Rock loves them white women. Once he sees one there ain't no stopping him."

He said this with a hint of sarcasm, but still. And did he really name his genitals? I guess I shouldn't judge, seeing as how I did the same. Something was stirring underneath the bed sheets, starting to rise. Something bear-sized. I braced myself.

"Now, don't you be alarmed. I just gotta hold him for a moment, you know, while he gets bigger. Otherwise—"

I couldn't believe it. A tent was growing underneath his sheets. A tent that could fit a family of four, plus the dog. Impossible, I told myself. It's obviously a trick. I stared in disbelief, as his manhood, now fully erect, stood as tall as an elephant's trunk, reaching the top of my head.

He read my face, frowned.

"Shit. I used to think the ladies would love the Rock. And they did, for a while. But you know. Ain't no woman on earth want to come near me now. I mean, It's too damn big."

He tore off the sheets.

To my amazement, he was wearing three-legged track pants, which he clearly needed. His ginormous joystick was standing long, tall and proud. I rolled my eyes. This was not how I wanted to spend my Dirty 30. I turned around, heading for the door.

"No, no, no! Nora, girl, don't you go just yet. *Please.* At least lemme look at those titties! We could make a porno!"

"I'm leaving."

"Wait! Nora. It was jokes. Shit, I know I ain't funny. I'm just lonely. Nothing ever going on around here no more. I'm just excited, that's all."

I stopped.

He leaned forward, pried his third leg over to the side, then spoke earnestly. His gold-toothed display was charming, but his eyes were steeped in sorrow. I felt pity. This was all for show.

T-Bone was trapped, confined to his bed, and this was his coping mechanism. He was just another sad sack like me, struggling with a curse he notably deserved. A curse he desperately needed getting rid of.

I'm going to help this three-legged laughing stock, I told myself right then. Not because I want to, but because it's the right thing to do. Besides, I've been a bitch. Lord knows I could use the brownie points. That said, this situation was highly unorthodox. The guy's sporting a cock that would make Ron Jeremy blush.

"Anyway, you know, the real reason I wanted you here was to ask you something." He cleared his throat. "Did you bump into him? The old wizard?"

"Who?"

"Don't you lie to me," he said, studying my face. "Did you or did you not bump into the old wizard?"

"Wears a nice suit? Cool hat?"

"That's him!"

"Then yes."

My mood was improving. It was nice talking to someone about the old man in the hat, someone who understands. Besides, this guy was kinda cute, in a dipshit sort of way.

His relief was obvious.

"So, I ain't the only one. That's wild. You know, I used to have a tiny dick. Barely anything. Just a twig shoved between two raisins. My woman used to say shit like, 'What? Is that all ya got? I thought you was black!' Shit, I wouldn't go near no locker rooms. And now I can suck my own dick. It's easy. Wanna see?"

He reached for his third pant leg, still fully erect, slowly and carefully pulled it off. I gulped. His dick looked like a bulldozer with an extended crane and shovel. It looked like furniture; something to hang something else on. In fact, his penis was so large that if he was masturbating, it would look like a wrestling match. No wonder he named it the Rock.

I almost fainted. "Good god no! Why would anyone want to see that?"

"You'd be surprised."

A moment passed where nothing was said. We were at a standoff. A disturbing thought arose, one I could've done without: This was how people regarded me. I was him. My mind anguished.

All the while, T-Bone Chappelle was checking me out. His disappointment was as obvious as the boner he was sporting.

"What happened to you anyway? A while back, you said you had the biggest boobies in town. Now look atcha. I'm mean, they're alright, don't get me wrong, but—"

I checked myself out in the mirror beside his bed. My breasts were nowhere the ridiculous size they once were. The curse was lifting more and more each day. This brought a wave of joy, which I did my best to suppress.

With both hands, he groped his gargantuan genitals. His testicles were giant sand bags, swooshing to and fro. His hands were puny in comparison.

He shot me his best grin. "C'mon girl. Aren't you at all curious?"

I was.

He smirked. His gold teeth glistened under the dim light of his lamp.

"I got beers, yo."

He pointed to the beer fridge in the corner of the room. It was covered in decals.

"Well," I said, suddenly feeling optimistic. "I could certainly use a drink." I wiped my brow to prove this.

"Go on," he said. "Help yourself."

Alcohol, I thought mockingly, the cause and solution to all life's problems.

"Maybe I'll have one quick drink before I go," I said.

"Atta girl," he said, with more sleaze than a rapper. "Go grab us some brewskies."

The thought of cracking an ice-cold can of beer seemed better than sex. It was my Dirty 30, after all. I *deserved* it. I licked my lips in anticipation. This would make the entire trip worthwhile. I'll enjoy a cold beer or two, then I'll help T-Bone lift that crotchety curse of his. Telling him to repent his sins and to get his life in order requires liquid courage.

I wondered what kind of beer he's got. Surely, a man of T-Bones stature drinks decent beer. In fact, I bet he's got a variety. I hoped this was true. I was parched.

Barley and hops danced in my brain as I went to the fridge. The anticipation was inexorable. I could taste that beer already. The fridge door swung open in a fury.

Disappointment came fast and furious. I was heartbroken. So much so, I nearly cried. Inside that rinky-dink fridge were two measly cans of discount light beer.

They were warm.

"What?" my voice smeared in sarcasm. "Is that all you got?"

Epilogue

Well, that's my story thus far.

Who would've imagined I'd end up in sunny Florida, awaiting the opening of my very own beach bar? Not me, that's for sure. It wasn't all wine and roses. I got burned to a crisp my first day. Lesley says that's my initiation. Same thing happened to her. My friends back home are jealous, and for good reason. It's amazing here. Even my mother seemed proud of me when I told her.

Well, almost.

After many drinks and much consideration, Lesley and I decided on a name for our watering hole: Beach Bum's Bar & Grill. We have a snappy sign and logo; and not to disappoint, the B's look like butt cheeks. Classy, right? Tell me about it.

Keeping with the spirit of the Cock & Fiddle, we'll be providing live music seven nights a week, twice on Sundays.

Before leaving, Blaze handed me that framed picture of Kate. It's placed behind the bar, so she can watch over us, while we pour drinks. Her picture is a beacon of joy. Whenever I'm feeling low, I'll look up at her freckled face and smile.

The music will be fantastic. The acoustics are second-to-none. Let me tell you folks, I've got that stage all jazzed up and ready to rock. I've even scratched my name into the back of the stage.

Opening Night will be the cherry on top. Who is performing, you ask?

Well, after much begging, pleading, finagling and coercing (not to mention a hefty down payment), we've secured the one and only Ray Wylie Hubbard.

Yes, the Texan troubadour himself will grace our stage, telling stories of snake farms and redneck mothers, chick singers and badass rockers. I'm so stoked it hurts.

Word travels fast. Susie St. Pierre contacted me, begging for the Nashville Rejects to open the show; and as luck would have it, Ray agreed. In fact, he asked us to be his backing band. Like, yes please! Turns out, all those stories about her and Ray were true. Who would've known?

Susie and Trish arrived late last night. They brought Cesar Rodriguez with them, who loves this balmy weather, not to mention the bikini-clad women and sandy beach.

We've been sipping Margaritas all day, rehearsing for Ray's set. "Gotta get it right," Susie's been saying, all afternoon. I've never seen her so nervous before. It's kinda cute. As a bassist, I'm not worried about making mistakes. If I make any flubs during Ray's set, I'll look hastily toward the drummer. (This is what musicians call: Diversion of Blame.)

What ever became of T-Bone, you ask? Well, you can ask him yourself, if you ever make it down to Beach Bum's. He's our Door Guy. Yes, in case you are wondering, T-Bone Chappelle is 'back to normal'; and no, I didn't have sex with him. How could I? Him having genitals large enough to warrant their own zip code, and all. But I digress.

So, all's well that ends well, right?

Except for one minor detail: There's a nightclub opening up directly across from us. As luck would have it, tomorrow is their Opening Night as well. Apparently, it's a hot jazz joint in the tradition of the once-famed Cotton Club.

"At least they won't be stealing any of our clientele," Lesley said, after her seventh margarita. "It's too hoity-toity."

This is true. It's a grandiose ballroom with a gang of motley-looking roadsters parked out front. T-Bone, who's knowledge of such vehicles is quite extensive, says the jet black 1937 Mercedes Benz 26OD is worth a pretty penny. Parked next to it is a classic Ford Model B Roadster that looks eerily familiar.

Much mystery surrounds the venue. In fact, up until this morning, the name of the nightclub had been kept a secret. A modern miracle.

They just unveiled their marquee. The sucker is huge. It's as big and bright as a Las Vegas skyline. It's like nothing I've ever seen before.

The sign boasts a well-tailored cartoon man wearing a fancy top hat. The man is tipping his hat: Hat goes up, hat goes down, hat goes up, hat goes down, and repeat.

This is not what scares me. No, what scares me is the club's name. Just reading it sent a shockwave scorching through my body. For the first time in over a year, a sickly breath is percolating from my head to toe; blood dripping from my nose like a leaky faucet.

I can hardly breathe.

My mind is flooded with questions. How could this be? Am I still cursed? What comes next?

I reread the marque—just in case—glaring at those wicked words with rightful suspicion. The name of the club stabs me in the heart each time I read it.

Thus, I've made a promise to myself. One I plan to keep for the rest of my life: I'll never set foot inside that club. Not in a million years.

Not happening.

Alas, the nightclub has the name: BIGGER *IS* BETTER.

About the Author:

Marcus Starr is a musician/songwriter and private music instructor, having performed in an assortment of bands/artists and solo projects, with numerous recordings and albums. His music spans blues rock, funk rock, jam rock, country blues, fingerstyle blues and more.

Marcus Starr earned a diploma in Jazz Guitar, having completed the Applied Music Program at Mohawk College in Hamilton ON. During the pandemic he focused his creative efforts on writing a novel, while penning horror stories on Reddit under the pseudonym u/CallMeStarr.

His efforts quickly paid off. Marcus Starr won the prestigious ODD & CRYPTIC 2022 award.

Marcus Starr is currently residing in the GTA, and is set to embark on his sophomore novel: House of the Hungry Ghosts. For more information regarding Marcus Starr, please visit: marcusstarrmusic.com.

Manor House
www.manor-house-publishing.com
905-648-4797